Chenoa's Spiritual Journey

By
Becky Jane Dice

Airleaf
Publishing

airleaf.com

ISBN: 1-60002-065-8

DEDICATION

To my husband Fred for his love and support through all the years.

He is one of God's blessings.

Pauline Anderson who did the final editing.

PROLOGUE

The White Mountain Apache Indian Reservation, Whiteriver, Arizona-1998

Thirteen-year-old Chenoa Fawn Gray Owl paused in the cool August dawn, exhausted after participating in her coming of age ceremony, commonly known to the Western Apache as the Sunrise Dance. As she tried to catch her breath, she sighed.

I made it, she thought. I didn't know if I could dance four days, dancing day and night. I made it!

Although she was tired, she felt good about herself. She was no longer a child.

Glancing at the crowd of family and friends gathered in the grassy clearing, she saw her best friend Erica Lupe. Chenoa grinned knowingly because Erica would soon follow in her own special ceremony.

She spotted her parents in the gathering, both of them beaming proudly. Her little brother River waved at her. She smiled and nodded.

Isabel Tinilzay, her grandmother, stepped out of the crowd and stood before her. Short and stout, Isabel smiled proudly, her dark eyes misty. As the north wind blew, it rippled through her long, snow-white hair.

"Granddaughter, come with me," she said in fluent Apache; she spoke very little English.

With apprehension, Chenoa slipped her hand into her grandmother's as they walked through the dew-covered grass to a special teepee about twenty yards away. She knew her grandmother would share bits of wisdom and instruction, as was the custom.

"*Shiwoye*,* am I woman now?" Chenoa said in a soft voice.

Isabel squeezed her hand. "Yes, you are a woman now."

When they reached the teepee, Isabel drew back the flap over the entrance and they walked inside. A blue blanket lay on the ground; they sat on it. Chenoa waited patiently as Isabel gathered her thoughts and prepared to speak.

Finally Isabel took Chenoa's hand and squeezed it for reassurance. "Remember, always help those in need and give of yourself," she said in an authoritative voice.

I have always done this, Shiwoye," Chenoa gently reminded her.

Isabel smiled and nodded. "I know but now you must reflect on how to be an even better person, the person you were meant to be. You are on a spiritual journey and you must follow a new path. Never look behind you, because what has happened is in the past and cannot be recaptured, but always look ahead because that's where your destiny lies. Always be ready to meet the challenges sent your way because it will make you stronger."

As Isabel's gentle instructions continued for the better part of the morning, Chenoa couldn't help but wonder how she could do all this. I am one person. Why is so much expected of me when I am so young? When you stop being a child, why does life get complicated?

* *A glossary of Western Apache language appears at the back of the book.*

CHAPTER 1

"I weep with grief; encourage me by your word."
[Psalm 119:28, New Living Translation Version]

Friday, November 30, 2001
Dear Diary,

Moving! My parents want to move to Ohio, and I can't imagine why they'd want to move so far from Whiteriver. I mean the White Mountain Apache Indian Reservation has been home all of my life. I guess it's all about the money, but it doesn't seem fair to me. I don't want to move away from the only home I've ever known. River is only four years old and he'll adjust quickly, but I'm not sure about myself. After all, I am almost sixteen. Ohio seems like a million miles from Arizona.

Chenoa Fawn Gray Owl laid her pen down and glanced out the window of her small bedroom. She was a dark, sloe-eyed beauty with high cheekbones that accented her proud Native American heritage. Her small shoulders slumped slightly and tears burned her eyelids. She fingered the hole in the right knee of her jeans and tried to make it bigger. When she couldn't tear the denim, she gave it up.

I ought to tell them I don't want to go, she thought. Yeah, that's what I'll do!

Chenoa wiped the tears from her cheeks with the sleeve of her blue sweatshirt and got off the bed. She marched out of the bedroom and found them in the living room discussing their trip to Ohio.

"I don't want to leave the rez, because it's my home." Chenoa grumbled She looked at them hoping they'd accept her appeal and let her stay in Whiteriver.

Anna Gray Owl reached out and gently drawing her down beside her on the sofa, "Chenoa, when you're a parent you'll have to make important decisions that not everyone will find favorable."

"But, Shimaa!" she whined, using the Apache term for mother.

Victor, her father got out of his recliner, his mouth quirking in annoyance. "Chenoa, we've talked about this over and over. Why can't you understand our point of view? Your mother and I are thinking about our children's futures." He ran his hand through his long jet-black hair, which he kept in a short ponytail. At age forty-seven, his hair had only begun turning gray within the past year. "This is something we must do. We're not doing this to be mean."

"But my family is here on the rez. How come you've changed your mind about helping the Indian?" Chenoa wanted an answer to that question because her father's main goal in life was helping their people.

Victor sank down into the recliner, removed his glasses, and rubbed his tired eyes. "Your mother and I are thinking about your futures," he said in a stern tone. A muscle twitched in his jaw, but he seemed oblivious to it. That twitching muscle occurred at times when he was under stress. "We want something better for the both of you. Please try to understand that," he added, his tone strained.

My father's being unreasonable, she thought, sitting back and folding her arms. Life isn't fair. It sucks!

"But my family is here," Chenoa grumbled through clenched teeth. "How come you said you cared about the Indian and you wanted to help them? How come you changed your mind about that?"

Victor put his glasses back on, "Your mother and I are in agreement about the matter and that's all that needs to be said about it. We're going to Ohio and I'm going to talk to Douglas Ream about my working in his clinic with his son-in-law. Besides, I wanted to move closer to my mother now that my father has passed away. My sister and brother aren't in a very good position right now financially to help out and my mother needs help."

It sounded like a lot of mumbo jumbo to Chenoa. She looked at her mother in mute appeal. "Shimaa," she whined.

Anna gave Chenoa's shoulders a reassuring squeeze, "Child, you just have to understand that what we're doing is for the best."

"It's not fair!" Chenoa blurted and stormed out of the room. She ran into her bedroom, flopped down on the bed, and propped her head up with her hands. Over the years, her father never put much emphasis on money, but the past several months he had sure changed his tune. He didn't care what she thought.

River, Chenoa's little brother, burst into the room, jumped onto the bed and asked, "Are Mommy and Daddy mad at you?" He was cute. His large dark eyes were so expressive, that she could see deep into his inner soul. When he was happy, his round smiling face lit up the whole room. However, his eyes looked haunted by some inner anxiety, and her heart started to shrivel when she saw the uncertainty in his eyes.

She got a big lump in her throat and mumbled, "No." Her voice sounded like a lifeless monotone. "No, they're not mad at me."

River brushed Chenoa's hair back from her face and peered into her eyes. "Are you gonna cry?"

Chenoa flopped onto her back, stared at the ceiling, and mumbled, "No." However, she wasn't so sure of her own answer. She tried never to take her anger out on her little brother, but she knew if she lie there, he'd pester her until she said something mean and hurt his feelings.

River lay beside her and was quiet for a minute or two, which was a first for him. "Are we going to move?" he asked his voice small and afraid.

Hot tears burned her eyes as she sat up not facing him. "I need some air," she mumbled. She fumbled for her coat on the chair by the window, put it on, and left the doublewide mobile home by the backdoor.

The bitter north wind hit Chenoa like a cold slap in the face and wildly whipped her long, jet-black hair. Low, thick snow clouds hung heavily in the sky and looked as if they could spew snow at any moment. She pulled her coat collar up and trudged through the deep snow that blanketed the ground, plodding on with no destination in mind.

I don't want to leave Whiteriver, she thought. I want to grow old and die here and let my soul walk with my Indian ancestors. I don't want to go to Ohio where there's no fresh air or miles and miles of quiet.

Chenoa heard a car horn honk behind her. She turned to see her grandfather's blue '80 Ford pickup truck with the familiar black exhaust pouring from its rusted tailpipe.

Lou Tinilzay pulled up beside his granddaughter, cranked down the window and smiled. "Daant'ee [how are you]?" he said in Apache.

"Doo dansht'ee da [I am fine]," she responded.

"Good." He nodded, his dark eyes shining. Lou Tinilzay was seventy-five years old and the flannel shirt and faded blue; bib overalls covered his stocky180-pound frame. "Where are you headed, Granddaughter?"

Chenoa shrugged. "Nowhere."

"It's a cold day for a walk to nowhere. Climb in and we'll talk."

She walked around the front of the old pickup and climbed into the passenger side. The cab was warm but the oil smell made her eyes burn, so she cranked down the window.

Lou shifted the pickup into drive and the engine whined like a cat with its tail caught in a window. The truck lurched twice and they were on their way.

Chenoa stared out the window for a few minutes and watched the snowy scenery that stretched for many miles. "Shichoo?" She began, using Apache term for grandfather, "have you heard my father wants to leave the rez?"

Lou shifted the truck into second gear and nodded. "Yes, I've heard."

"Shichoo, I don't want to go," Chenoa stated with a heavy sigh. "This is my home." She hoped he'd understand and talk some sense into her father.

"Sometimes we must do some things we don't want to do, Granddaughter."

"Why?" Chenoa asked. She hoped he'd tell her she didn't have to go and that she could live with them forever and ever. Just whose side was he on anyway?

"Life is full of uncertainty. We knew when Anna went to college she would be free to make the choice to leave the rez. She told your grandmother and me that if she ever found her place in the world, she would go. However, she didn't and she returned to us. When she married your father, who was not from this area, we knew that leaving would still be possible, but we didn't know when. Sometimes our paths change and we go off in different directions."

"But…" Chenoa began.

"Granddaughter, in order for people to live together in peace, they have to respect one another," he said with a firm tone. "The old are respected for their wisdom and the young because they are the future of the people. Chenoa, the outcome of this respect should keep peace within the family. Understand your father is making a great sacrifice. It's the gift of self and it's the most meaningful thing a person can give. Victor has told me he loves the Apache but he knows he cannot stay. He's making this move to keep his family strong. Although he is an Indian and not touched by materialism, he knows he is letting his children down and it hurts him here." Lou closed his fist and held it over his heart. "A broken spirit isn't a pleasant thing. I won't stand in his way and you shouldn't either."

Chenoa glanced out the window again and sighed. What if I leave the rez, she thought, and never return? Will my spirit be broken by the absence of my people? What if I am gone so long my family forgets me or I forget them?

With hot tears burning her eyelids, Chenoa looked at Lou and asked, "Shichoo, if I moved away from the rez would you forget me?"

She had to know the answer. After all, they had fished together, and she had listened to his Apache folk stories. If he said yes, her heart would break.

"No, Granddaughter, I'd never forget you," he said, his voice firm. "I would never do that to a part of the family. We'll keep in touch and your father promised that you and River can visit us during the summer. Nothing is definite because he hasn't had a job offer yet."

Chenoa's grandfather was right. Her father didn't have a solid job offer. Maybe he wouldn't have one for a long time, and they'd be able to stay on the rez for another one or two years. She could only hope that would be the case.

"Shichoo, if I get my parent's permission, could I stay with you and Grandmother?"

Lou looked at Chenoa and smiled. "If you get their permission, you'll be welcome in our home."

"Thanks!"

"We are nearing your home. Would you like me to drop you off?"

Chenoa's grandfather was a sly one. He had managed to drive around the block, and she hadn't noticed it.

"Yeah, I guess so."

Lou pulled up in front of Chenoa's home a few minutes later and parked the pickup at the side of the road. Chenoa jumped out and waved good-bye to him. When she went inside Anna was standing by the range making fry bread and acorn stew. It smelled delicious and Chenoa couldn't wait for supper. Victor stood at the counter preparing coffee in the percolator. He carefully measured the ground coffee into the paper filter and closed the lid. He added water and made sure the pot was in place so the coffee could drip into it.

Anna looked up and smiled; her dark eyes sparkled. "Did you enjoy your walk?"

Chenoa walked over to the small round table covered by a red and white-checkered tablecloth and sat in her usual chair. "Yeah, I guess so," she mumbled. "I ran into Grandfather and he gave me a ride around the block."

Victor sat at the table with his cup of coffee and asked, "Did Lou have anything interesting to say?"

"Yeah," Chenoa answered. Carefully she told her parents what Lou said and waited for their reactions, which were slow in coming. Then she said, "I want to stay with Grandfather and Grandmother. You can take River with you to Ohio but I'm not going."

Anna and Victor exchanged uncertain glances.

8

"Chenoa, when we go to Ohio, we'll go as a complete family," Victor said in a stern voice. "We're not going to leave you behind to live with your grandparents."

"Why?" Chenoa whined. She just couldn't win any arguments with them. Why couldn't they meet her half way in this and give her some freedom to make her own choices?

Anna stepped away from the stove and sat beside Chenoa at the table. "Chenoa, we cannot leave you behind because my parents are too poor to take care of a child." she said, her voice firm. "They barely have enough for themselves let alone taking in a grandchild. Even if my father said it would be all right for you to stay, it would be too much of a hardship for them." Anna put her arm around Chenoa's shoulders and gave a reassuring squeeze. "And if I didn't have my little girl right beside me sharing new adventures with me, my life would have no meaning whatsoever."

Chenoa hated being referred to as "little girl" because she felt it reflected her size. Standing 4'10" and weighing 90 pounds, Chenoa was smaller than most girls were her age. Her baggy clothes hid what little figure she had.

However, her mother was right about life having no meaning if they weren't able to share new adventures together. As much as Chenoa hated the idea of leaving the rez, the miles between them would be hard. If she couldn't be with her mother, she'd rather die.

Chenoa felt a renegade tear slip down her right cheek and she quickly wiped it away. "I don't want you to leave me behind, Shimaa. I'd rather have old Rusty Massey the shaman tie me to a post and skin me alive, slowly." She shuddered when she thought about Rusty because he gave her the creeps. When he looked at her with his one good eye she got the feeling he knew what she was thinking before she even thought it. Chenoa tried to avoid him whenever she was in town because he was too weird.

Anna kissed Chenoa's cheek and smiled. "I wouldn't let Rusty skin you alive, nor will anyone else if I have anything to say about it." Her mother sounded like a mother lioness protecting her young to the death. "We'll be together as a family and that's all that matters. Honey, if you're anxious about leaving the rez then you must take this concern to Jesus and talk to Him about it. He's a special friend you can always talk to and He'll listen to you."

Anna always called prayer "talking to Jesus". However, Chenoa wasn't yet "saved" like her parents. So, even if she did talk to Jesus, would He listen to her? Anna always seemed to have the right answers, but Chenoa found little comfort in this one.

Anna's gentle hand closed over Chenoa's and she said, "You think about that, Honey. I know you'll feel better when you've made the right decision and stick with it." She smiled brightly and patted her hand. "Now, I need you to do me a big favor and set the table for supper. Okay?"

"Okay," Chenoa said, and then got up to do as her mother asked her.

After supper, Chenoa stared out the window of her small bedroom. The twinkling stars dotted the blackened sky like little pinholes in a black velvet canvas. It was cold and windy outside the mobile home, and her room felt chilly.

The mobile home was all Chenoa's parents could afford. Although her father was a doctor and her mother was a teacher, they weren't rich, just comfortable by rez standards.

Maybe being just comfortable persuaded her father to leave the rez. Born and reared in Kill Buck, New York, a small town on the Allegany Indian Reservation, Victor became the first person in his family to go to college. After earning his medical degree, he could have gone anywhere and made a decent salary at any hospital in the country, but he wanted to help the Indian.

Victor met Anna at the annual White Mountain Apache Tribal Fair during Labor Day weekend in 1982. Victor said it was love at first sight, and they were married five months later. Then, after trying to have a baby and having two miscarriages, Chenoa came kicking and screaming into the world in 1985.

I guess I can't fight my parents about the idea of moving to Ohio, Chenoa thought. My father has pretty much made up his mind and he's moving forward with his plans. If we have to move away from the rez, why can't we move to Phoenix or Tempe? What's so great about Ohio anyway?

Chenoa sighed and walked out of the room. She found Anna sitting alone at the end of the sofa, her legs tucked under her. She was reading her Bible. After she put River to bed at 8:30, this was her quiet time.

Plopping down on the other end of the sofa, Chenoa hugged a small, frilly pillow. "Shimaa, can we talk?"

Anna looked up from her reading and smiled. "Of course. What's on your mind?"

"If we move to Ohio, can we still visit the rez? Maybe I can spend the summer here and…"

Anna put her arm around Chenoa. "Yes, child, your father and I have been considering everything. We've been praying about this together and letting the LORD be our guide. Nevertheless, you mustn't worry about all these things, Chenoa, because your father hasn't really discussed this with Douglas Ream. We must take life one day at a time and not worry needlessly. You shouldn't be anxious for nothing, but only pray about the matter."

"What happens if Dad doesn't get a job offer from Dr. Ream?" She hoped this was the case and they would get to stay in Whiteriver.

"Well, if Douglas isn't able to offer your father a position in his clinic, then he'll have to search for a good offer someplace else."

Chenoa sighed in exasperation. *I'll never get a break at this rate. I'll just have to do as Mom suggested and talk to Jesus. Maybe if I tell Him how much I want to stay here He'll throw a monkey wrench in my father's plans.*

CHAPTER 2

Saturday, December 1, 2001
Dear Diary,
*   Last night I prayed about my father asking Dr. Ream for a position in his clinic. I kind of made a deal with God and told him if He makes it so Dad can't find a job off the rez and we get to stay in Whiteriver, that I'd go to church without making a big fuss about it. I know you aren't supposed to make deals with God but I made this with a sincere heart.*

Chenoa closed her diary and leaned against her pillows. The afternoon turned colder. She grabbed her afghan from the nearby chair and put it around her shoulders.

I know I should be happy because it's my sixteenth birthday, she thought, but I'm not in a celebrating mood.

They were supposed to have a quiet celebration that night and Chenoa's best friend, Erica Lupe, was coming over. She wouldn't be happy when she heard they'd probably be moving.

River burst into the room, jumped on the bed, and threw his arms his around Chenoa. "Happy birthday!" he exclaimed with a bright and cheery face.

"Thank you!" Chenoa said, giving him a kiss on his cheek. She tucked his yellow sweater into his jeans and kissed his chubby cheek.

River bounced up and down on the bed. "Are we going to have cake and ice cream?"

Becky Jane Dice

"You'll have to ask Mom."

"What do you want to ask me?" Anna asked, from the doorway with a smile on her happy face.

River bounded off the bed and jumped into Anna's waiting arms. She gave him a big bear hug and kissed his cheek.

"Are we having cake and ice cream?" River asked.

Anna smiled. "Maybe, if you're a good boy. Your father's in the kitchen; go find him. I think he has some milk and cookies for you."

"Cookies!" River exclaimed. "Mmm!"

River reminded Chenoa of Cookie Monster from Sesame Street. He really loved his cookies and they were the perfect things when she wanted to bribe him.

Anna turned to Chenoa. "Now what would you like for supper, Chenoa? Since it's your birthday you can have anything your heart desires."

Chenoa perked up. "Anything?"

Anna's beautiful dark eyes sparkled. "Yes."

"Pizza! I'd like pizza!"

Anna sighed. "I had to ask. Would you like to go to the store with me? Mr. Alchesay has frozen pizzas in Whiteriver."

"Yeah, let's go!"

"Now that your father has River occupied we can sneak out and talk."

Her mother was sly. She and Victor had a system worked out. When Anna and Chenoa wanted to have their mother/daughter outings, her kept River distracted.

"Get your coat, and let's get going."

Chenoa grabbed her coat from the foot of the bed and put it on. They sneaked out the back door, climbed into her mother's blue '92 Chevy, and headed toward town.

"Can we get the usual? I'd like the vegetarian pizzas."

"Yes."

"Can we get pop? Mr. Alchesay always has Dr. Pepper in stock."

"Of course." Anna nodded as she steered the car around two dogs fighting over a rag in the middle of Fort Apache Road.

As they drove toward town, they were quiet. With a population of 5,200, Whiteriver was the largest town on the rez. Small inadequate houses lined both sides of the road, many without electricity.

The Apache, although proving long ago to be survivors, still faced daunting social and economic problems, including unemployment and poor housing. Poverty had been the greatest obstacle. Few businesses had opened on the reservation and many found it difficult to make ends meet.

Anna and Chenoa passed an old burned out mobile home, a charred shell from a fire last August. A newborn baby perished in the blaze.

"Isn't that the old Tall Tree place?" Chenoa asked.

Anna nodded. "Yes. I wonder how Marge is doing since she lost Timothy in the fire."

Chenoa shrugged. "I don't know."

Turning left on North Power Line Road, they drove further into the small town. Chenoa saw Sheriff

Daklugie pull someone from his white patrol van parked in front of the police station. He hustled the unwilling man inside the one-story brick building.

Except for a post office with the U.S. flag flying out front, only one small grocery store stood in town. Several souvenir shops were sandwiched between two churches. Outside the Saint Francis Church, the priest stood directing several boys as they shoveled the snow from in front of the building. Whiteriver Baptist Church stood several doors down and that is where Chenoa's family attended. Pastor William Monday stood out front and waved at Chenoa and her mother as they drove by. An old run-down laundromat stood around the corner.

Anna turned right on South Supermarket Drive and pulled the car into the Bashas Market parking lot. It was half full of cars. As they got out and approached the building, Chenoa saw Mr. Alchesay hanging a Christmas wreath on the front door. He looked at them and smiled.

"*Daagot'ee* [greetings]!"* he said in Apache. Otto Alchesay had short black hair and his big belly spilled over his belt. Nearly every button on his red and blue-checkered flannel shirt were strained and threatened to pop off.

"*Daagot'ee,*"* Anna said.

He opened the door for them and they walked into his grocery store. Chenoa noticed the floor was swept clean and everything was in order. Mr. Alchesay liked everything neat.

"It's nice to see both of you," Mr. Alchesay said.

"Thank you, Otto. How are Millie and the twins?" Anna asked.

"They're growing up but Millie is growing rounder everyday. The doctor said it might be a Christmas baby. We'll have to wait and see."

As Chenoa walked further into the small market, she saw Paul Alchesay, Otto's son sweeping the floor at the end of the snack aisle. A tall, thin boy of sixteen, he had one long braid down his back. A light brown stain was on the lower right side of the white apron he wore over his jeans and gray tee shirt.

"Hi." Paul acknowledged her presence with a nod and a wink.

Chenoa felt the heat rise in her cheeks. "Hi!" He always winked at her. Erica told Chenoa that Paul had a crush on her. Chenoa told Erica she was crazy and Erica just laughed.

Paul winked again and disappeared into a back room.

Mr. Alchesay straightened several cans of peas on a shelf. Once he had the front of the can showing he was satisfied. He turned back to Anna. "How can I help you, Anna?"

"I'm just looking for your best frozen pizzas."

Mr. Alchesay smiled. "The best! What's the occasion this time, Anna? Did Chenoa get straight A's on her report card again? Since you're a teacher I'll bet she gets plenty of coaching."

"It's too early for report cards. Today is Chenoa's sixteenth birthday."

"Oh!" Mr. Alchesay's eyebrows arched up. "Well, happy birthday, young lady!"

"Thank you," Chenoa said shyly, not expecting any congratulations.

As Chenoa and Anna went on with their shopping, Chenoa turned to Anna and asked, "Shimaa, when can I start dating?" She knew the question came unexpectedly because she never really showed much interest in dating.

Anna stopped and gawked at Chenoa in disbelief. "Huh?" That was an unusual response from Anna. She was usually more lady-like. Only Chenoa would have given a response.

"When can I start dating?" Chenoa asked, expecting an answer. Butterflies fluttered in her stomach as she waited for an answer that seemed to take an eternity coming.

Anna took Chenoa gently by the hand and led her over in front of the windows. "Honey, your father and I've never really discussed dating," she said, her dark eyes shining with pleasure. She cupped Chenoa's chin in her gentle hand and she smiled jauntily. "But I have a feeling we'll be discussing it soon. Who is it that has caught your eye?"

Chenoa stomach felt all knotted up at the thought of telling her mother she might be interested in any one boy. "It's just a boy," she mumbled, her voice cracking.

Anna's one eyebrow rose in a questioning slant. "Hmm! Could my daughter be interested in-let me guess-Paul Alchesay?"

Her eyes were downcast. Chenoa swallowed the lump in her throat. How could she guess the right boy the first time?

Anna lifted Chenoa's face until their eyes met and she saw her face brighten. "Your secret is safe with me. However, if he's who you want to date you must remember if we move your time with him may be short."

Chenoa nodded and her body slouched. "I know," she barely whispered. Her chin sank dejectedly into her chest.

Anna kissed Chenoa on the forehead and said, "Your father and I will discuss it, I promise."

By the time, they finished their shopping Paul walked up to Chenoa and smiled. Up close, he was cute with deep dimples. "I'll talk to you at school," he said.

"Okay," Chenoa replied, studying his facial features. His dark skin was free of pimples and had a bit of razor stubble on his chin.

Paul nodded and a silver thunderbird earring swung from his left earlobe. "See you in church tomorrow," he said, his dark eyes dancing.

I wish he wouldn't smile like that, Chenoa thought, because it makes me feel like Jell-O inside. Could he really have a crush on me?

Anna walked up to Chenoa and touched her shoulder. "Let's go home, Chenoa."

"Okay," Chenoa answered. She smiled at Paul, and then followed her mother out of the store.

Chenoa's best friend Erica Lupe joined the family for supper. Chenoa could tell she enjoyed the pizza as much as she did!

"Erica, would you care for another slice of pizza?" Anna said.

"Yes, Mrs. Gray Owl," Erica responded eagerly. Erica had high cheekbones and reddish brown eyes that reminded Chenoa of the color of autumn leaves. Her long hair was one thick braid that always seemed to rest on her right shoulder. She wore a pair of faded jeans with frayed bottoms and an old white sweater.

Anna gave Erica a large piece of pizza and her dark eyes grew large. Anna immediately tried to ease Erica's concern. "We have plenty," Anna said.

"Thank you, Mrs. Gray Owl." Erica bit into her slice of pizza. "Mmm! We didn't have pizza for my birthday a few weeks ago. Mom made venison stew. My father shot the deer on his last hunting trip."

Erica's parents didn't have a whole lot of money and pizza was a real treat for her. When Chenoa invited her for supper, she practically begged her parents to allow her to come join them. They had been friends since the age of four and it wouldn't have felt right without her.

"Hey, what are you doing for Christmas?" Erica asked Chenoa. "There's going to be a Christmas party at church. I suppose you'll be there."

"No," Chenoa said. "We're going to visit some friends of my parents in Ohio. My father is going to ask Dr. Ream for a job at his clinic."

"Oh?" Erica asked. "What are you saying?"

"We may be moving away from the rez."

"No!" Erica cried, throwing her arms around Chenoa. "You can't leave me, Chenoa. I'd be so lost without you. You can't leave!"

"I'll be back, Erica."

"When, Chenoa? When are you coming back?"

"We're coming back on New Years Day," Victor said. "Hopefully we'll be back home before school starts again."

"Who is Dr. Ream?" Erica asked.

"Douglas Ream and his wife are my childhood friends," Anna said. "We grew up on the reservation a long time ago, and we've kept in close contact. Every year we visit them around the holidays."

"Are they Apache?" Erica asked.

"No, they are white people," Anna answered. "Their parents lived and worked in Whiteriver for a time."

"Oh," Erica said.

They ate most of the pizza and then Victor helped Anna cleared the table.

"*Shimaa**, Erica and I are going to study in my room," Chenoa said.

"All right, Honey," Anna answered. "We'll have cake and ice cream about eight o'clock."

"Okay, Come on, Erica."

Chenoa led the way to her bedroom and shut the door.

Erica sat in the chair by the window. "Will you tell me about any adventures you have in Ohio?"

Chenoa plopped down on the bed. "Sure," she promised. Chenoa saw her history book lying on the foot of the bed. She hated the book because history wasn't her best subject. "I heard the test is going to be hard."

"Yeah, I guess so," Erica said reluctantly. She didn't sound like she was looking forward to taking the test either.

"Do you think you'll pass it?"

Erica shrugged. "Maybe."

"I saw Paul this afternoon," Chenoa said, hoping to put a spark in the conversation. She knew Erica's interest in getting Paul and her together ran high the past several months.

Erica perked up. "Yeah! Do you like him?"

"I don't know. I think he's cute though." She smiled and softly snickered.

"If he ever gets the nerve to ask you out would you go out with him?"

Chenoa shrugged. "I don't know. How do I know he'll like me anymore after he really gets to know me?"

"Like what?"

"I'm not very lady-like. I'd rather ride my grandfather's pony than dress nice to impress a boy. I don't think I'm pretty and I'm too skinny."

"Oh that," Erica said, making a vague gesture. It was so slight Chenoa didn't realize she had made it. As she spoke, she played with the end of her braid. "Don't be insecure, Chenoa. I mean Paul must think you're special if he's showing an interest in you. If you're worried about being a-"

"Tomboy," Chenoa finished the sentence for her. "I'm a hopeless tomboy."

"If you want to get Paul to notice you put on a pretty dress. Find out what Paul's favorite color is and wear that color. My sister June said it worked for her."

"If you want the honest truth, Erica, I feel weird in a dress. When I put on a dress, I cease being me. I can't explain it, but that's how I feel sometimes. If that's how you get a boy to notice you, then I'm doomed."

"I'm sure Paul likes you because you're nice."

Chenoa didn't want to talk about her insecurities and grabbed her history book. "I think we'd better study," she said, changing the subject.

They sat back on the bed and took turns reading each paragraph aloud. Then they asked each other the questions at the end of the chapter to test their knowledge. They always did that together. It was their special method of studying and had helped them ace tests for the last three years.

By the time they finished, it was eight o'clock. They walked into the living room and sat on the sofa. River was sitting at the other end coloring in a coloring book. In his favorite recliner located in the corner, Victor sat watching a football game on the television. When he was home, he rarely wore his shoes. His shoes had been discarded and set beside the chair. Anna served everyone cake and ice cream.

After they'd eaten their fill of cake and ice cream, Chenoa's parents gave her a present.

When Chenoa tore off the blue tissue paper and white bow, she saw it was a new diary. She remembered looking at the diary with her mother at a mall in Show Low last month.

"Wow!" Erica exclaimed. "A diary!"

"Yeah!" Chenoa said. "I love writing in a diary. It helps me figure out the answers to many of my problems. It's something I've done since I first learned to write."

"Really?"

"I've kept all my diaries since the age of seven."

"I guess she takes after me in that respect," Anna said. "I have quite a collection of journals-about forty years worth. I told Chenoa that when I die, they're hers."

"Are you going to be a writer someday?" Erica asked. "You could write your life story or something."

Chenoa shrugged. "I want to go to college and become a teacher at the reservation school. Mom and I have talked about it quite often and she thinks it's a great idea."

"Gee, you have your future all planned out," Erica said. "I don't even know what I'm doing tomorrow let alone three years from now."

"It's always best to have a goal to work toward," Anna said.

At nine o'clock that evening, the party was over. When Victor drove Erica home, Chenoa rode along.

CHAPTER 3

Chenoa was never so glad to have one of Pastor Monday's sermons end as that day. His sermon on the evils of gossip was boring. He must have dug down to the bottom of the barrel for that one.

As Chenoa walked out of the sanctuary forty minutes later, she made her way through the crowd toward the coat rack to get her coat.

"Psst!" someone called. It sounded more like a car tire going flat. "Chenoa!"

Chenoa looked around and saw Paul Alchesay standing by a doorway leading into a Sunday school room. He motioned to her. Chenoa pointed to herself. "Who, me?" she asked.

"Yeah," Paul said, "Come here."

Chenoa walked over to Paul and they stepped into an unoccupied classroom. Several posters were on the wall, one being an image of Christ with an Indian chieftain behind it. The other picture was of Christ hanging on a cross with thunderbirds in the background. On a long table was a stack of Sunday school lesson books entitled "The Indian and God".

Chenoa thought Paul looked handsome in his dark suit and tie. He carried a black Bible under his left arm.

"What is it, Paul?" Chenoa asked. Maybe this is it, she thought. Maybe he'll ask me out.

"Our Sunday school class is having a Christmas party and I was wondering if you would go with me."

Becky Jane Dice

"I won't be here for Christmas," Chenoa said with a heavy heart.

Paul's facial features fell. He had a hangdog expression and his dark eyes looked haunted by some inner pain. "Where are you going?"

She told him about the trip to Ohio and why they were going. "We'll be returning on New Year's Day."

"Oh. When are you leaving?"

"On the sixteenth."

"On Saturday there'll be an indoor powwow at the high school; would you like to go with me?"

"Sure! I think I'd enjoy that."

Paul smiled and his dimples deepened. "Great! I'll drive by and pick you at eleven-thirty. Don't eat lunch because we'll get something to eat later."

"Okay," she said. Is he taking me out on a date or are we going as just friends? she wondered. Maybe if I go with him to the powwow it will break the ice between us.

Paul glanced toward the door. "I'll see you later, Chenoa. We'll get together in school sometime." He smiled and left the room without looking back.

When Chenoa walked out of the room to get her coat, Erica walked up to her and took her arm. "I saw you and Paul talking. Did he ask you out on a date?"

"I don't know," Chenoa answered.

"Huh?" Erica had a puzzled look on her face.

Chenoa knew that was a dumb answer, but Paul didn't use the word "date." "He's taking me to the powwow on Saturday."

26

"Wow!" Erica cringed when she realized she spoke loudly in church. She glanced around to see if anyone was looking at them. However, the crowd of people gathered was talking as loudly as she did. "Great!" She lowered her voice. "At least it's a start."

"Yeah, I know."

"Chenoa," Anna called as she, Victor, and River stood at the front door. "Come on, we're leaving."

"I'll see you in school, Erica," Chenoa said, as she joined her family, and walked out to their station wagon.

After lunch, Anna and Chenoa piled the dishes into the sink to wash later, because they were going to visit Chenoa's grandparents.

As they drove to their grandparents' home, a two-room structure, she saw the two majestic pine trees that stood behind it like sentries guarding the small homestead. A wisp of gray smoke rose from the chimney, curled into the crisp air and disappeared. About 200 feet on the eastside of the house stood a small barn that housed two horses and an old cow. An old wooden fence in need of repairs encircled the barnyard.

When Victor pulled up out front and stopped, Chenoa and River jumped out of the station wagon and raced into the house.

"Shiwoye!" Chenoa called out.

Isabel Tinilzay stood by the cook stove stirring a simmering pot of venison stew. The delicious aroma of deer meat and vegetables mixed with herbs filled the room. As her grandchildren hugged her, Isabel laughed softly. "I'm glad you came!" she said. She kissed Chenoa and then River.

Anna and Victor came in and greeted Isabel. The family sat wherever they could find a seat. Chenoa plucked a big yellow and white male cat off the chair so she could sit. She left the old uncomfortable sofa for her parents. River sat on the floor in front of the sofa.

"Where's Father?" Anna asked in Apache.

"He's feeding the horses," Isabel answered. "He'll be in shortly."

Just then, Lou walked in the front door with a big smile on his face. He nodded, took his coat off and joined them.

"What have you decided about the move to Ohio?" Isabel asked.

"We've not made definite plans, *Shimaa*," Anna said. "Victor has to ask Douglas Ream if he has a position open first. That's why we're going to Ohio."

"And will Chenoa be going along?" Isabel asked. "Lou mentioned she asked about staying with us."

"Chenoa will be going with us," Victor said with a firm tone and looked at Chenoa. "She is my daughter and I will provide for her."

Chenoa didn't say anything. She petted Chester the cat and he purred. She wished she hadn't said anything to her grandfather about staying with them because it made Victor's statement seem awkward.

Chenoa thought about her meeting with Paul Alchesay that morning and wished the situation were better. I finally get a boy to notice me and it's for nothing, she thought. Life isn't fair!

"Well, you must look ahead because that's where your destiny lies," Isabel said. "Never look behind you because the mistakes you've made are in the past. The only time to reflect on the past is to see how you solved a problem."

"Yes," Anna said, with a nod, "I left the rez once, but I returned to begin my family here. I never thought I'd be leaving it again."

"One must stop and consider that their walk through life will always take different paths," Isabel said. "It may not lead them back to the starting point. You must do what you have to do. Your life must go that direction. It's so ordered by the Great Spirit."

Anna nodded as if she understood Isabel's reasoning. She glanced at Victor who also smiled. It was as if they were saying to one another: "It's okay, we're doing the right thing. We have their blessings and we can move ahead with our plans."

Chenoa wasn't comfortable with that line of reasoning. She hated the thought of leaving the rez behind. What if I have a relationship going with Paul Alchesay and I wind up leaving? What if I hate Ohio so much and I want to come back here, will they let me?

"*Shichoo*,* please tell us a story," Chenoa said hoping to change the subject to a lighter topic.

Lou's dark eyes shone with pleasure upon hearing Chenoa's request. He liked to tell stories. The little children in Whiteriver called him *"na go dihii"** which meant "storyteller."

Lou began his story telling. "A long time ago, White Painted Woman lived on the earth. Four monsters also lived there. The monsters killed many people White Painted Woman gave birth to a son and his name was Child of Water.

One day, a monster tried to steal their food. Child of Water wanted to fight the monster. He and the monster agreed to a contest.

"Both fighters had a chance to shoot four arrows. Child of Water picked up a blue rock. The rock was a good luck charm. The monster shot its arrows at Child of water. None of the arrows hit him. Child of Water's fourth arrow hit the monster's heart.

"As Child of Water grew, he killed the other three monsters. Ever since, the world has been safe for humans."

Lou continued his story. By the time, he finished the last of the story it was suppertime. Isabel served them venison stew. Lou had to light the small kerosene lantern on the table. Chenoa's grandparents couldn't afford electricity and the lantern was the only source of light in the evenings.

After the meal, the Gray Owls headed for home. By the time they arrived, the snow was falling heavily.

If it keeps snowing like this, Chenoa thought, there won't be any school and no school means there won't be a history test.

"I have to finish grading my papers," Anna said.

Chenoa went to her room, pulled her diary from under the pillow and flopped onto the bed. She penned these words on the pink pages of the diary:

Dear Diary,

Suddenly, I have some new feelings, and I'm trying to figure them out. It seems like the minute I turned sixteen something inside me kicked in and I started noticing Paul Alchesay in a new way. I'm afraid of what I'm feeling because I don't understand what is going on inside me. Why am I feeling this way? How do I stop it?

In addition, there is the possibility of moving away and leaving all this behind: my home, my family and my friends. What do I do if I really start liking Paul the way he likes me? What if he's the only boy I'm meant to be with and I have to move away? What if...

Chenoa didn't finish writing the sentence, whatever it might have been. Gee, she thought, life sure does turn on you sometimes.

Chenoa needed to talk to Anna. She found her seated at the kitchen table, test papers spread out and her red pencil flying across the pages.

A transistor radio set on the table and a weather report came on. "This is Leo Dillon from KVWA 970 AM, Show Low, with a weather alert. Stay warm, folks, because the snow is falling. It may become one for the record books in this area with six to eight inches to be expected and..."

Chenoa sat at the table. "*Shimaa,* can we talk?" She saw the plate of chocolate chip cookies on the table and took one.

Anna looked up, put her pencil down and smiled broadly. "Sure, Honey," she said, giving Chenoa her full attention.

"Have you and Dad talked about me dating?"

"No, but I promise I will," she answered. Usually when she gave Chenoa her promise to do something she did it. She gently caressed her chin and asked, "What's the hurry, Chenoa? You'll be dating soon enough."

"How come some things change overnight? Last week I didn't even notice boys…" She didn't finish her train of thought because she didn't know how to put her thoughts into words.

"I understand how you feel, Chenoa."

"Huh!" Chenoa said giving a start of surprise. "You do!" She wished her mother had told her why she was feeling this way because she was clueless.

"My dear, once you become a teenager so many changes take place both physically and emotionally. Suddenly, you have all new feelings, and it is up to you to figure them out. You start liking the opposite sex and think you're in love."

Cheona felt a rush of heat into her face. "I don't love-ah-anyone," she stammered. "I just…"

Anna put her arm around Chenoa and said, "I know, I'm just saying how teenagers think. It's a difficult time in a young person's life. Emotions can seem like they're out of control."

"Sometimes I feel like someone put a magnifying glass in front of me and I see every single thing that is wrong with me."

"And what do you think is wrong with you?"

"Nobody understands me."

"Well, you're not the only girl who has felt that way," Anna said. "Other girls, even boys feel that nobody understands them. Believe me, Chenoa, I went through my teen years as if I was on a continuous roller coaster and I thought it would never end. Then when I was sixteen I found a relationship with Jesus Christ and that eased the growing pains. I still had some problems, but I learned to love myself because I was who God had made me."

"So, will you ask Dad about me dating?"

Anna kissed Chenoa's forehead and nodded. "Yes, of course, child. I promise."

Victor walked into the kitchen and asked, "Anna, would you like some hot chocolate?"

"Sure!"

"How about you, Chenoa?"

"All right," Chenoa mumbled, munching on a cookie.

As Victor put water in the teakettle, he asked: "Chenoa, have you made a list of what to take on the trip to Ohio?"

"No," Chenoa answered. She hated lists, but her father made lists for everything. He wasn't spontaneous like Anna and her.

Victor squinted at Chenoa as he always did before giving her a stern lecture. His dark eyes looked like

Becky Jane Dice

tiny slits. He wagged his finger at her. "We're leaving here on the 16th and you need to be ready. You need to start packing!" he said.

"I don't know what I want to take," Chenoa said, with an indifferent shrug.

Victor pushed back the sleeve of his green sweater and shook his head. "You take after your mother," he sputtered. "Just take enough clean clothes for everyday and one or two dresses for church."

"Aw, Dad," Chenoa grumbled. "Dresses!" She hated dresses and she hated dressing up even more. Chenoa was a tomboy, and wearing jeans and sweatshirts suited her just fine.

Victor squinted even harder and continued his lecturing. "I don't want a daughter of mine wearing pants to church. It's not proper. Women are supposed to wear dresses and men are supposed to wear suits and ties. While I was growing up on the rez my father told me that women should wear modest clothing and act like ladies at all times."

"Yes, Dad," Chenoa mumbled in obedience. Her pride severely bruised by his stern words, she jammed the rest of the cookie into her mouth.

"Anna, you need to help her," Victor said. "You know how she waits until the last minute."

"Yes, Victor, I'll help her."

"Can I go to the powwow at the school on Saturday?" Chenoa asked.

"May I?" Victor corrected.

"May I?" Chenoa asked.

"Who are you going with?"

34

"Paul Alchesay," she said, deciding to be truthful. She hoped Victor didn't give her grief over it because she was going with a boy.

Victor's eyebrows arched up. "Is this a date?" he asked, his voice stern.

Chenoa didn't know, but she wished it were a date. "No, we're just going as friends." She hoped he wouldn't find fault with that as he did about the way she dressed.

"Yes, you may go but you'd better be on your best behavior. See to it that Paul doesn't try anything indecent."

My father is too strict about everything, Chenoa thought. Why can't he trust me? I'm sixteen years old. I'm not four anymore.

CHAPTER 4

Monday, December 3, 2001
Dear Diary,

The snow, which began falling gently yesterday, turned into a fierce winter storm. School was cancelled for the day because the roads were too icy and snow covered. Mom said we'd have to make the most of our time indoors. I'm glad we have plenty of games like Scrabble, Checkers and a few others to play.

Chenoa put her diary aside and glanced out the window. She could see the snow coming down by the bucketful. It didn't show any sign of stopping.

She got off the bed and walked into the living room where River was standing on the sofa looking out the window. A frilly pillow lie on the floor, so she picked it up and placed it back on the sofa.

"What's so interesting out there?" she asked.

"Snow! Snow!" River exclaimed, jumping up and down. The big snowflakes always held him in fascination.

Chenoa took a step and felt something small and hard under her right foot. Looking down she saw a purple crayon. She picked it up and put it with his coloring book on the end of the sofa then went to the window and looked out. She saw the Goseyun's shaggy, brown mutt scampering around in the snow. He was trying to eat the falling snowflakes. River giggled when he saw it. Chenoa watched until she became bored, which took less than two minutes.

"Do you want to build a snowman later?" she asked.

"Yeah!" he exclaimed, his eyes wide open and sparkling.

Anna walked into the room and asked, "Would you like some hot chocolate with marshmallows?"

"Yeah!" Chenoa and River exclaimed simultaneously.

Anna made hot chocolate and added big fluffy marshmallows. As they sat drinking their hot chocolate, they talked.

"I'm glad I have my children," Anna said as she put her arm around Chenoa and gave her a gentle squeeze. "In a way, Chenoa, we're all born of God. We're His children and He loves us very much. Someday you'll grow up and have a little daughter with whom you can share all the things I've taught you."

Chenoa smiled. She wasn't sure if she wanted a child, but the idea of having special times between her daughter and herself seemed appealing. Anna was a good teacher and had taught her well.

"I told you about your little sister, Sage," Anna spoke with sadness in her voice. "How she was stillborn."

Chenoa nodded, but she didn't say anything. She was eight years old at the time, but she remembered Anna was sad.

"There had been no breath in Sage to prove she was ever alive," Anna continued. "The day before she was born, she was active. She kicked me like she wanted to burst out right then."

Anna was quiet for several seconds. "My people in ancient times dreaded the ghosts of the dead," she explained. "They seldom spoke the dead persons name, and just said, 'He's gone.' Although your dad and I are saved, we wanted to do something special. We wrapped Sage in a blanket, and said a prayer that she might have a safe journey to Yaa ka'yu, heaven. Then we sprinkled ashes and pollen in a circle around the grave."

"Shimaa, even though you're saved, you still observe our people's traditions. Is that wrong?"

"God wouldn't hold it against me, Chenoa. God loves us all no matter if we're Indian or white. He hears us all. I was raised with Indian beliefs but I also follow Christ's teachings. Even so, I can still acknowledge my Indian heritage and participate in some of my traditions. If God wanted people to be the same he would have made us all Indian or all white."

After they finished their hot chocolate Chenoa went to her bedroom and penned these words in her diary:

I feel like I'm caught between two worlds, that of my Indian culture and the white man's beliefs. Mother says God loves us all no matter what race we are. Mother has faith in God, but where did she find that faith? Where did she find all the answers to her questions? When did she start believing in God? Did she feel any different after she accepted Christ?

By mid afternoon the road crew had the roads cleared.

Chenoa was bored. River was taking a nap and she was tired of just sitting around. She went in search of Anna and found her sitting in the living room reading her Bible.

"Shimaa, may I go visit Great-Grandmother? I wanted to say good-bye before we leave for Ohio."

Anna smiled. "Sure. Make sure you bundle up. I will send your father for you when he comes home."

Chenoa hugged Anna. "Bye!" Chenoa got her coat and put it on. She slipped out the back door and started walking. The north wind was sharp and cut through her like a knife.

A car horn honked behind her. Chenoa turned and saw a green Volkswagen pull up beside her. The occupant rolled down the window and she saw it was Pastor Monday.

Pastor Monday gave her a big smile. "Hello there! Where you off to on such a cold day?"

"I'm going to see my great-grandmother."

"Oh! Hop in and I'll take you there."

Chenoa shrugged and climbed into the warm car. It was cold and she didn't relish the thought of becoming an icicle before she got to her great-grandmother's trailer. The old woman lived a mile and a half away on Holly Grape Road.

"I hear you may be leaving us soon," Pastor Monday said.

"I guess so."

"You don't sound very enthusiastic about it."

Chenoa looked at him oddly. "Did you want to leave your home to come to the rez?" She hoped her tone didn't sound too critical. Most whites didn't like leaving the comfort of modern living to live among the Indians.

Pastor Monday chuckled. "I go wherever the Good LORD instructs me to go. I do it willingly because He wants everyone to hear His Good Word."

"Why is going where He wants you to go so important?"

"I'm just His obedient servant, Chenoa. My only desire is to stay in the center of His will and let Him use me where I can do the most good. That is all He asks of us."

Chenoa didn't comment on that. She fell silent for the rest of the trip. As Pastor Monday turned down Holly Grape Road, she pushed his words into the back of her mind.

Pastor Monday pulled up in front of an old house trailer and stopped. "Give Sweet Grass my best. I would stop in myself but I have an appointment."

"Thank you," Chenoa said. She got out and headed toward her great-grandmother's trailer. As she opened the door, she saw the old white-haired woman huddled in a rocking chair by the small stove. Her arthritic back was hunched over and she held a cup of steaming broth in her gnarled fingers. Chenoa knelt beside the old woman and smiled. *"Daa got'ee, Shiwoye! Daant'ee?"**

The old woman gave Chenoa a toothless grin and her dark eyes twinkled. *"Doodansh,"** she answered in Apache. The old woman didn't speak a word of English. Although she was part Lakota, it had been a long time since she spoke her mother's tongue. Her true name was also Chenoa, for whom she been named. However, everyone on the rez knew her as Sweet Grass.

"There wasn't any school today. We're going away and I wanted to come and say good-bye."

Sweet Grass nodded. "I heard a rumor you might be leaving."

"I don't want to go, Shiwoye. I don't want to leave you or my people."

Sweet Grass made a sound. "Child, you must not be so close minded that you miss an opportunity to grow. I have found that out in my one hundred winters. You go wherever the Great Spirit sends you and experience life."

"I don't want to leave you." Chenoa wiped a tear from her eye.

Sweet Grass chuckled softly and caressed her hand. "Shh, child. Some day you will return. You will be different but wiser. The world never stops changing. People and circumstances change. The old ones die as the news ones are born."

Chenoa threw her arms around the old woman's thin frame. "No!" she sobbed. "I don't want you to die. Never!"

Sweet Grass pulled back and looked Chenoa in the eye. "Child, I will live to see your first born. That is a promise."

"But…"

"I feel this in my heart. Don't fret."

"Why must there be change? Why must people die?"

Sweet Grass looked thoughtful. "A generation goes, a generation comes. The sun rises and the sun sets. The wind goes southward, and then turns to the north, it turns and turns again back to its circling goes the wind. So goes life."

"How do I find my way from my home, Shiwoye?"

"That answer lies here," Sweet Grass said pointing to Chenoa's heart. "Only you can answer that. You alone know the answer and that answer is deep within your heart. There you will find peace."

Chenoa didn't understand Sweet Grass's philosophy of life. "How do I find this peace?"

"First love everyone. Respect your brothers and sisters. Never quarrel with one another. Be good to others and always be friendly to whomever you meet, wherever you meet them. The generous person is the one who is respected."

"Grandmother has said our moccasins must walk a different path."

Sweet Grass nodded. "This is true. Remember, Child, let The Great Spirit be your guide, and He will take care of all you need. He will lead you to restful waters and refresh your spirit.

He will guide you along a good path, and when you are afraid, your heart must be brave because He is there. The Great Spirit will always feed you and you will have many good things because of Him."

Sweet Grass's words reminded Chenoa of the passage in the Bible that Anna always read, 'the LORD is my Shepherd.'

Chenoa wanted answers to some of life's questions. "Shiwoye, there is a boy who is interested in me, and I'm not sure if he's the one for me. How can I be sure?"

Sweet Grass smiled. "There is someone for each of us. You will know in your heart when the right boy comes along. Who is this boy?"

"Paul Alchesay."

A sigh escaped Sweet Grass. "I know the boy. Child, he's not the one you will share your life with."

"What? How do you know?"

"I just know he isn't the one."

Chenoa knew her great-grandmother was very intuitive and understood life and people. She should trust her judgment. "Then does that mean we will never be together?"

"Forever? Perhaps not, Child. But that doesn't mean you and he will never have a special relationship."

"When you married Great-Grandfather did you really know he was the one for you?"

Sweet Grass nodded. "Nachi was a good man and we shared fifty-five winters together. Back then marriage was arranged by the young man's parent's, and then the couple courted. When Nachi wanted to marry me, he asked my aunt to approach my family. He offered my father several good horses and blankets, and my father accepted.

Our people didn't have a wedding ceremony. My parents, according to custom, built a dwelling and Nachi came to live in our camp. Our own wickup faced away from my parent's home, out of respect for a long standing taboo that a man should never look at and talk to his mother-in-law."

"Why couldn't a man look at or speak to his mother-in-law?"

Sweet Grass shrugged. "Perhaps to avoid conflict and insure harmony between households. Some still practice this, but not many."

For the time remaining, Chenoa listened to her great-grandmother talk about life and how The Great Spirit fit into it. By the time Sweet Grass finished, Victor came to get Chenoa.

"Are you ready to go, Chenoa?" Victor asked. "It's starting to snow again."

"Like last night?" Chenoa hoped that wasn't the case.

"No, but it's cold. Let's go."

Chenoa and Victor went out to the car. A cold wind chilled Chenoa as she climbed into the car.

As Victor drove toward home, he hit something in the road and skidded a little. "Whoa!" he exclaimed and stopped the car.

"What was that?"

Victor grunted. "I don't know." He got out and looked around the car. When he got to the front, he stood shaking his head.

Chenoa got out and pulled her coat tighter. "What's up?" By the frown on his face, she wasn't sure she wanted to know.

"Flat tire!"

"Oh."

"I'll get the spare." Victor hurried to the back of the car, opened the trunk, and pulled out the spare tire. He looked it over and shook his head. "This one isn't much better."

"Can you use it?" Chenoa knew nothing about tires; she just wanted to go home.

"It's worn down and may not hold the road."

"It looks okay to me. Put it on."

Victor looked at Chenoa and frowned. "Chenoa, don't be so impatient. I'm thinking about our safety."

Chenoa stuffed her hands in her pockets and asked, "Can't you put it on before we freeze too death?" The cold air stung her nose and cheeks. She didn't like the way her father always thought about the situation because he took too long in deciding to take action.

"We need to get home safely."

"Dad, I'm cold. Do you need any help putting the tire on?" She didn't know how much help she could be but at least she offered.

"No, I can do it," he replied reluctantly. "Get in the car."

Chenoa sighed and got in the car. She waited as her father struggled with changing the tire. Finally, she got out to see what was taking so long. "What's taking so long?"

"The nuts are on too tight and my hands are ice cold."

"You should have put gloves on."

"You sound like your mother. Go back in the car where it's warm."

Chenoa stood watching her father fight with the nuts and grunting something under his breath. She glanced around and saw a shadow slinking up the road. She wasn't sure if it was a dog or a wolf. She'd heard a report the other day that a wolf had killed a farmer's chickens.

Chenoa shook her father's shoulder and asked, "What's that Dad?"

He looked up. "Huh?"

"There!" Chenoa pointed on down the road where the form was moving toward them. Victor muttered something in his native Seneca, and Chenoa thought it meant "Oh my God!" He usually didn't say something like that and she sensed urgency in his voice.

"Get in the car!" he snapped. He practically pushed her into the car and got in on the driver's side.

"Is that a wolf?"

"Probably." Victor turned the lights on illuminating a big, gray wolf in the road. Its eyes glowed in the car light.

"Beep the horn, maybe it'll go away."

Victor grunted. "Yeah, right. Just sit tight, it'll go away."

"Do you still have your gun?"

"It's in the trunk."

"Rats!"

"Chenoa, just sit still! It'll go away."

"I thought you kept the gun in the glove compartment."

"Not with my children in the car. I can't take a chance in someone getting hurt."

"Why don't you run over the wolf?"

Victor sighed impatiently. "Hush, silly girl. It has a right to live because it's one of God's creatures."

"What makes it more important than the chickens it's killing?"

"You ask the strangest questions."

"Is it more important than the chickens?"

"I doubt it," Victor mumbled.

The wolf moved within a few feet of the car and stared at them.

Chenoa cranked the window down an inch and hollered, "Go away! Get!"

Victor pulled her away from the window. "Stop that! It's not a dog."

"Nothing else is working."

A few minutes later, truck lights came down the road and the occupant beeped the horn. The wolf jumped and dashed off into the brush at the side of the road. After the vehicle stopped, the occupant got out and walked toward the car. As he walked over to the driver's side, they could see that it was Lou Tinilzay.

"What's got you stranded out here?" Lou asked.

"Flat tire," Victor answered. "The nuts are on too tight and I couldn't get them loose. The wolf rather sneaked up on us. Thanks to Chenoa's keen eyesight, we were able to get to safety."

It's good I get credit for some thing, Chenoa thought.

"The wolf looked hungry," Lou said. "Once it starts killing livestock it needs to be put down. I'll help you change your tire."

"All right." Victor looked at Chenoa. "You stay in the car. I don't want that wolf getting you if it decides to come back."

Victor got out of the car and Lou helped him change the tire. He threw the old tire in the trunk and climbed back inside.

"May you way home be safe," Lou said.

"You, too," Victor said. He waited until Lou was safely back in the pickup before he drove away. "Ready?" he asked Chenoa. She nodded.

They drove home without incident.

CHAPTER 5

Tuesday, December 4, 2001

It's back to school as usual. The history test has been pushed back until Wednesday. That doesn't make me sad because I wish they'd push the test back until December 5, 2110.

A big bang startled Chenoa. She jumped, looked up, and remembered she was in study hall. She saw the boy in front of her pick his book up off the floor. Glancing across the crowded room, Chenoa saw Paul Alchesay watching her. He smiled, and then pretended to read his textbook.

After class, Chenoa met Erica in the cafeteria for lunch. She had a big Cheshire Cat smile on her face. She must have been in one of the dress down moods because she wore old jeans and a purple sweatshirt. Today her hair hung in two long braids and was tied with yellow ribbons.

"What are you grinning about?" Chenoa asked. Erica had her curious and silly grin on her face. She always looked like that when she had some choice bit of gossip she wanted to share. "Well, tell me, Erica!"

"Paul Alchesay asked about you," Erica answered.

Chenoa grabbed Erica's arm. "He did? Tell me what he said!"

Erica giggled. Chenoa hated it when she did that because it seemed so dramatic. She wanted the facts, not drama. She wanted to shake the information out of her but chose not to, this time. She waited with as much patience as she could muster.

"Yeah!" she said, both braids bounced with every nod. "He seemed pretty interested in talking to you."

"He was watching me during study hall." Chenoa hoped she didn't sound like she was complaining. It was hard to believe that he could be interested in her.

"See!" Erica said, grasping Chenoa's hands and giving them a reassuring squeeze. "I told you he has a crush on you. What did your parents say about him taking you to the powwow on Saturday?

"My dad said it was okay if we went as just "friends". I'm going!"

"Great!" Erica squeezed Chenoa's hand and her dark eyes crinkled like half moons. "Fill me in on every juicy detail."

"Okay," Chenoa promised.

After school, Chenoa was studying in her bedroom. As she looked over her history notes, she came across a notation: "write a report on the Revolutionary War."

"Rats!" she muttered. "I don't want to write it." She shut her notebook, and threw it on the bed. I hate history, she thought. I hate it! However, if I don't get a good grade Dad will ground me and I won't be able to go with Paul to the powwow.

With a sigh, she got off the bed, went in search of her mother, and found her searching in a kitchen cupboard.

"Shimaa, can I go to the library? I have a history report to work on."

Anna smiled. "Of course. Would you like for me to drive you?"

"Sure!"

"Let me wake up River, and…"

"No, don't wake him," Chenoa protested knowing when River's nap was disrupted he was a cranky child the rest of the day. "I'll walk. It's not that cold."

"Okay. Make sure you bundle up."

"Okay." Chenoa hugged her and Anna kissed her cheek.

"Be careful. Call me when you're ready to come home."

"All right."

Chenoa put on her coat and backpack and headed out the backdoor. As she walked up the road, she heard a car horn honk behind her. It was Paul Alchesay in his old blue Nova.

Paul cranked down the cracked window and smiled out at Chenoa. "Hi! Where are you headed?"

"The library."

"Would you like a ride?"

"Sure!" Chenoa hurried over to the passenger side, opened the door and climbed inside. "Thanks!"

They headed toward the Whiteriver Public Library.

"Erica told me you were…ah…asking for me," Chenoa stammered. *Very smooth, she thought. Stuttering isn't cool. I'm such an idiot.*

"Yeah, I was just wondering if you're still going to the powwow with me on Saturday."

"Sure! I asked my father if it was all right and he said yes."

"Great!" He reached over and held Chenoa's hand. "I wanted to talk to you about something important but not now." He squeezed her hand. "Maybe we'll talk about it on Saturday during the powwow. Okay?"

"Okay," she said, wondering why he was being so secretive.

Soon they arrived at the small Whiteriver Public Library. Several cars were in the parking lot and Paul parked beside an old, black pickup truck.

"Are you coming in?" Chenoa asked.

Paul merely nodded. He took her hand again and they walked through the glass door. He led her into the room with well-stocked shelves. "What book are you looking for?"

"I need to write a report about the Revolutionary War."

"Oh! Come with me." Paul led Chenoa to an aisle and began looking at the books on the top shelf. He reached up and removed one book, looked at it and handed it to her. "This one might be helpful." He began searching some more and pulled another book off the shelf. "This one might be better."

"Thanks!" Chenoa took both books over to a table, sat, and began leafing through the first book.

"What exactly are you looking for?"

"One of the battles. I hate history!"

Paul sighed but didn't comment on her statement. "I'm thinking about applying for a job at the Fort Apache Timber Company."

Chenoa gave Paul a hard look. "What do you know about working with lumber?"

Paul shrugged. "Next to nothing. But it beats sweeping floors and stocking shelves at Bashas Market."

"What about school?'

"What about it?"

"Are you going to finish?"

Paul shrugged. "I need to do something else."

"Like what?"

"Have a job and a girl."

"You're not going to stay in school?"

Paul shrugged again. "A lot of kids on the rez don't finish high school. It's no big deal, Chenoa. Besides, I've learned all I can."

"But…" Chenoa protested.

"It's no big deal."

"What does your father say about it?"

"I haven't told him."

"Are you going to?"

"What is this, Chenoa, twenty questions? I haven't decided anything. Let's drop it, okay?"

Chenoa sighed and dropped the subject. She opened the book and scanned a few pages. After several minutes, she found something interesting about the Revolutionary War…if that was possible. She took her notebook out of her backpack and began writing. She had barely finished the first paragraph when Paul plucked the pen from her left hand.

"Is homework all you think about?" he grumbled.

Chenoa blinked. "I just want to get a good grade."

"Who are you trying to impress, Chenoa?"

"No one. I just think education is important."

"Why, because your parents were lucky and got a higher education? They're stuck here on the rez. Not many leave and those who do they forget who they are."

Chenoa had no clue about where he was going with this line of reasoning. "What are you talking about?"

"Simple, your father's planning to uproot your whole family and take you all to Ohio. Once you live around white people, you'll change. I don't want you coming back to the rez not knowing who you are."

"Huh!"

"Yeah, I care. I wasn't going to ask this until later but if your father's plans fall through and you get to stay maybe we can…ah…maybe you can agree to be my girl?"

"Uh…" she stammered. "My parents and I haven't discussed dating but I could ask."

Chenoa hoped he didn't think she was a baby because she couldn't date at sixteen.

Paul grinned from ear to ear. "Sure!" he exclaimed. "Whatever! I hope when you ask them they say yes. I mean…well…I hope they say yes."

"I'll ask. I hope they say yes, also."

From the big grin on his face, he must have thought she had promised him the Universe. "Great!"

After Chenoa finished the first page of her report, she decided to check out the two books. She was about to call her mother and tell her she was ready to come home but Paul offered her a ride.

As Paul parked in front of the house, he gave Chenoa's hand a gentle squeeze. "I'll see you in school tomorrow."

"Okay!"

Paul pulled Chenoa close and kissed her tenderly on the lips.

Chenoa felt a spark flow through her as they kissed. When their lips parted, he stared into her eyes and smiled. Chenoa felt the heat rise in her face and all she could do was smile weakly.

When Chenoa finished studying in her bedroom that evening, she penned these words in her diary:

Paul Alchesay asked me to be his girl! Wow! Now I'll have to stay in Whiteriver. I have to! I'm hoping my father won't get a job in Ohio so I can stay and date Paul. I like Paul. However, not the way he likes me yet.

I don't know who has influenced him about dropping out of school. Although many kids on the rez do drop out of school, that doesn't mean he has to. He needs a good role model...someone he could look up to. My parents always told me education is important and I don't know what to do or say to help him to stay in school.

Chenoa closed her diary and went in search of her mother. She found Anna lounging on the sofa reading her Bible.

"Shimaa, how important is education?" Chenoa asked.

Anna closed her Bible. "It's important to get all the education you can. It will help you get a good job."

"A lot of kids on the rez don't finish school."

"I'm aware of that. However, you must stay in school."

"What happens if we live in Ohio...among white people...I change? What happens when I come back and I don't know who I am?"

Anna grunted and hugged Chenoa. "What prompted such talk, Child? Who's been trying to scare you with these ideas?"

"I-I was talking to Paul Alchesay and..."

"Well, if he's going to plant negative ideas in your mind..."

"But, Shimaa, he wants me to be his girlfriend."

"And how do you feel about this?"

Chenoa shrugged. "If we stayed here maybe..."

"Chenoa, you mustn't allow any boy to influence your decisions. You must be the person you were meant to be. I've always encouraged you to do whatever you set your mind to do."

"But Dad wants to..."

"Child, many of our people who enter professions as teachers, doctors and such have done so and must leave the rez to pursue their chosen field. I love your father and I respect his decision to relocate. I thought you were okay with that."

"Paul wants..."

"Paul Alchesay wants many things but he doesn't have my daughter's best interests in mind. If he's given up on school and doing something with his life, that's his concern; it's not yours. You shouldn't give up everything for the sake of a boy. I'm not saying this to be mean, Chenoa. Once you become an adult, you'll understand these things. One must choose their partner wisely. Guard your heart or you will lose it."

Chenoa thought about what her great-grandmother said about Paul…he wasn't the one that she'd share her life with, and that she may be right. "I don't want to date a white boy. That's all there is in Ohio; if there is a Native I'd never find him."

Anna smiled and squeezed Chenoa's shoulder. There is someone out there for you. Trust me, Child, I know. He will find you." Anna kissed Chenoa on the temple.

Chenoa went back to her room and sat on the bed. As she touched her lips, she remembered Paul's kiss. She took out her diary and once again penned words within the pages:

Paul kissed me! I remember the warmth of his kiss. I wish I didn't.

How can Mom be against him? In addition, Great-Grandmother also was against her dating Paul. Paul is a wonderful boy and I will always wonder what might have been. What if there is never anyone else out there for me. Will I be spinster like Mildred Fox? Heaven forbid! What do I do?

CHAPTER 6

Saturday, December 8, 2001
Dear Diary,

I haven't seen or talked to Paul Alchesay for three days. I've not sorted out my feelings. I'm not sure how I should feel about Paul. Sometimes I'd really like to start dating him, and then there are times when I question whether it would work out. Whenever Erica asks me about Paul, I don't know what to tell her. As far as I know, Paul is still taking me to the powwow.

Chenoa laid her pen down, and looked out the window. The morning dawned bright and clear for a winter day in Arizona, but it was cold.

With a sigh, Chenoa got ready to go to the powwow. By the time she was ready, Paul showed up at the front door wearing old jeans and a blue sweatshirt. When Chenoa opened the door, he smiled and said. "Hi! Are you ready to go to the powwow?"

"Yeah," Chenoa said. She grabbed her coat from a chair and put it on. He opened the car door for her like a perfect gentleman, waited as she got in and closed the door. Paul wasn't very talkative as they drove to the school. Chenoa listened to a Joanne Shenandoah cassette.

"Do you always take Joanne's music wherever you go?"

Paul nodded. "Yeah! She's a good singer."

Once they arrived at the school, he parked the car and they went inside. As they headed for the gymnasium, they heard laughter and many voices. The gymnasium was crowded with spectators and she saw many of her classmates but did not see Erica. Paul managed to find seats and they sat and waited for the powwow.

A man stepped up to the microphone and started the activities. He began with a prayer and then several of the elders stood and gave speeches.

Paul leaned over to Chenoa and whispered in her ear. "These two give Indian time a new meaning. If Thomas doesn't talk for an hour his brother will make up the difference and then some."

Chenoa giggled behind her hand and nodded. "His brother is an old bag of wind."

"If he owned a watch the battery would've run down an hour ago."

Chenoa giggled again.

After forty-five minutes, the last speech ended and the powwow began.

Paul pointed to two young boys in dancing. "Those are my brothers, Donny and Ronny. They wanted to dance so Mom made their costumes."

"They dance well," Chenoa said trying to be heard over the drums. The ten-year-old twin seemed to be having a good time dancing in the shadows of the taller dancers around them.

"Yeah!" Paul said looking at his brothers with pride. He slipped his arm around Chenoa and pulled her closer. He kissed her and gave her shoulders a gentle squeeze.

"Paul, are you going to stay in school?"

Paul glanced at her and shrugged. "I don't want to talk about it. I want to enjoy the powwow. Okay?"

Chenoa nodded reluctantly. She wanted to encourage him to stay in school and get an education. She liked him and she didn't want him quitting school and becoming another statistic on the rez.

Paul leaned over to Chenoa and asked: "Do you want to get something to eat?"

"Yeah," she said feeling her stomach grumble.

They found the food stands in the next room. The different aromas made her mouth water. She saw fry bread, Indian tacos and corn soup.

"What would you like to eat?" Paul asked.

"The Indian tacos look good, and the corn soup."

They put Indian tacos on their plates, scooped out corn soup into bowls, and went to an empty classroom.

"How come you've been avoiding me in school?" Paul gave her a wondering look and waited patiently for her answer.

"I haven't been avoiding you." That was only a half-truth. After their conversation Tuesday afternoon at the library, she wasn't sure what she'd say to him.

"What's going on, Chenoa?" he asked between bites of corn soup. "Do you still want to be my girl?"

"Yeah, I guess so…if we come back to the rez to live." Chenoa shrugged. "If not…" her voice trailed off and she didn't finish her train of thought.

"You don't sound too sure of yourself."

Chenoa sighed. "I'm not sure of anything. It depends on what happens in Ohio." She hoped he'd accept that explanation for now. What could she say?

It was the truth. Everything depended on what happened in Ohio.

"I know when a girl changes her mind. I want to know why you're hesitant, Chenoa."

Chenoa shrugged.

Paul cupped her chin in his hand and forced her to look at him. "Talk to me. I want to know what's bothering you."

"I don't know. Maybe you should stay in school. After you graduate you can get a better job."

Paul grunted. "On the rez? Are you crazy? Look around you and see there are no good jobs. Why are you so bent on me staying in school?"

"Education is important."

"Oh, you just want an educated man and not an ignorant savage. Is that the case?"

"No, I didn't say that."

"You might as well have. If I didn't like you so much I'd go find someone else."

Paul's harsh words cut into Chenoa's heart like a knife. She didn't want the day to end like this, with Paul angry with her. Maybe she should apologize to him and tell him she didn't mean what she said. However, deep down that would have been a lie and she couldn't live with herself if she wasn't honest.

"If you liked me as much as you say you do, you'd promise me you'd at least try."

Paul looked at her and frowned. "I'll try for you." His voice sounded tight and Chenoa knew he wasn't being honest with her or himself.

"Don't do it for me, but for yourself."

Paul sighed in exasperation. "Girls!" he spat. "I don't understand them."

After they finished their meal, they went back to the gymnasium to watch the Indian dancers. The powwow lasted two more hours. Paul took Chenoa home and parked in front of her house.

"I hope everything gets settled soon," he said. "Let me know as soon as you can."

"Okay,"

"I'll see you in school on Monday."

"All right."

Paul leaned over and prepared to kiss her on the lips and she stopped him. "You need to talk to Mr. Sundry, the guidance counselor, about school."

"Don't you ever give up?"

"No! Don't you give up either." Chenoa didn't wait for a kiss good-bye. She opened the door and got out of the car.

She sat on her bed that evening wishing she had the answers to her questions but she was clueless. One part of her wanted to be with Paul, yet the nagging questions taunted her. She trusted her mother's intuition but Paul wanted her to be his girlfriend.

This is a mess, she thought. What do I do? Erica said we'd make a nice couple. How can she see it and nobody else can? Is she wrong and everyone else right?

A knock on the door made her jump.

"Sorry to startle you, Chenoa," Anna said, "Would you like some hot chocolate?"

"No," Chenoa answered quietly.

Anna looked concerned. "What's wrong, Chenoa?"

Chenoa shrugged. "Nothing."

Anna sat down on the bed. "I don't believe it. I'm your mother and I know better."

"What does it mean to fall in love?"

"That's hard to say. If you ask ten people what they think it means to fall in love, you would get ten different answers. I consider falling in love as uncorking your imagination and bottling up the common sense."

"What?" Chenoa looked confused.

"I've been in love a few times. Unbelievably your father wasn't my first love. Each time there is a sense of losing control. It's wonderful and frightening at the same time. When I fell in love with your father, I wondered how it would turn out. Would he love me the way I loved him. Would it be forever? Would I get hurt? Child, there are a thousand questions and no guarantees."

"Erica says we'd make a nice couple."

"Hmm," Anna mused. "Does Erica know what's deep in your heart? I venture to say no."

"What do I do, Shimaa?"

"You must decide for yourself what you want. Our decisions must be our own even if we make a mistake. Don't undermine your feelings. Love, no matter what course it may take is a precious gift. The love that you feel for a boy is something special." Anna touched Chenoa's chest with a gentle finger. "Let this be your guide, daughter."

After Anna walked out of the room, Chenoa penned these words in her diary:

Dear Diary,

Maybe Mom is right. Maybe I should decide what I want…even if I make a mistake. Paul is cute but…What if I find out he's not who I want? Should I care about what Erica thinks…just because she thinks it's a great thing? What is scary is that I don't really know what I want. Maybe I should wait to make a decision about Paul until after our trip.

CHAPTER 7

Sunday, December 9, 2001
Dear Diary,
I didn't hear a word the pastor said during the church service because I was thinking about Paul and the decision I have to make. I guess I should stop beating myself up because I can't see the answer clearly. Am I afraid of being honest with myself? I want to put my thoughts and feelings on a dark dusty shelf where all indecisions lurk.

Chenoa glanced out her bedroom window and sighed. What do I do? Maybe I should draw straws… the longest one gets Paul.

Anna came to the door and said, "Come on, Honey, we're going to see my parents."

"Okay!" Chenoa exclaimed. She hoped Lou would tell stories so she grabbed her coat and climbed into the family station wagon.

When they arrived at her grandparent's home, the aroma of corn soup greeted them at the door.

"It's been cooking since early this morning," Isabel said, gesturing emphatically. "Eat! Eat! I have plenty!" She walked over to the wooden stand where she kept her dishes, picked up five bowls and set them on the table.

"Mmm!" Chenoa said, dishing some of the corn soup into her bowl. She chased Chester the cat off the chair so she could sit down.

"Meow!" Chester protested, looking back at Chenoa. Then he crawled into the corner, curled up but with a watchful eye on her.

The rest of the family filled their bowls, and sat. While they ate, they listened to Lou. He didn't share any interesting historical Apache folklore, but he did share something with the younger children, something Chenoa would probably appreciate later in life. Right then she only considered it one of his pep talks.

"Dear grandchildren, one must be generous in this lifetime, one must share." He spoke slowly with authority in his aged voice "You, my grandchildren, must share for it is something an Apache would do. A real Apache will provide for his family and his relatives as well as those who are in need."

"Why, *Shichoo*?"* River asked.

"Why?"

Lou smiled in his kind way, laid a large, calloused hand on River's shoulder saying: "Because it's better to help others, then good will come to you, but you shouldn't count the cost or ask what you will get in return. You must help each other. It is better to give away than to keep it all for yourself. If a man calls you `stingy' it's the worst kind of insult they can say against you." Lou lovingly patted River on his head.

"But, Shichoo," River spoke up, "what if I don't have enough for myself, then what?"

Chenoa knew then that River didn't really understand what Lou was talking about, but he surely did ask a very important question. Chenoa sat there wondering what the full meaning of Lou's answer to that question might be.

Lou smiled. "It doesn't matter. He must still help that one in need. Be generous! In addition, my grandfather taught me about courage. I always looked up to him because times weren't easy but he didn't complain."

"Was he a good man?" Chenoa asked.

Lou nodded. "Yes. He faced the hard and difficult times with his head held high. He faced danger and didn't run away, but faced death with dignity. In the old day, counting coup meant you had courage. But today, grandchildren, you must have courage to face bad thoughts and desires."

"How?" Chenoa asked.

"Guard your heart, Granddaughter," Lou answered. "Be careful about what goes into your heart and what comes out. It takes courage to make changes instead of running away. Be courageous! Always be strong here," he added, closing his fist over his heart. Lou smiled and his dark eyes reflected patience and wisdom.

The next week Chenoa and her family were busy preparing for their trip to Ohio. Chenoa packed her suitcase. On Saturday the 15, Anna did the laundry so they wouldn't leave dirty clothing behind.

River burst into Chenoa's room and grabbed her hand. "Shichoo is here. He said he wants to talk to you. Come!" he added pulling on her hand.

"Okay! Okay!" Chenoa put her diary aside and went out to the living room. Lou was standing by the door and he smiled slightly. "Did you want to see me about something?"

"Your grandmother sent me here to get you," Lou said slowly. "She said it was important and for you to hurry."

"Okay," Chenoa answered. She put her coat on, and followed Lou out to the old pickup. "What does Grandmother want to talk to me about?"

Lou shrugged. "I don't know." He turned the key in the ignition and that familiar 'cat with its tail caught in the window scream filled the cab. He put the pickup into gear. It lurched and sputtered, and they were on their way down the road. Lou was silent all of the way to his home and Chenoa thought that was strange. He wasn't talkative by nature but he usually didn't clam up completely.

When they pulled up in front of the house, Lou said, "Your grandmother is waiting inside. I'm going to chop some wood."

Chenoa nodded. She took her time going into the house. As she opened the door and walked in, she called out, *"Shiwoye?"* Chenoa didn't receive an answer so she sat on the old sofa.

She looked toward the small bedroom and noticed that the old white wool blanket hanging over the doorway was still. Maybe Isabel was in there. Chenoa wondered what she could be doing. Her grandmother prayed in her bedroom at times and didn't want to be disturbed. Therefore, Chenoa waited patiently.

Chester lay curled up on the chair watching her with inquisitive yellow eyes. Chester was a lazy cat and paid no attention to the little, gray field mouse that hid behind the rusty pail used for gathering water from the pump outside. The mouse stuck its tiny, twitching nose out in defiance, as if daring the cat to chase him. It scurried under the wooden stand where Isabel stored her plates and cups.

Although the day grew colder, the cook stove kept the house toasty warm. There was enough light so Isabel didn't need to light the kerosene lamp.

Chenoa glanced toward the bedroom again; and wondered what was keeping Isabel. She must have been cooking up something special if it was taking her that long to invite her in or her to come out. She said it was important because Grandfather said to hurry. That was strange because Isabel never rushed important conversations.

Chenoa heard a noise in the bedroom. Isabel pushed the old blanket aside and emerged from the room. The hem of her traditional Apache dress stirred up the dust.

Isabel sank down beside her on the sofa. Her dark eyes looked haunted by inner anxiety. Isabel grasped Chenoa's hand and sighed as if she had a heavy heart.

Chenoa wanted to look away but she couldn't. Isabel always looked serious when something bothered her. However, this look, although she'd seen it many times, stirred something deep in Chenoa's stomach and it hurt. Something bad must have happened, but what was it? Chenoa chewed on her fingernail as she waited for Isabel to speak.

Isabel sighed again. "Chenoa, the Great Spirit came to me in a dream. Long and hard I prayed for understanding but each time the answer was the same."

"*Shiwoye,* what was the dream about?"

"Chenoa," she said her voice tight and her face twisting with anguish. "The Great Spirit is sending you on a journey. It's a journey not of your choosing. Your moccasins must walk this path alone."

Chenoa's heart bounced into her throat. "What! Why, *Shiwoye,* what have I done?"

Isabel squeezed her is hand. "It's required!" she stressed, "but there's more, Granddaughter. The Great Spirit said you must teach your brother River the ways and traditions of his people because your parents won't be there to do it. You must keep the stories alive in his heart and mind as well as your own."

Chenoa tried to process Isabel's words. What is she trying to tell me? Why can't my parents teach him? Why do I have to do it?

After a cleansing breath, Chenoa began, "What do you mean, I don't understand, *Shiwoye?* What's going to happen to them?"

A tear formed at the corners of Isabel's eyes and her sorrow deepened. "They're going to die," she reluctantly said. Her bottom lip quivered and the tears slipped down her cheek, to her chin and dropped onto her dress. Chenoa knew her heart was breaking.

It felt like a trapdoor had sprung open in Chenoa's stomach and she wanted to throw up. They can't die, she thought. I'm only sixteen years old; I can't be orphaned.

Chenoa hated Isabel's dreams. Isabel began having dreams at an early age. She told Chenoa that the Great Spirit gave many people gifts. During vision quests, people had found their way or solved a problem. She knew many of Isabel's dreams had been fulfilled. This knowledge made Chenoa's heart thud against her chest.

"You'll have to learn to stand firm in your beliefs, or you'll risk losing your identity. Isabel said. "It's a spiritual journey, Chenoa. The Great Spirit requires it of you."

A whole host of butterflies tickled Chenoa's stomach and threatened to take flight. "Why must my parents die in order that I learn a lesson, *Shiwoye?*" Chenoa sobbed.

Isabel remained silent, as Chenoa knew she would. Isabel was very intuitive and had dreams that foreshadowed the future. She didn't share her complete knowledge of the dream in order to let it play out. That would allow the person to find his or her way through the right course of action.

"The Great Spirit will tell you when He chooses. He has chosen this path for you, Chenoa, and some day you'll understand. Remember, when He talks you must listen with your heart." She pointed to Chenoa's heart. "And see with your mind," she added pointing to her head. "Learn well! I can't tell you anymore it's forbidden!" Chenoa started to say something, but she waved off all further questions with a gesture. "It is said."

Chenoa belched and a sour taste rose up into her throat. The news of having to go on a spiritual journey not of her choosing, but that of the Great Spirit, was difficult for her to digest. Having to have her moccasins follow a different path than the one life already had chosen came as a shock and wonderment. During the journey, she would have to see with her mind and listen with her heart if she was to understand. It sounded like a riddle to her, at least for now.

Before Lou came to take Chenoa back home, Isabel took her hands and gently squeezed them. "Granddaughter, when you travel with your family to Ohio I want you to stand firm." She placed something cold and hard in the palm of Chenoa's right hand. "When you need to pray keep this prayer stone close and you'll find your answers."

Chenoa opened her hand and saw a piece of turquoise. She closed her hand hoping it would give her courage.

Isabel hugged Chenoa close and kissed her cheek. She pronounced a blessing over. "May the Great Spirit go with you and watch over your heart. Keep it pure. Guide your footsteps that you do not fall, reward your spirit with all good things, both now and hereafter." Isabel kissed Chenoa's cheek and added: *"Nadistinyu bikeh hi daa* [follow the right path]. *Ni at e' hii nlt' eego antee Le'* [be true to your heritage]."

CHAPTER 8

Thursday, December 20, 2001
Dear Diary,

Courage! A lot can be said about the word "courage". Grandfather said it takes courage to face the changes in your life instead of running away from them. Nevertheless, as we get closer to Hartville, I can't help but be anxious. Isabel told me about her dream and I can't seem to get her words out of my mind. Its message hangs over me like a black storm cloud hosting a powerful tornado.

Chenoa glanced out the window of the small diner in Canton, Ohio and wished her heart wouldn't race like a runaway train. It seemed like the closer they got to Hartville the harder her heart pounded like tribal drums.

They stopped at the diner for lunch because Victor had been driving since 5 A.M. and he needed a break. He had taken several bathroom breaks but he was tired. After eight hours of driving with his hands locked on the steering wheel, they practically had to pry his hands open. During the meal, Victor almost drained the coffee pot hoping the caffeine would keep him awake. Anna suggested opening a vein in his arm and putting in the coffee intravenously. After drinking all that coffee, he went to the restroom and took River with him.

Chenoa thought about Isabel's dream, and didn't tell Anna what Isabel said and Anna never asked. She dreaded this trip and her grandmother's dream didn't make it any better.

She watched the big snowflakes fall as she caressed the turquoise prayer stone in the pocket of her jeans.

Anna, seated to Chenoa's left, put her arm around her shoulder and said, "Chenoa, worry is a burden that God never meant for us to bear alone."

Chenoa, looked at Anna stupidly. How could Anna know her troubled thoughts? She placed her hand over the entry she had just written in her diary, and thought Anna had read what she wrote.

Anna smiled. "As we travel this road of life things like tests and illnesses keep us from enjoying life. We only create more worry by thinking of all the bad things that might happen but never do."

Does Mom know me that well? Chenoa wondered.

"When you're anxious about something what do you do?" Chenoa asked, wanting to know. She didn't want to tell her what Isabel said about her death. If Anna thought she meant being anxious about moving away from the reservation, she wouldn't tell her anything different.

"I talk to Jesus and He helps me deal with it."

Before Chenoa could respond to that statement, Victor and River came back from the restroom. "Let's go," Victor said, "we've still got a long way to go."

Victor paid the check; they left the building and climbed back into the station wagon. When they reached Hartville, Chenoa concentrated on the scenery out the car window.

The area was originally the home of the peaceful Delaware Indians. They were driven from their home in the Delaware Bay area by the British along with help from some hostile Indian tribes in the mid-1700s.

They passed a factory and the sign on the front of the building read: Schumacher Lumber Company. As they drove down North Prospect Avenue, Chenoa saw many stores lining the street. She saw The Chocolate Factory and The Hutch on the right side of the street, a jewelry store and the post office on the other side. When Victor stopped for a red light at the town square, she saw The Pantry Restaurant at the intersection of North Prospect Avenue and Maple Street. It was established in 1829. Chenoa remembered the Reams took them there for breakfast one morning last year. The food was delicious.

Chenoa looked to her right and spied Tessmer's, which reminded her of a general store from the olden days. As they waited for the light to turn green, an Amish resident driving a horse and buggy passed through and headed west on Maple Street. The horse was just plodding along, with breath vapors puffing from its nose, and then disappearing in the crisp air. The people in the buggy didn't seem in a hurry.

"Wow!" River exclaimed pointing at the horse and buggy. He watched it with fascination until it disappeared down the road.

Once the light turned green, they continued until they crossed over the railroad tracks that cut through town. To Chenoa's left beyond the snow-laden crab apple trees lay the golf course, which now stretched out beneath a foot of snow. About 100 feet up the road a sign on the left side, read: CONGRESS LAKE CLUB-PRIVATE in big black letters. Victor turned into the entrance and stopped at the gate.

A security guard stood in a small guardhouse and opened the window. "May I help you?"

"The Reams are expecting us," Victor said. "We're the Gray Owls."

The security guard checked his rooster. "Okay," he said. "Have a nice day, folks." He pushed the button that swung the gate wide open, allowing the Gray Owls inside.

"Thank you," Victor said. He drove on. The road split off onto East and West Drives. As Victor turned right onto East Drive, they drove past the impressive Congress Lake Clubhouse. Its parking lot was full of cars.

"Look at that!" River exclaimed, pointing at the large, red brick building.

To their left stood the most beautiful homes they'd ever seen. They could have passed for small mansions that cost hundreds of thousands dollars to build. Congress Lake, a natural lake, bordered the backyards of all the residents. At the end of East Drive, the Ream's stately home came into view, proudly shrouded by trees. Big white pillars stood on the front porch and a Christmas wreath hung on the front door.

The family climbed out of the station wagon and walked up to the front door. Victor rang the doorbell as they waited to be let inside. Dr. Douglas Ream, dressed in jeans and a blue sweater, opened the door and greeted them with a friendly smile.

"Come in," Douglas said with a deep voice. Standing six feet, five inches tall, he weighed nearly 250 pounds and had a muscular build. His big biceps bulged beneath his blue sweater.

"Thank you, Doug," Victor said and shook Douglas' big hand. "Hello, Anna," Douglas said with a nod. "Chenoa, it's nice to see you again."

Chenoa forced a shy smile and said, "Hello, Dr. Ream." When she looked into his pale blue eyes, she could see kindness reflected in them.

As Douglas brushed at his small gray-flecked beard, he said, "Chenoa, you may call me Doug or Douglas. There is no need to be so formal among friends."

"If it's all right with you," Chenoa said politely. Turning to Anna, she asked, "Is it all right?" Anna nodded.

As they stepped into the foyer, Chenoa smelled a mixture of baked apples and cinnamon and she knew someone was making pies. Her mouth watered at the thought of sinking her teeth into a warm piece of pie with a generous dollop of whipped cream.

The sounds of Christmas music came from somewhere and put her in the Christmas spirit.

Douglas looked at them and smiled. "I'm happy you could make it for the holidays. I hope your stay will be a pleasant one. As he spoke, he kept running his fingers through his gray-flecked hair and squeezing the ends between his fingertips. Chenoa thought his hair was too long for a man of fifty-two.

Barbara Ream soon joined them. "Hello!" She hugged Anna and Victor. When she hugged Chenoa, she caught the scent of Moon Wind perfume that Barbara always wore. "Hello, Chenoa. It's so wonderful to see you again."

"It's nice to see you again, Mrs. Ream," Chenoa said, trying to sound cheerful. She didn't want Barbara to know how uncomfortable the hug made her. Chenoa didn't know her as well as Anna did.

Barbara smiled and Chenoa noticed she had a lopsided smile. It was a nice smile though for she had taken good care of her teeth. They were white and straight. "You may call me Barbara," she said. When she smiled, her dark blue eyes sparkled and became half moons.

"Okay."

Tamara, the Ream's daughter, a tall, slender, blonde-haired girl in tight jeans and a red cashmere sweater, bounded down the stairs with a big smile. She was the same age as Chenoa and had a shapely figure, which made Chenoa envious. Tamara gave Chenoa a big bear hug. "Hi, Chenoa! We have a lot of catching up to do."

"Yeah," Chenoa said, thought she wasn't in the mood to talk because she wanted to sit by herself.

They walked into the living room, which was as big as a cave and had lush blue carpeting. The room was furnished with an antique outfit that consisted of a sofa and three matching chairs. A glass-topped coffee table that set in front of the sofa had the Lord's Supper painted on the glass, and a big black Bible lie in the center. A fire blazed in the stone fireplace, it's embers sending snappy sparks up the chimney. In one corner stood, a real Christmas tree decorated with red velvet bows and icicles. On top of the tree set an angel, which seemed to watch over the home. Christmas cards from family and friends hung around the high archway leading out into the carpeted hall.

When they entered the room, a large black French poodle dashed in and barked at them. Chenoa wasn't afraid, but River nearly climbed up Victor's leg as if he were a tree.

Victor quickly picked up River and held him close. "I've got you, Son," he said, trying to make the boy feel safe.

"Bach, lie down!" Douglas ordered with a firm voice. Bach crept over to a small blue oval rug in front of the stone hearth and curled up on it, still keeping a watchful eye on them. "Sorry, Bach didn't mean to startle River. He's easily excitable."

"No harm done," Victor said.

Before Chenoa sat on the white plush sofa, she removed the blue brocade pillow, sat down and hugged it. It was an old habit and she hoped nobody noticed. She glanced up at the oil portrait of Douglas and Barbara above the mantel, and thought it gave the room added emotional warmth. On the mantel, decorated with holly leaves, set a row of photographs of the Reams four children.

Tamara sat next to Chenoa on the sofa and everyone else chose his or her own seats.

Barbara sat in an old fashioned rocking chair with a red cushion that seemed totally out of place among the beautiful furnishings. "I've made coffee and sandwiches," she said.

"Coffee's fine, Barbara," Anna said with a sigh. "We just had lunch."

"Nothing for me," Victor said politely declining her offer. "I'm still feeling a little jittery from all the coffee I drank while we were on the road."

"Okay. We'll have the sandwiches for dinner."

Tamara tugged on Chenoa's sweater and said quietly, "Come with me."

Chenoa followed Tamara up the stairs and down to the end of the hall. She opened a door on the left and as they stepped into the room, it was like stepping into a fairytale.

Oh brother, Chenoa thought.

It looked like someone had a pink fetish and splashed it all over everything, from the walls to the sheer curtains to the dust ruffle on the bed. Chenoa hated pink; blue was her favorite color. The antique dresser with the gold-framed mirror was much too dainty for her taste. Silly Raggedy Ann and Raggedy Andy pictures were above the make-up/desk combination. She cringed. The hideous pink fuzzy rug beside the four-poster bed with its pink canopy, made her furious and she wanted to push it under the bed.

"How do you like it?" Tamara asked.

Chenoa wasn't sure how to answer that question without offending her. "Uh…It's…Uh…" It was so sickly sweet Chenoa was speechless.

"Yeah!" Tamara grinned. "I hate it, too! I wouldn't let Mom decorate my room. Carissa Ann and I are as different as night and day."

"Come to my room and we can listen to my CDS," Tamara said.

Chenoa didn't get a chance to decline. Tamara grabbed the sleeve of her sweater and led her across the hallway to her bedroom. It was a blue room, with a single bed and a purple boom box at its head. She glanced at all the books in the small bookcase and saw several she'd read like "Little Women" and "Heidi". She didn't recognize some of the books by several of the young adult authors. In the upper right corner of the dresser mirror she saw a photograph of a Native boy and boy oh boy he was drop-dead gorgeous!

Wow! I'd sure love to meet him, she thought. Mmm! Boy!

"Who is that?" Chenoa asked pointing to the picture. She hoped she hadn't sounded too interested in case he was Tamara's boyfriend.

Tamara gazed fondly at the photo. "Dakotah Little Eagle. He's my neighbor. His father is some big shot attorney in Hartville. The Congress Lake committee held a vote and there was some questions about letting the family move in. I guess it had to do with the fact that he's Native American or something."

"Is he your boyfriend?"

Very subtle, Chenoa chided herself. I might as well ask: "Can I have him?"

"I wish!" Tamara exclaimed and her face flashed. "Can you keep a secret?" Chenoa nodded yes. "And you won't tell a living breathing soul?" Chenoa shook her head, no. Tamara shut the bedroom door. "I have a big crush on Dakotah, but he doesn't know I exist.

"Oh," Chenoa said. It was more of a statement than a question. Chenoa was curious, but not for long.

"Talk around Lake High School has it that he's about ready to break up with Janie Long, his girlfriend She is a horrible creature and doesn't deserve such a wonderful guy." Tamara looked at Chenoa and asked: "Do you have a boyfriend?

Chenoa felt the heat rise in her cheeks. "No, not really."

"Me neither. Nevertheless, I'm hoping and praying Dakotah will notice me. I'm keeping my fingers crossed."

Chenoa didn't respond to that because she didn't know what to say.

Tamara pulled a CD case out of the top dresser drawer and opened it. She took out a CD and put it in the boom box, pushed the play button, and the music started. "This is Janet Jackson's latest CD. Mom and Dad gave me five CD's for my birthday last Monday."

They listened to the CD for a few minutes, and then Tamara walked over to her computer hutch by the window and sat down. The desk was clean and orderly. A new Gateway computer and an Epson ink jet printer set on the right side of the desk.

"I'm going to check my e-mail messages," Tamara said, turning on her computer.

Chenoa was computer illiterate. The school on the rez couldn't afford computers. After a few minutes, she was forgotten. She went back into of the fairytale bedroom but it was too stuffy and boring. Grabbing her coat, she went outside for some fresh air.

The wind chilled Chenoa as she walked through the woodsy backyard. As she trudged through the deep snow, she thought how beautiful this place was, and then paused by a tall green pine tree to admire the snowy scene. Suddenly, she noticed a Native boy, who looked to be about seventeen years old, skating on the frozen lake. He glided with graceful ease across the ice. The wind blew through his long jet-black hair but he didn't seem to mind. His beautiful hair reached down to the middle of his back and it looked clean and well groomed.

Mmm, Chenoa thought with a wistful sigh.

The boy stopped when he realized he was being watched, and flashed her a big smile. He was a dark-eyed hunk and had a smile that would make an orthodontist jealous. Standing six feet, two inches he was taller than most Native boys around that age. For a moment, she felt their souls connect. Her heart pounded so hard she gasped to catch her breath. From the startled look in his dark, gentle eyes, he felt something too.

He glided toward shore and quickly came to a graceful stop. The blade of his skate dug into the ice, sending up a shower of ice chips. "Hi!" he said in a soft voice.

It was then she realized he was Dakotah Little Eagle, the boy in the photograph taped to Tamara's mirror. Chenoa turned to go, but Dakotah reached out and touched her arm. He didn't try to restrain her. "Don't go, please," he said. He looked unsure of himself, as if he didn't know what his next move should be. His large Adam's apple moved up and down so many times Chenoa thought he'd swallow it completely. "What's your name?" he practically whispered.

He was drop-dead gorgeous. That thought must have affected Chenoa's brain because it stopped functioning and nothing felt connected. She was struck dumb.

"Uh...I'm...Uh..." Chenoa stammered feeling awkward and for the second time this day; she was speechless. Her first instinct was to run, but her feet wouldn't obey her either. I must be retarded or something, she thought and finally managed to speak. "My name is Chenoa," she blurted out loudly.

He smiled. "I'm Dakotah Little Eagle."

She felt awkward. Her heart flip-flopped in her chest and her stomach hurt. She turned and ran back to the house, and felt stupid for doing it. Dakotah must have thought she was retarded for sure. She didn't understand what she was feeling or why she was feeling it.

She walked into the house by the back door; Anna was in the kitchen giving River a glass of water.

"Where did you go?" Anna asked.

"Just out," Chenoa answered and her own voice sounded strange to her. Anna looked at Chenoa strangely and shooed River out of the kitchen. "Just out," she repeated.

"Well, if you go out don't wander too far away."

"Okay." Chenoa felt shaky over her meeting Dakotah Little Eagle and she hoped it didn't show. She didn't want to explain her feeling to Anna.

Anna put a comforting arm around Chenoa. "Are you sure everything's all right? Did anyone try to hurt you?"

"No. I'm just tired and I want to rest."

"Okay," Anna said, giving Chenoa a kiss on her temple, "you go ahead and rest and we'll talk later."

"All right." Chenoa was relieved Anna didn't press the subject. She walked up to her room and stayed there until suppertime. Afterward she went back to her room.

Chenoa decided to write a letter to her friend Erica. As she lie across the bed, she poured out her thoughts and feelings.

Dear Erica,

Hi! I wanted to write and let you know we made it to Ohio safely. I wish I were back in Whiteriver. I really miss you. The one great thing about this visit, I know I'll be returning to the rez.

Congress Lake is beautiful. I bet the fishing is great in the summer. My grandfather loves to fish. I'm sure he'd catch a basketful.

I had something weird happen today and I don't know where to start. I met a Native boy that set something within me stirring, something I've never felt before. I've never really analyzed my feelings for any boy, not even Paul Alchesay. I don't feel any emotional attachment toward him and I've known him all my life. However, what I felt when I met Dakotah Little Eagle, I really don't understand and I'd only known him a few minutes. Erica, when I looked into those dark, dreamy eyes, I felt our souls connect. I'm confused as to what that means. I'm clueless."

I'd like to get to know Dakotah better before I go back. Tamara says he has a girlfriend but they're about to break up. When they do; Tamara wants to get together with him.

How can I be interested in two boys at the same time? Granted, my interest in Paul is only mild. Sometime-I'd like to fall in love, but I don't know much about love.

Mom and I haven't really talked about the subject of boys or dating. Mom and I are as close as two people can be, but I break out in a cold sweat when I think about this stuff. I guess I'm just being silly.

I know, Erica, you must be shaking your head by now and thinking. I've finally lost it!" However, you know me. We've talked about this stuff. Sometimes I wonder and try to figure it out but I drive myself crazy. I guess I'd better stop it.

It's getting late, Erica, so I'll close and get this in the mail tomorrow. I'll see you after the New Year.

Your friend, Chenoa

CHAPTER 9

Friday, December 21, 2001
Dear Diary,

I don't know what's on the agenda today, but it can't be any worse than hanging out in this bedroom or listening to grown ups rehashing old times. Tamara is glued to her computer screen and she's not very good company. If I sit here and think about Dakotah, I'll feel guilty about it because Tamara's interested in him. Nevertheless, he so darn cute.

Chenoa closed her diary and laid it beside her on the window seat. What would happen if I start liking Dakotah the way Tamara does? she thought. What if we become friends and we fight over him? She mentally shook the questions from her brain. Get a grip, Chenoa Fawn Gray Owl, she chided herself.

Chenoa looked out the window and sighed. She could see the lake and it looked gray as it reflected the overcast sky. The morning sun tried to peek through the low, thick snow clouds, but it had a hard time. The surrounding area was beautiful with a deep snow blanketing the ground as far as the eye could see. A cold wind blew against frosted windows.

River burst into the room and grabbed Chenoa's hand. "Can we go out and play in the snow?" he pleaded.

"Okay. Let's get our coats." Chenoa didn't really want to go outside, but she didn't want to stay inside either. She took him by the hand and led him down the stairs to the hall closet. Anna and Barbara were sitting in the living room talking. They heard Chenoa and River laughing, looked up and smiled.

"Hello, Honey," Anna said with a smile. "What are you two going to do?"

"We're going outside," Chenoa answered.

"I want to play in the snow!" River squealed.

"All right," Anna said. "Make sure River keeps his mittens on."

"Okay."

"We're going to the mall later," Barbara said. "We can look around and you may pick out something you'd like for Christmas."

"Oh!" Chenoa looked surprised. She looked at Anna; Anna smiled and nodded. "Anything?"

"Anything," Barbara promised.

River tugged on Chenoa hand. "I want to go out!"

Chenoa reached into the hall closet and got their coats. They bundled up and went out the backdoor.

The air was crisp and a light wind blew as they strolled toward the lake. Bach romped playfully in the snow. Reaching down Chenoa scratched his ears, "Good boy," she said. He sniffed her hand as if he wanted to be friendly. "Come on," Chenoa coaxed. Bach nuzzled her hand with his cold, wet muzzle and then licked it.

River patted the poodle on the head. "Good doggie," he said.

Bach sniffed River's hand, suddenly lost interest, and scampered off toward the front of the house.

They continued their walk to the lake. Chenoa glanced about, but didn't see Dakotah ice-skating. She half wished he'd be there, yet, she was relieved that he wasn't. She stood by the tall pine tree and looked out over the lake wondering if it was as beautiful in the summer as it was now.

She felt someone's hand on her shoulder and she looked around with a start. Dakotah Little Eagle smiled down at her. "Hi!"

"Hi!" Chenoa said. Her heart quickened as she stared up into his dark, dreamy eyes.

"Where are you from?"

"I'm from the White Mountain Apache Indian Rez in Arizona. I live in Whiteriver."

"Oh! You look like Maggie Gray Owl. She lives beside my grandparents in Kill Buck, New York."

"Maggie Gray Owl is my paternal grandmother. You see, we're visiting the Reams. My mother and the Reams are old friends." Chenoa hadn't intended on giving him that much information, but for some reason she kept babbling. It was embarrassing.

"The Reams are nice people. My sister Mary is about your age. I know she'd really like to meet you."

Chenoa didn't know what to say. She kicked at the snow with the toe of her shoe.

"Since you're staying with the Reams, will you be coming to the Christmas Eve program on Tuesday? I'm singing several solos," he said, with a gentle smile.

"Yes," Chenoa said hoping for a chance to get to know him better. It would be interesting to hear his voice when he sang.

"Good, I'll be looking forward to seeing you in church." His dark eyes seemed to dance as he spoke to her.

"Chenoa!" Anna called from the house. "River! Lunch is ready!"

"I have to go," Chenoa said, hating the thought of leaving Dakotah.

"Okay! Bye!"

"Bye!" she said. They had started walking back to the house when Chenoa said to River, "I'll race you."

"Okay!" River exclaimed. He liked it when she made everything a game.

"Go!" she said playfully and gave him a little push.

River raced ahead of Chenoa as fast as his little legs could go. She let him have a good lead then ran after him. Before they got to the back of the house, she scooped him up into her arms and he howled with laughter.

"You win!" Chenoa also laughed.

After lunch, Anna, River, Tamara and Chenoa climbed into Barbara's big blue Thunderbird and she drove them to Belden Village Mall in Canton. It was crowded with holiday shoppers. They went into Walden's Bookstore where Chenoa saw journals on display. One of the journals that caught her eye had a summery scene with fluffy white clouds.

Barbara put her arm around Chenoa's shoulder and asked, "Would you like the journal?"

Chenoa really wanted it, but it was pricey. "But it costs so much."

90

"It's all right," Barbara whispered in her ear. "After all it's Christmas and I want to get you something special." She gave Chenoa's shoulders a gentle squeeze.

"Okay," Chenoa said, feeling guilty over her decision.

They shopped a little more, and then decided to eat an early dinner. When they arrived at the food court, it was crowded with holiday shoppers who were also hungry. Several mini restaurants made up the food court: McDonalds and Taco Bell to name a few. A small pizza shop stood at the end of the line and the smells of hamburgers and pizza mingled together.

"What would you girls like to eat?" Barbara asked shouting to be heard over the many voices.

"Pizza!" Tamara and Chenoa said simultaneously.

"What would you like to drink?" Barbara asked.

"Dr. Pepper!" Chenoa said.

"Diet Coke!" Tamara said.

"Shimaa," River said, "can I have fries or onion rings."

"We'll see," Anna said, picking River up and kissing his check. He moved his knee and her blue skirt bunched up baring her thighs. She pulled her skirt down without making a fuss. Her blue flowered blouse was tucked neatly into the top of her skirt. When she looked at River, her dark eyes sparkled and danced and it was evident how much she adored him.

"We'll go order the food," Barbara said." You girls can find us seats."

Barbara and Anna walked off with River while Tamara and Chenoa looked for seats. As they walked toward the tables many voices and children's laughter greeted them. Finding a seat for five people wasn't easy but they did manage to find an empty table. Under the burden of their shopping bags, they shuffled over to the empty table in the center of the court and sat down.

"I'd love to get a Christmas present for Dakotah," Tamara said. "I don't know what to get him and I don't have the nerve to ask his sister."

"I've met him several times."

Tamara's mouth formed a perfect "Oh. Where?"

"By the lake." Chenoa didn't want to sound too interested and make her jealous. "The first time was yesterday, he was ice skating. The second time was today just before lunch.

"What do you think about him? Isn't he a fantastic hunk?"

Chenoa thought Tamara was trying to bait her for a reaction, but she wasn't falling into her trap. "I guess," she answered once again trying not to sound too interested.

"Well, duh!" Tamara sputtered. "He's not exactly the Hunchback of Notre Dame! He's so gorgeous I could...I could...Well..." She sighed wistfully. "He's mine. Once he dumps the Wicked Witch of the West I'm moving in."

What did she mean by "moving in"? Chenoa didn't think Tamara was his type.

"Before I became interested in Dakotah," Tamara continued, "I had a crush on Mr. Parker, my eighth grade English teacher. He was a real doll. He had us read poems for several weeks then asked us to write some of our own. I was a real idiot and wrote one about Mr. Parker."

"What happened?" Chenoa asked. Chenoa was interested in knowing what kind of if she got into trouble.

"Mr. Parker called my parents in and talked to them," Tamara answered and her cheeks turned a nice shade of pink." My parents sat down with me and told me nice girls don't go after married men or write poems like that."

"What happened after that?"

Tamara made a face and turned a deeper shade of pink. "They made me apologize. I hated that. When I got a crush on Dakotah I decided I'd find a better way to tell him than poetry. Maybe I'll pretend I'm interested in something he likes and he'll fall in love with me."

Oh brother, Chenoa thought. How shallow can she be?

"Hey, look at what I found in Walden's Bookstore," Tamara said changing the subject and lifting one of the bags off the floor. She pulled out several books on the field of nursing and leafed through them. "I'm trying to choose a career. It's a toss up between teaching and nursing. You know Mom and my sister Carissa Ann are teachers, but I'm more interested in nursing."

"I'm going to college after I graduate," Chenoa said. "I want to be a teacher like my Anna. She's the only one in her family to go to college."

"Really?"

"Yeah," Chenoa nodded. "She received a grant and attended the college in Phoenix."

"I want to be a pediatric nurse. There are enough teachers in the family."

They changed the subject and talked about boys again. Chenoa listened to Tamara plot and plan how to get Dakotah to notice her. When their mothers returned with the food, they dropped the subject.

CHAPTER 10

Friday, December 21, 2001
Dear Diary,

Why do I sit here thinking about Dakotah Little Eagle when I know Tamara Ream is interested in him? I can't seem to get him out of my mind and it's making me crazy. I don't know him but from the conversation I had with Tamara, I'm beginning to get to know him. However, I'd rather talk to him and get to know him that way. Tamara doesn't know everything...not deep in his soul.

Chenoa glanced out the window and looked toward the lake hoping she could catch a glimpse of Dakotah. She didn't see him out on the lake.

Tamara burst noisily into the room and grabbed Chenoa's arm. "Come with me!" she said with breathless excitement. Chenoa had no choice but to follow her into the room. She pointed to the glowing computer screen, "Look!" she exclaimed, "I was searching for information on the Seneca Indians and I found all kinds of information on them. Wow! I can't believe it! I've printed a lot of information and I plan on reading every bit of it." Her printer was still humming. "I want to learn all I can about the Seneca Indians before Dakotah asks me out."

Oh brother, Chenoa thought.

"You need to go to the rez and live there a couple years," Chenoa said, firmly believing it. If Tamara thought she could read something about Indians, and that it would make her an expert, she was badly mistaken.

Tamara blinked. "Huh?"

"If you're serious about getting to know about Natives, you need to go live with them, like your parents did. Even then you might not learn everything."

Chenoa didn't know why she was telling Tamara all this. If Tamara thought any computer printout would work, she was in for a rude awakening.

Tamara looked at Chenoa as if she were green with white polka dots. "Wow!" she exclaimed disbelievingly. "I mean this material is just a start... well; maybe I can get my mom and dad's permission to spend the summer on the reservation. Are you really sure?" Chenoa nodded, once again. "Thanks, I think."

"Yeah," Chenoa said and walked out of the room.

Anna met her in the hallway. "Honey, you have a phone call from some young boy who said his name is Dakotah Little Eagle. I don't know who he is but he sounds nice."

"Dakotah's the Reams neighbor."

"Yes, that's what he said on the telephone. If it's important don't keep him waiting."

Chenoa hurried to the telephone. "Hello?" she said into the receiver. Chenoa could hardly breathe; her heart was pounding so hard.

"Hi, Chenoa," Dakotah said his voice full of cheer. "This is Dakotah. My sister Mary wants to meet you. Are you free to come over? If your parents say, no, we'll understand."

"I'll ask," Chenoa said. "Hold on." She held her hand over the receiver and told her parents what Dakotah said. "Can I go over to Dakotah's home?"

"May I?" Victor corrected.

"May I? Please?" Chenoa wanted so much to get their permission that she nearly held her breath.

"Who's Dakotah?" Victor asked.

"Dakotah Little Eagle is a very nice boy," Douglas said. "He and his family are good Christians."

"Yes," Barbara said from her rocker. "The whole family is active in church. Dakotah often plays the guitar during the service and sings songs."

"As a matter of fact Jeffery Little Eagle is from your hometown, Victor," Douglas said.

Victor's eyebrows arched up. "Really? I went to school with Jeffery. I haven't talked to him in years."

Chenoa sighed. "Dad, may I go?"

"Yes! Yes!" Victor nodded. "You may go, but be back by nine o'clock."

"Thanks!" she said, happily. Chenoa spoke to Dakotah again and told him she was allowed to go to his home.

"Great! I'll come get you. Bye!"

"Bye!" Going to the hall closet, Chenoa took out her coat and waited for Dakotah.

Within several minutes, a car pulled into the driveway and Chenoa heard the door bang shut. She held her breath until the doorbell rang.

"I'd like to meet this young man," Victor said. He followed Douglas and Chenoa toward the door.

Douglas opened the door and Dakotah looked surprised to see three people standing in the foyer. "Come on in," he said.

"Thank you," Dakotah answered.

"Dakotah," Chenoa said, "this is my father Victor Gray Owl."

"Hello!" Dakotah said, shaking Victor's hand. "I know your mother quite well. I'm from Kill Buck."

"So, I've been told," Victor said. "I went to school with your father."

Chenoa tugged on Victor's sweater. "Dad," she said, "nine o'clock will be here before you know it."

"Oh! Right!" Victor moved aside. "Have fun, Chenoa!"

Dakotah and Chenoa climbed into his yellow `94 Chevy Nova. A faint pine smell came from the air freshener hanging on the rearview mirror. When they got to his home, he invited her in. She walked into the Little Eagle's home, heard Native music playing from the stereo in the corner of the living room, and recognized Carlos Nakai's voice. The house was furnished with plush, white sofa and three matching chairs. A coffee table set in front of the sofa and a big white family Bible lie in the center. Next to, it set a clay pot with Native designs. On the walls hung several pictures of Native pottery and various Southwestern designs. In addition, a large, Native American dream catcher hung on the wall. Spread out on the floor in front of the stone hearth; lay a homemade rug with a blue thunderbird.

Mrs. Little Eagle, a small, thin woman with short, black hair met Chenoa in the living room. She had dark eyes that sparkled. "Hello," she said with a smile. "You're welcome in our home any time."

Chenoa smiled. "Thank you."

Mr. Little Eagle said, "Would you care for some eggnog, Chenoa?"

Chenoa nodded. "Yes, please."

"I'll be right back." Mrs. Little Eagle left the room.

"Where's Mary?" Dakotah asked.

Mr. Little Eagle walked to the hearth and bent over to pick up a small log. "Mary will be down in a minute, Son," he said, placing the log in the fire. He straightened up and was almost as tall as his son. His lanky frame filled out his red cardigan sweater and dungarees with no room to spare.

"Did I hear my name mentioned?" Mary asked from the doorway. Her voice was as gentle as her mother's was. She was as beautiful as an angel and smiled as she walked into the room. Her cheeks were dimpled and her dark eyes danced with pleasure. High cheekbones reflected her proud Indian heritage and beauty. She wore blue sweat pants and a yellow sweater with an Indian maiden on it. A white scarf kept her long black hair pulled back away from her face.

"Mary," Dakotah made the introductions, "this is Chenoa Gray Owl. Chenoa, this is my sister Mary."

"It's nice to meet you," Mary said, her dark eyes reflecting her happy nature.

"Hi!" Chenoa didn't know what else to say.

"So, tell us about yourself," Mr. Little Eagle said taking a seat in the big easy chair.

Chenoa told them where she was from and about her family. She also informed Mr. Little Eagle that he and her father had gone to school together. By then, Mrs. Little Eagle returned with four glasses of eggnog on a silver platter.

"What grade are you in?" Mr. Little Eagle asked.

"I'm a freshman," Chenoa answered, accepting the glass of eggnog his wife offered.

"Really?" Mr. Little Eagle said. "What courses are you studying?"

"Mostly English, history and a few others. I don't really like history."

"Most people don't, except for me because I liked the subject."

"Me, too!" Mary said.

"I think after I graduate I'd like to become a teacher like my mother, and work on the rez."

"That's interesting." Mr. Little Eagle nodded.

"Do you like to read?" Mary asked. "I do."

"Yeah," Chenoa answered, "but I also like to write in a diary. It helps me figure out my problems."

Mary made a face. "Oh, I tried to write in a diary but I never keep it going. It takes too much discipline," she added with a dismissive gesture.

Chenoa shrugged. "I kind of enjoy it."

"It's all right," Mrs. Little Eagle said. "Journaling isn't for everyone."

"I keep a journal," Dakotah confessed. "It helps me stay focused on life, my relationships with others' needs and most by all my relationship with God."

Chenoa wondered what kind of stuff Dakotah wrote in his journal and how he stayed focused. "I don't know any boys who write in a journal."

Dakotah smiled. "Journal writing isn't exclusively for girls. I just try to stay sensitive to others need and to be used by God; He directs our steps and we have to be willing to listen."

Chenoa realized how sensitive Dakotah really was and her heart went out to him. She wished she wouldn't feel so drawn to him, but she couldn't help herself.

Why does he have to be so irresistible? she thought. Would I be drawn to him if he were ugly and fat? Nevertheless, he's not and I can't think that way about him.

"Chenoa," Mrs. Little Eagle said, "I'd like to invite you to dinner tomorrow night, would you please come?"

"I would have to ask my parents, and then let you know."

"Good, we'll plan on it." Mrs. Little Eagle glanced at her watch and changed the subject. "Dakotah, have you picked up your paycheck at Giant Eagle yet?"

"Oh! No, I haven't!" Dakotah stood up and looked at Mary and Chenoa. "Would you girls like to go along?"

"Sure!" the girls said simultaneously.

Chenoa put on her coat. She was glad he invited them to go along. She hoped she'd get to sit beside him and…Stop it; she chided herself. You're being silly.

They walked out to the car and piled into the front seat. Chenoa got her wish and got to sit in the middle, almost tight against Dakotah.

This is cozy, she thought.

As Dakotah started the car, Mary leaned forward and looked at him. "Is Janie coming to hear you sing Christmas Eve?"

Dakotah shrugged. "I don't know."

"Did you ask her?"

"Yeah," he said in a quiet voice. Chenoa didn't think he wanted to talk about it.

Mary sat back. "She likes to mess with his mind. She's wenoih!" Mary used the Seneca word for crazy and made the crazy motion with her finger. Chenoa heard her Aunt Lisa use that word often. "She doesn't understand Dakotah because she's not a Christian and I don't think she's right for him."

"It's not that she doesn't…" he began.

"Don't defend her. You should consider what she's been doing lately."

"What did she do?" Chenoa asked. She didn't want them to think she was trying to be nosy, but she liked Dakotah and it would help her understand him.

Dakotah was quiet for a minute. "She's really changed in the last two months. I'm not sure why, but lately she's like Dr. Jekyll and Mr. Hyde. She doesn't trust me as she used to do."

Chenoa heard the hurt in his voice and she felt his pain. "Isn't there any other girl you'd rather be with?" She was fishing for information and hoped it wasn't obvious to him.

"No, not really," he responded. "I mean...well... Hmm!"

Mary nudged Chenoa. "He does that when he's put on the spot. Good one, Chenoa." She giggled behind her hand.

"No, my little sister, it isn't what you think. I don't want to say anything because I don't know much about this girl. Until I do I'm keeping a lid on it."

"My curiosity burns within me," Mary said.

So does mine, Chenoa thought.

"Your curiosity will be charred black in no time," Dakotah said. He pulled the car into the Giant Eagle parking lot and easily found a space. As he put the car into park, he added, "I don't know how long this will take so you girls better come inside."

As they walked toward the building, She trudged through the parking lot feeling as if a ball and chain dragged her down. She wished she'd never asked that last question; it would have been better not knowing if Dakotah was interested in someone else.

Mary and Chenoa stood inside the front of the store, and Dakotah disappeared into the office.

"What does Dakotah do here?" Chenoa asked.

"He bags groceries, and sometimes he runs one of the registers."

"Oh."

Chenoa wondered if Mary really knew her brother the way she let on. She was dying to ask her if she had any inkling if, he was interested in any other girl. Maybe he let a name slip out in casual conversation, then again; maybe Dakotah didn't discuss his feelings for a girl with his sister.

Cut it out, Chenoa chided herself. Don't get bent out of shape over a boy you barely know. Just stop it right now!

Five minutes passed before Dakotah came out. When he did a red haired girl walked up to him and handed him a card. After exchanging a few words with her, he headed their way.

Is it her? Chenoa thought. Stop it, for Pete's sake!

By the time he got to them, half a dozen girls had wished him Merry Christmas. Chenoa wondered if Dakotah had feelings for any of those young girls.

As they headed toward the door, a tall, good-looking white boy about seventeen came in from outside. He spotted them and smiled broadly.

"Hey, Greg!" Dakotah exclaimed happily and clapped him on the shoulder. "Are you working tonight?"

"No, I'm just picking up my check."

"Me, too! Hey, you remember my sister, and this is Chenoa Gray Owl. Her family is visiting for the holidays."

Greg's green eyes reflected his friendly nature. "Hi!" he said, then asked, "Are you a cousin of Dakotah's?"

Chenoa shook her head, no. "I'm here with my family for the holidays. We're staying with the Reams."

"Cool!" Greg exclaimed. "I've got to run. See you guys in church tomorrow night. Right?"

"You bet!" Dakotah grinned. "See you!"

"A good friend of yours?" Chenoa asked, as they walked out the door.

"Yes! Greg Martin and I have been close friends since my family and I moved here four years ago."

They were silent on the way home. When Dakotah pulled into the Ream's driveway, it was nearly eight-fifty.

As Chenoa climbed out of the car, she said, "Thanks for the ride."

Dakotah smiled. "You're welcome."

"I'm looking forward to you joining my family for dinner tomorrow night."

"Yeah, me too. Bye!"

"Bye!" Dakotah and Mary said simultaneously.

When Chenoa walked in the front door, her parents were sitting in the room with the Reams.

"How was your little visit?" Anna asked from the sofa.

"All right," Chenoa said. "Mrs. Little Eagle said if it's all right with you and Dad I could go to their house for dinner tomorrow."

"It's all right with us."

"Thanks," Chenoa went up to her room and got ready for bed. After she got in bed, Anna came in and sat on the bed.

"Your father and Douglas talked today about the possibility of him working in the clinic. Douglas has said he'd take your dad into the practice and said he can start February 1. It looks like we'll be busy for a while getting ready to move."

When Anna left the room Chenoa grabbed her diary scribbled this words:

Life sucks! I'm doomed! I don't want to leave my home on the rez. However, I'd give it all up, if that meant I could be close to Dakotah. He's so sweet and I'd love being near him 24-7.

CHAPTER 11

Saturday, December 22, 2001
Dear Diary,
Last night's news has left me feeling numb and all day I've felt like the earth is going to open up and swallow me. How can I leave the rez? God didn't keep His part of the bargain and I don't feel like I can trust Him. How can I trust God when he doesn't listen to me when I talk to him?

Chenoa sighed and glanced out the window. From on the window seat, she could look down at the frozen lake. It had been overcast all day. The lake looked sad, like her. At four o'clock in the afternoon, she had no energy for anything. Dakotah would be coming to get her in an hour and she would have to get ready.

I wonder if Dakotah and his family would be offended if I showed up in jeans and a sweatshirt. she thought.

Chenoa went to the bathroom and took a quick shower. She brushed her hair thinking about Dakotah, and wondering if he thought about her and, if he thought she was pretty. What would happen if they moved to Ohio and he asked her to go out on a date? He'd have to break up with his girlfriend first, but what if...

At five o'clock Chenoa was finally ready. She stepped out of the room and nearly bumped into Tamara coming out of her bedroom.

"I hear you'll be moving to Hartville now that my dad has agreed to take your father into the practice," Tamara said, her blue eyes haunted by some inner anxiety that matched the tone of her voice. "I think it was nice that my father did that and we can be friends."

"Yeah!" Chenoa said. She didn't know what to make of Tamara's statement because she seemed worried about something.

"Are you interested in Dakotah?" Tamara questioned.

"Just as a friend." Chenoa knew in her heart that wasn't true. She was interested all right, but she didn't know how he felt about her. "His sister Mary is nice and I'm hoping we can become friends."

"Oh," Tamara said with a nod and walked away.

What's with her? Chenoa thought as she walked down the hall toward the bathroom. I wonder if she could be jealous of me.

The doorbell rang downstairs. Chenoa ran down to the living room in time to see Douglas let Dakotah into the house.

Dakotah smiled and nodded. "Hi, are you ready to go?

"Yes." Chenoa got her coat out of the hall closet and Dakotah held it up as she slipped her arm into the left sleeve and then her other arm. She said good-bye to the grown ups in the living room and walked out to Dakotah's car.

"I hope you like Indian tacos and corn soup," Dakotah said as he opened the car door for Chenoa."

"Mmm! Yummy!" Chenoa said, her mouth almost watering.

As Dakotah ran around the front of the car, Chenoa noticed in an upstairs window, Tamara looking down at them, motionless as a statue. She put Tamara out of her mind as they drove away.

When they arrived at Dakotah's house, his mother took her coat and hung it in the hall closet. "Dinner will be served in five minutes."

Mrs. Little Eagle was very punctual and served dinner within five minutes. Before anyone ate, Mr. Little Eagle asked a blessing for the dinner. The meal was delicious and Chenoa ate her fill.

Mary took Chenoa to her bedroom and they became better acquainted. She showed Chenoa her collection of stickers.

As they looked through the first of three books, Mary pointed to one and said, "This is my favorite." It had a smiling sun with the words: "Be happy."

"It's nice. Whenever I see the sun it makes me happy."

"When I see the sun, it reminds me of God. If you have the love of God in your heart all your days are bright."

"Yeah." Chenoa pointed to the eagle sticker and changed the subject. "What's the story about this one?"

"It's kind of like our family crest. It's a little eagle. Do you collect anything, Chenoa?"

Chenoa shook her head. "No, I don't, but I like to read."

"So do I. It's always fun to see someone else's adventures. I'd be interested in hearing about your adventures in Arizona. I've never been there."

"I rode my grandfather's pony. I like to ride out to the meadow, especially in the summer when it is in bloom. I can't see the green grass because of the scarlet and yellow flowers. I sometimes lie under a tree and daydream about falling in love."

Mary perked up and smiled. "Do you have a boyfriend?"

"No." Chenoa wished she did have a boyfriend so drop-dead gorgeous that she didn't have to think about Dakotah. "There is a boy that's interested in me, but we're just friends."

"Mmm, just friends?" Chenoa nodded. "I have a crush on Mike Webster. He has the dreamiest blue eyes and cute dimples when he smiles."

"Really?" Chenoa wondered why she would think about a white boy that way. Perhaps there wasn't a large Indian population in Hartville.

They continued looking at Mary's sticker collection and she was able to explain how she got them. After a while, Chenoa went to use the bathroom. On her way, she heard guitar music. She followed the music to a room where she found Dakotah strumming away. Chenoa stood watching for several minutes before he looked up at her. He smiled and his face brightened.

"Come on in," he invited, laying his guitar beside him on the bed. He opened the door wider and let Chenoa in.

As she stepped into his room, she was amazed how neat it was. She always thought boys were messy housekeepers but everything looked nice and orderly, even his desk that held his computer was clutter-free. She noticed a clock on the wall that didn't have any hands on it.

"That's interesting," Chenoa said pointing to the clock.

"It's for Indian time. My grandfather made it for me."

"Oh!"

Chenoa noticed his CD collection in a large CD rack that would have held a couple hundred. "What kind of music do you have?" Chenoa asked pointing to the collection of CDS.

"Mostly gospel," he said, walking over to the rack, "but I also collect Native American music." He pointed to the second shelf. "I have 50 or 60 CD's. I send away for them or I buy them in the stores."

"Wow!" Chenoa was amazed at the size of the collection and impressed that he stayed in touch with his Indian culture. "Have you listened to all of them?"

Dakotah nodded. "Yeah, I've listened to them all. Would you care to hear them?"

"Yeah!"

Dakotah turned on the stereo that set on a wooden stand in the corner. He slid the CD in and they listened to a mixture of beating drums, flutes and chanting voices. They listened to the whole CD and then he replaced it with another one.

Chenoa settled down in a comfortable armchair and listened to the music. Before she realized it, they had listened to four CD's. Chenoa wanted to listen to more but it was getting close to nine o'clock and she had to go back to the Reams' home.

"I'll take you home," Dakotah offered. "It's a cold night and wouldn't want you to get sick."

"Thanks." Chenoa followed Dakotah downstairs and into the living room. Mr. Little Eagle was reading the newspaper and his wife sat on the sofa heading a book. Mary was also reading a book in a chair.

Mrs. Little Eagle looked up and smiled. "Are you leaving already?"

"Yes. I wanted to thank you for the dinner, it was very good."

"You're welcome, dear. I'm glad you enjoyed it. Now, you know you're welcome over anytime."

"Thank you."

Mrs. Little Eagle got Chenoa's coat out of the hall closet and hugged her. "Good-bye."

"Bye." Chenoa followed Dakotah out to his Nova and they got in. After they were sitting in the Reams' driveway she said, "I enjoyed listening to your CD's. I like the music but it kind of makes me homesick for the rez."

"I know what you mean," Dakotah said, with a nod.

"Thanks for the ride home." Chenoa got out of the car and went inside. She was glad she didn't meet anyone as she walked to her room because she wanted to write in her diary. Chenoa flopped on the bed and penned these words on the pink pages:

How many times have I wondered if Dakotah likes me? I mean we just met two days ago and I feel... Ugh! I can't explain the feelings that are battling within me. Does Dakotah find me attractive? Is there a chance for us to be together? If there were no one special in his life, would he like me?

Wouldn't it be great if I had a magic crystal ball that held all the answers? Think of the time that would save if I did. But I don't have all the answers and, truthfully speaking, not knowing makes being in love that much more exciting.

CHAPTER 12

Monday, December 24, 2001
Dear Diary,

I've never looked forward to attending a church service before but tonight is different. I want to listen to Dakotah sing because he has a beautiful voice and it just makes me swoon.

I wonder if he notices me the way I notice him.

Chenoa's train of thought was interrupted when Anna came to the door and said, "Honey, we're ready for church. Hurry along now as Dad and River are waiting in the car." She was dressed in a white dress that had a wide black sash around the middle.

"Okay." Chenoa slipped her stocking feet into her good loafers. She bolted out the door and down the stairs. Since she was the last one out, she slammed the front door shut making sure it was securely latched.

She climbed into the family station wagon and told Victor, "All right, let's go!" Down the road, they went to meet the Reams at their church. The Church of the Brethren looked nice and cozy there in the woods beneath a couple of towering alders.

Barbara greeted them at the door and introduced them to Pastor Charles Heritage, a stout, balding man with friendly green eyes. He sported a gracious a smile.

Thrusting out his hand he said, "Hello!" and shook Victor and Anna's hands. "Welcome to our little church in the woods. I'm so happy you could be with us."

As Chenoa walked toward the coat rack filled with coats, she saw Tamara hanging up her coat.

"Hi there, Tamara," Chenoa called out just as she felt a hand settle on her shoulder. It was Dakotah.

"Chenoa, how would you like to sit with me and my family?" Chenoa could see by the look in his dark, dreamy eyes that he wanted her to say, yes.

Mary walked up about then and almost pleading said, "Please, say yes, Chenoa."

"I don't know if..." Chenoa sensed Tamara watching her with a critical eye. She threw caution to the wind and blurted out, "Wait right here, I'll go ask my parents."

Chenoa found her parents standing near the sanctuary doors conversing with the Reams. Without waiting or thinking she butted in and asked, "Can I sit with Dakotah and Mary Little Eagle? Please?"

"May I?" Victor corrected.

"May I?" Chenoa retorted.

"Yes," Victor said, "but behave yourself and act like a lady."

"Thanks! I will." Chenoa smiled, turned and walked toward Dakotah and Mary, grinning like a little kid with a penny in a candy store. "My dad said it's okay."

Dakotah smiled. "Good!"

"I want to hang up my coat." Chenoa turned and headed for the coat rack. As she slipped her coat on the hanger, Tamara touched her arm.

"Are you interested in being friends with Dakotah?" Tamara asked, her voice edged with tension and her mouth formed into a tense line.

Chenoa had no idea where she was going with this line of questioning or why. She didn't know why Tamara looked so uptight, but it showed because she continued to chew on her bottom lip. If she kept it up much longer, her lip was going to turn into mush.

"Yeah," Chenoa finally answered.

As Tamara stared at Chenoa with a fixed look, a look of confusion flickered in her eyes. "I wouldn't get involved with him if I were you. Janie won't like it if a girl comes between her and Dakotah. She doesn't like anyone that weasels in on what she considers her private territory."

"Huh?" Chenoa was thoroughly confused. She didn't know whether Tamara was talking about Janie Long or herself.

"Janie isn't right for Dakotah," Tamara continued choosing her words carefully. "She doesn't know how to treat him. I've been as close as I dare in the last four years and I've gotten to know him pretty darn well. I know what he needs. I don't think you're his type, either."

I'm not his type, Chenoa thought. As far as I am concerned, I'm more in tune with his emotions and feelings than she could possibly think. I don't care if she knew him for twenty years, that doesn't mean she knows Dakotah. Just what did they talk about anyway? Mostly trite things! Huh, not his type!

"Hey, Chenoa," Dakotah called out as he walked up with Greg Martin. "Greg's going to sit with us, too."

Chenoa saw Tamara look at Dakotah, she sighed as if she wished she could join them. Her bottom lip trembled when Dakotah didn't include her and he led Chenoa away.

As the small group walked into the sanctuary, Dakotah, Mary, Greg and Chenoa found seats in the fourth row and they sat together. With a little luck, Chenoa managed to get the seat next to Dakotah. She wasn't in the sanctuary. She wasn't in the church. She was in her own little bit of heaven.

Mary leaned forward, looked at her brother and stated, "Janie didn't come."

Dakotah just shrugged and said in a flat tone; "Guess not." If Janie's absence bothered him, he didn't show it.

After the congregation had been seated, the Pastor opened the service with prayer and then turned the proceedings over to the choir. They opened their part with "Away in a Manger" followed by three other songs. Then came the moment Chenoa had been waiting for as Dakotah picked up his guitar, went to the front and sang two songs; "The Little Drummer Boy" and concluded with "What Child is This?" in the Seneca language.

Chenoa understood some of the words because her Aunt Lisa was teaching her the Seneca language. Several times during his singing their eyes met and all Chenoa could do was sigh.

After the service had ended, Dakotah invited Greg and Chenoa over to his house for a visit. Mrs. Little Eagle served eggnog and Dakotah played Christmas songs on his guitar while they all sang. Greg and

Dakotah harmonized on a couple of their favorite songs as the others listened, enthralled.

After the singing was over Dakotah placed the guitar in its case and walked back to his seat.

Greg set his empty cup on the stand and stood up. "I have to leave. Mrs. Little Eagle, thank you for the eggnog. It was good."

"You're welcome, Greg," Mrs. Little Eagle said. "Do drop by when you can."

"Okay. Bye!" Greg left the house.

Dakotah glanced at his watch and noted the time. "I'd better get you back to the Reams house," he said breaking the spell, "I don't want to get you in trouble keeping you out too late, or myself for that matter."

Dakotah drove Chenoa over to the Reams and they parked in the driveway. "I've had a fun time this evening."

His dark eyes looked into Chenoa's searchingly. At that very moment, very briefly, she felt okay but felt a spark of sorts. Chenoa could not explain the experience. She tried to speak but only a whisper left her lips, "So did I."

"I hope that we can get together again, at least once, before you have to go back to Whiteriver."

"I'd like that, too," Chenoa's stomach fluttered at the thought of spending more time with him, it's something that she really enjoyed doing. She sat there wishing that he'd kiss her.

Just then, they were surprised by the big bright porch light coming on. Nuts, she thought. Darn the rotten luck of mine. She hoped Victor wasn't looking out the window especially if her dream came true and Dakotah kissed her.

"I'd better go in before one of them comes out." Chenoa was a little disappointed that her parents didn't give her a little more time alone with Dakotah. She was more interested in him, more than she thought she should be.

"Okay," he remarked and smiled cheerfully.

Inside the house, Chenoa heard Dakotah start the car and drive away. Nobody was in the living room so she tiptoed up to her room. Just as Chenoa was ready to write about the evening's happening in her diary someone knocked on the door. When Chenoa opened it, there stood Anna with a half smile.

"Hi, Honey. How did things go?"

"All right."

Anna quietly closed the door and remarked, "It's nice that you're making friends for the short time we'll be here. Dakotah seems like a nice boy and his sister seems nice also."

"Yeah, they're nice." Chenoa tried to be careful how she worded her responses. She didn't want Anna to think she had anything to hide.

"Do you like Dakotah?" Anna asked directly.

Chenoa could feel her cheeks start to get warm. She couldn't believe she would just come right out and ask her such a personal question. Either Anna had ESP or Chenoa was transparent.

"He's nice, *Shimaa*." Chenoa answered carefully. She didn't want to admit to Anna how deep a crush she had on Dakotah, so she walked over to the bed and laid her diary on the pillow.

Anna caressed Chenoa's chin in her gentle way and looked deep into her eyes, "Uh huh!" she remarked firmly, "just as I thought."

"Huh?" Chenoa didn't have a clue about what Anna thought, but she was somewhat leery.

"My daughter is growing up," she stated with a broad smile, "and right before my very eyes."

Chenoa's mouth was agape. "What do you mean?"

"You more than like this young man. I'd venture to say you're well on your way to a crush."

Wrong, Chenoa thought, I'm already well into its grip. As to how Anna knew that, Chenoa was clueless. "I didn't want it to happen, *Shimaa*. Maybe when I get back to Whiteriver I'll get over it."

"Honey, it's not an illness that you get over in a week or so. This is something you don't take a pill for and it goes away. Sometimes it takes a long time for the heart to heal. Trust me, Chenoa, I've been there."

"What do I do, *Shimaa?*" Chenoa asked, feeling helpless as a tear rolled down her cheek. She quickly wiped it away. The thought of going back to Whiteriver with these strong feelings for Dakotah unabated tore at her heart.

Anna held Chenoa close and sighed. Chenoa knew she was getting ready to give her some more motherly wisdom. "That's up to you. You must deal with it and then go on with your life; this is all part of growing up. Maybe you can write a good-bye letter to Dakotah in your diary. I did that when I had a crush on a boy when I was your age, and it helped me; I'm sure it can help you." Anna hugged Chenoa tighter and whispered in her ear, "Your secret is safe with me."

Respectfully Chenoa asked, "Who was the boy, *Shimaa?*"

Anna drew back and smiled. "His name isn't important; the importance is the fact that we remain friends after all these years." She paused, kissed Chenoa's cheek and continued, "I'm going to let you in on a little secret. You will definitely know when the right boy that God has planned for you to share your life with makes his appearance. You'll know deep within your heart," she added pointing to Chenoa's heart.

After Anna left the room, Chenoa flopped on the bed, gathered up her diary and penned these words:

I'm not really in tune with God right now or on to what He has in store for me. I know that Dakotah is special and if I'm destined to fall in love with him, I wish I wouldn't have to go back to Whiteriver. I don't know much about love but somehow I know this won't go away without a big struggle. I wish I knew how Dakotah feels about me. Maybe if I did it would be harder to go home and function, wondering what might have been.

Therefore, God, if you're listening, give me a sign that Dakotah and I are meant for each other. I mean, to have or let me develop a crush on a boy who lives halfway across the country would be somewhat cruel.

CHAPTER 13

Christmas 2001
Dear Diary,

Last night I cried myself to sleep and thought about my time getting to know Dakotah. Although we'll be returning in February, it hurts not knowing if Dakotah is interested in me. How do I deal with that, and my mom's idea of writing a good-bye letter in my diary is crazy. I can't seem to bring myself to write a pretend letter. Just how did I get to this point and how do I stop it?

This is Christmas Day and I should be happy about that, but all I can do is analyze my feelings for Dakotah. All I wanted was to be friends, but that backfired. If Anna can see it, it must be true. What do I do? Should I avoid Dakotah? If I have to, how do I do that. When I look into his gentle, dark eyes I seem to get lost. When he tells me his problems I really want to listen and help him solve them. It kills me inside that I can't come up with decisions that will make things better for him.

Who is the weird person I've become? Chenoa thought. *I let my heart wander and it turned into a stranger. Do I slap some sense into it and tell it to get a grip. Yes, I have to recover control.*

Bach began barking excitedly downstairs, signaling the family's arrival. Chenoa walked down to the living room to meet the Reams' children. Samuel and his wife arrived first followed shortly by Carissa Ann

Carter and her husband Jackson. One other son and his wife couldn't make it.

They gathered in the living room where Barbara served coffee; then opened Christmas presents. Aside from the diary, the Reams gave Chenoa a set of satin ribbons for her hair. They were pretty and soft to the touch; she looked forward to using them.

River got a collection of six Dr. Seuss books from Anna and Victor.

Chenoa didn't see what the others received because she sneaked out of the room to be alone.

Barbara served dinner at one o'clock. She had prepared a big turkey dinner with all the trimmings. During the dinner, there was much conversation, except Tamara, who acted like the ice queen toward Chenoa.

Afterwards the men gathered in the family room to watch a college football game on the big screen television. From their happy shouts and cheers, Chenoa assumed it meant their favorite team was winning.

Chenoa sat in her room for a while, but that got boring so she decided to go outside.

She grabbed her coat, and put it on, and went downstairs and outside. Carissa Ann and her husband were building an enormous snowman in the backyard. They looked up and smiled at Chenoa.

"Hi, there!" Carissa Ann said cheerfully her bright blue eyes sparkling, "Come join us!"

Carissa Ann was in her early twenties with long flowing blonde hair. She looked friendly and that made Chenoa feel at ease. Seven months pregnant, it looked like she had eaten the entire turkey. Maybe getting to know her wouldn't be so bad, Chenoa thought without feeling awkward.

River jumped out from behind the snowman and giggled. Jackson picked River up and the giggling continued. Jackson had a hearty laugh, which he added to that of River's.

"My son will be just like you," he said. "He'll be cute and cuddly." In his late twenties Jackson stood 6 feet. Dark hair stuck out from under his red stocking cap.

Carissa Ann laughed. "Jackson, behave yourself."

Jackson laughed heartily and put River down. "Make me," he teased, and a playful glint shone in his dark deep-set eyes.

Carissa Ann picked up a handful of snow, formed a snowball and threw it, hitting him in the chest. Jackson looking determined picked up a handful of snow and threw it at her. Carissa Ann managed to dodge the snowball, but Chenoa got a face full of cold wet snow, she shivered. After recovering from the shock, Chenoa giggled and the others laughed.

Chenoa scooped up a handful of snow and threw it at Jackson. He saw it coming, flopped playfully onto his back on the ground, and laughed when River jumped on him.

"Uncle! Uncle!" Jackson cried between howls of laughter.

"Great pitching!" Carissa Ann congratulated and patted Chenoa on the shoulder.

Jackson managed to get up and brushed the snow off his black coat. "It was a lucky shot," he said and gave his wife a conspiratorial wink.

"You're just getting slow, Jackson," Carissa Ann snipped good-naturedly.

Jackson had a smirk on his face. "Look at who's talking about getting slow. It takes you five minutes just getting to the bathroom in the morning."

Carissa Ann stuck out her tongue and gave him the raspberry. "Phhtt!"

"Hello!" Dakotah called out cheerfully as he walked toward them. "It looks like everyone's having fun." He reached down and ruffled River's hair. "Nice snowman." He looked at Chenoa and smiled. "Would you like to take a walk with me, Chenoa?"

"Ooh!" Jackson cooed in jest. "Cozy!" He grinned.

Carissa Ann took a playful swipe at him but missed. "Don't mind him, he never grew up."

Chenoa felt the heat rise in her cheeks, and butterflies gathered in her stomach as she coaxed her feet to move. To Chenoa's surprise, they obeyed her. As Dakotah and Chenoa walked toward the lake, they left the giggling trio behind with their snowman. Chenoa and Dakotah didn't talk until they reached the lake, just quietly walking hand in hand.

Dakotah turned to Chenoa, still holding her hand and asked, "Would you like to do something tomorrow? Maybe we can ice skate."

"Ah…" Chenoa's voice trailed off when she thought about Tamara having a crush on Dakotah. Then she decided since she was only visiting she wanted to have fun. Maybe she'd have something new and exciting to tell Erica when she got back to Whiteriver. "Okay." Chenoa needed something to do with her foot so she gently made circles in the snow with the toe of her shoe.

He touched Chenoa's shoulder, and she made the mistake of looking up into his eyes. His eyes, dark and deep-set, were so expressive they caused her stomach to flutter mysteriously. "You do know how to ice skate, don't you? I could teach you. Janie doesn't like to ice skate because she's afraid of falling through the ice."

"I'm not afraid. It looks pretty thick and solid."

"What size shoe do you wear?"

"I wear a size six."

"Great! So does Mary. We'll plan that for tomorrow."

"Won't Janie mind if you're with me?" Chenoa asked, still making circles in the snow with her foot.

"No, Janie won't mind," he answered. "She'll be busy anyway."

Chenoa's heart ached for him for some strange reason. She didn't want to make his girlfriend mad, yet she didn't like seeing Dakotah sad. "I'll ask my parents. They were talking about going for a drive but I'd prefer not to go, yet I don't want to be cooped up in the house either." Chenoa said more than she planned to, but his presence always seemed to draw her out of her shell.

Dakotah sighed and looked out toward the lake, lost in thought. He then looked at Chenoa and said, "I'll come over tomorrow and bring the extra pair of ice skates. Mary seldom uses them."

"Okay."

Dakotah looked like he had something on his mind, but he didn't say it. Instead, he said, "I have to go. My older brother and his family are visiting and I haven't seen them in a while." He touched Chenoa's shoulder and caressed it. "I hope you have a nice Christmas."

"Thanks," Chenoa said quietly. "I hope you have a nice Christmas, too."

As they went their separate ways Chenoa thought about Dakotah and his sweet smile. When she went into the house, she found Anna and Barbara sitting at the kitchen table drinking coffee and talking over old times.

"Hello," Anna said, "are you enjoying the fresh air?"

"Yes," Chenoa answered.

"It's cold outside. Don't get sick."

Anna was a worrywart. Chenoa wanted to ask her if it was all right if she could ice skate with Dakotah. Anna knew how she felt about him and Chenoa didn't want her asking a bunch of questions.

"Shimaa, Dakotah invited me to go ice skating with him tomorrow. I was wondering if it would be all right if I go. That's if we're not doing anything special."

As Chenoa reported this to Anna, Tamara walked in and took a carton of milk from the refrigerator. She scowled at Chenoa and Chenoa knew Tamara thought she was invading her turf. Tamara told her often enough that Dakotah was hers and she didn't want anyone coming between them.

Anna smiled. "I didn't know you could ice skate."

"I can't, but Dakotah promised to teach me. Can I go, huh, can I?"

Anna patted Chenoa's hand and said: "It's all right. Your dad and I are taking a drive; we're going to do some sightseeing. I trust Dakotah will take care of you and see that you don't break anything."

Chenoa gave Anna a big hug. "Thank you, *Shimaa!*" Chenoa went to her bedroom with a happy song in her heart. As she started to take her diary from under the pillow, Chenoa heard the door close behind her. Chenoa looked up and saw Tamara smugly glaring at her, arms folded across her chest. Her brow was furrowed and her face was hot and pinched.

"Are you moving in on Dakotah?" Tamara demanded.

Chenoa didn't have to answer her. What she did with Dakotah was her own business and she didn't feel she had to ask her permission. Tamara didn't own him.

"No," Chenoa said honestly. Chenoa didn't feel she owed her an answer but she wanted to keep the peace between them. "I just like him as a friend." Chenoa's heart told her differently. "I just..."

"Just what?" Tamara snapped, her blue eyes smoldering.

Chenoa flinched. "I just want to be his friend," she answered firmly. "I'd like to have a little bit of fun before I go back home. Maybe I can brag to my friends that I learned something new," Chenoa added, trying not to come off sounding too defensive.

"Well, see that you don't lead him on," Tamara grumbled. "I want Dakotah and I don't want someone in his memory to get in my way." She jerked the door open and left in a huff, slamming the door with a resounding thud.

Chenoa sat down on the bed and tried to sort out Tamara's words. It seemed Tamara thought she had a big chance of winning Dakotah's heart. Fat chance! It would take more than an attitude if she wanted to win him over. She'd have to be willing to give him his space and give him the right to choose between her and someone else. Chenoa knew that boys don't like possessive girls.

CHAPTER 14

Wednesday, December 26, 2001
Dear Diary,
I have an ice skating date with Dakotah this afternoon. I'm really looking forward to it and I hope I'm a good student. I like something new; also, I'll have some neat stuff to tell Erica and my other friends in Whiteriver. I'm not even going to worry about Tamara with all her insecurities and petty jealousy.

Chenoa saw the lake through the window and felt anxious, giddy, and excited all at once.

"Chenoa!" Anna called from the bottom of the stairs. "We're ready to go."

Chenoa jumped off the window seat and downstairs. She found her parents in the foyer and hugged Anna.

"I hope you have fun learning how to ice skate," Anna said. "Don't get hurt or break anything."

"I'll be all right, Shimaa," Chenoa said confidently. "You worry too much."

Anna didn't look the least bit offended as she smiled and said, "It's a mother's prerogative to worry about her children. I know Barbara and Douglas will look after you." Anna hugged Chenoa tightly and it seemed to last an eternity. "I love you, Honey," she whispered in her ear.

She felt something go through her that she couldn't explain and she couldn't shake off the feeling. It left her unsettled.

"I love you, *Shimaa.*" Chenoa didn't want to let go.

Anna kissed her cheek. "This evening after dinner you can tell me all about your little adventures on the ice."

"I will," Chenoa promised. She hugged Victor. "I love you."

"Have fun, Chenoa," he said.

Ten minutes later Chenoa's parents left, Dakotah showed up with a pair of white ice skates, dangling in his left hand. Tied together by their laces, a smaller pair of blue ice skates was draped over his right shoulder. He wore a big smile and looked truly happy. Chenoa didn't understand the change in him but she was glad for him.

"Are you ready to go?" he asked cheerfully.

"Yes."

Dakotah took Chenoa's hand and led her toward the lake. "When's your birthday?" he asked.

"I turned sixteen on December twelfth.

"Oh. Mine is September 15th."

"Okay!" Chenoa made a mental note of it.

"Do you have a personal relationship with Jesus Christ?"

Chenoa stopped and looked at him waiting for her answer. She didn't know how to answer that question. If she was truthful and told him she didn't, how would it affect their relationship?

"No, I don't," Chenoa said, deciding to be honest.

"Oh."

"I don't!" Chenoa got defensive about it. "Does it matter?" she challenged.

The kindest, sweetest smile came across his face and it caught Chenoa off guard. "No," he said. He took her hand again and led her to a white wrought-iron bench that encircled a birch tree. Dakotah brushed the snow off the bench and Chenoa sat down, she felt the cold through her jeans and shivered. "I'll help you lace your skates," he said as he dropped to one knee and slipped her foot out of its shoe. "They have to be tied correctly, snuggly, but comfortable, or they won't fit properly and you can't skate." He sounded like an expert on the subject and knew what he was doing as he put the skates on her feet and laced them. "How's that? Comfortable?" Chenoa nodded. "Not too tight?" She shook her head, no. "Good!"

Dakotah sat next to Chenoa and put an ice skate on his right foot. He began lacing the skates and looked at her. "Have you ever thought about praying and inviting Jesus into your heart?"

Chenoa didn't know how to respond. She shook her head no.

As Dakotah put on his other skate, he asked, "Do you mind if I put that on my prayer list?"

Chenoa nodded reluctantly not really giving it much thought. "Yes, go ahead."

When Dakotah finished lacing, his skates he stood up and helped Chenoa stand. "Come on," he instructed with much patience. "Lean on me until you get used to the skates." He never said anything more about being saved. Instead, he held Chenoa firmly. After a bad start she fell down and Dakotah followed. Although her butt was getting sore, she laughed.

Dakotah must have enjoyed their little teacher/student time because he laughed, also. She loved his laugh because it was gentle. After getting to his feet, he helped her up, Chenoa almost fell again but his arms tightened around her. "Stand still, until you can stand solidly."

It felt good to be in his arms. Chenoa wished he'd kiss her. His gentleness seemed to melt her heart and her legs felt like Jell-O. His dark eyes were so expressive that she could almost see into his soul as to what he was feeling. Her heart did flip-flops as she sensed his breathing change and he looked deep into her eyes.

"Do you think you can stand?" he asked, his voice husky.

"I think so."

They practiced some more. The last time Chenoa fell, Dakotah helped her up and suggested, "Let's sit down and put our shoes on." As Dakotah helped her back to the bench, Chenoa thought she saw something dark move away from the pine tree. Dakotah didn't seem to notice so she put it out of her mind.

After they put on their shoes, they strolled over to Dakotah's house, holding hands. Mrs. Gray Owl happily made them hot chocolate topped with big, fluffy marshmallows. As they sat alone in the kitchen Dakotah and Chenoa talked and God and Christianity.

"You've never thought about giving your heart to the LORD?" Dakotah asked.

Chenoa studied the marshmallows in her cup. "No."

Dakotah cupped Chenoa's chin in his hand and forced her to look him in the eye. "Why?"

She shrugged. "Too many questions," she answered trying to be honest.

"Such as?" Dakotah asked and waited for her answer.

He would have to ask that question, Chenoa thought. She had to search deep within her heart and ask the questions she never had the courage to ask anyone but herself.

"How do you know you are going to Heaven when you die? How can I put my trust in someone I cannot see?" She was interested in his answers.

"To answer the first question," he said with conviction. "I've accepted Jesus Christ as my Savior."

"What does it really mean to `accept Christ'?" Chenoa asked searching for a deeper explanation. "I know He's God's Son and all that, but do I know I can just turn my life over to Him and let Him guide me sight unseen."

Dakotah was a quiet for several minutes. Chenoa didn't know if he was thinking or praying. Then he looked at her, "The answer is simple, yet hard to explain. While we were on the lake, I was trying to teach you to skate. It's as if I'm preparing you so you will be able to skate from this side of the lake to the other side. Do you follow me, Chenoa?"

"Kind of," Chenoa said even though she wasn't sure. She thought she would be fair and listen to his explanation.

"To make it clearer," he said with patience, "I'm helping you learn how to ice skate. My teaching you is like I'm witnessing to you and telling you about God's salvation, helping you make a choice about accepting Jesus as your Savior. Now, I'm only human and I can counsel you but I can only help you chose to accept Christ as your Savior. If you follow Him, He'll take you to the other side of the lake."

Chenoa looked at him feeling like she'd missed something he said. "Why do I want to get to the other side of the lake? What's there?"

"I'm coming to that," he said patiently. "Think of this side of the lake as earth and the other side as Heaven. Although I'm helping you, I can't do it all and neither can you. Yet, if you really want to get to Heaven you'll need more than my help. You need a sled, Chenoa, Jesus is that sled."

"What?" Chenoa grunted.

Dakotah caressed her hand and smiled. "It's up to you to make the choice about climbing on the sled. God gave you a free will to either get on that sled or reject a free ride to the opposite shore. You may say, 'Yes, I believe in that sled and I believe in the opposite shore. However, Chenoa, it takes more than that. Unless you actually get on the sled, you'll never get there."

"Oh."

"I realize that's not the world's greatest illustration but I hope you understand what I'm trying to say."

Chenoa was sure his illustration helped, but she couldn't picture herself getting on the sled. "I understand it."

"Yes," Dakotah challenged, "Do you prefer to sit on this side of the shore because it's safe or you don't want to go to the opposite side?"

"I'll think about it."

As Chenoa sat in her bedroom, she penned these words in her diary:

Dear Diary:

I don't know how to take my conversation with Dakotah. I'm not ready to deal with his challenge. It seems scary trying to get to the other side of the lake when staying on this side is safer. What if there is a crack in the ice and it got bigger as I passed over it? What happens if I fall off the sled? Is that the end? Why can't I walk around to the other side?

Who can answer those three questions? Chenoa wondered.

Chenoa sighed and turned toward the window. The lake looked gray and was overcast, nothing like the place where Dakotah and she had had fun earlier.

If God doesn't talk to me, Chenoa thought, why should I talk to Him? If He wants me to believe in Him He has to do a better job at proving to me that He's there. Why doesn't He make Himself known to me?

Chenoa heard a noise and looked up to see Tamara glaring at her in the doorway. Her blue eyes were a stormy gray. "What do you think you're doing with

Dakotah?" she asked furiously, folding her arms across her chest.

"Nothing," Chenoa said turning her face back to the window.

"I saw you two together at the lake and you were having way too much fun. At least I thought so."

Chenoa glared at her. Therefore, she's spying on us now and she was the dark shadow at the lake.

"So!" Chenoa said, furious that Tamara had the nerve to spy on them.

"How dare you!" Tamara fumed, stomping her foot like a spoiled child. "You're having too much of a good time together. I don't stand a chance with you around. I confessed to you that I had a crush on Dakotah and you stabbed me in the back." A look of hurt and betrayal flashed in her eyes and her lower lip trembled.

"What does it matter, how he feels about me? I'm going back to Whiteriver in a couple days and I'll be out of the picture for a while. If you want him you can have him."

Tamara put her hands on her hips. "Yeah, right!" she sputtered clenching her fists. Chenoa thought she was being overly dramatic. "What if when you come back to live in Hartville, you both get together and start dating?"

Chenoa sighed in exasperation. "Boy, do you have a vivid imagination? Do you lie awake at night dreaming up dumb stuff like that?"

Tamara's mouth popped open but not a word came out.

The telephone rang somewhere downstairs but neither of them cared. They just exchanged angry looks, daring the other to speak the next word. Dagger and flames flew back and forth between them; still neither of them spoke.

Douglas burst into the room as if a hungry bear were chasing him because he had a jar of honey. His face was etched in desperation and the blood had drained from it. "Chenoa!" he said breathlessly, his voice full of urgency, "we have to get to the hospital right away!"

"Why?" Chenoa blurted out as she jumped off the window seat, "What's wrong?"

"Honey," Douglas said trying to stay calm, but his pale blue eyes had a haunted look in them, "your parents have been in an automobile accident. We have to get to the hospital, now! I'll explain on the way."

Chenoa gaped in stunned silence. "What!" she barely squeaked." Her heart slammed against her ribs. She thought her heart would burst out of her chest or explode trying.

"Chenoa, the doctors did all they could but your father didn't make it, "Douglas said, his voice thick with emotion.

Chenoa didn't want to believe what he told her, she just felt numb and couldn't move.

"Come on, we have to go!" Douglas urged pulling Chenoa toward the stairs.

"Can I come too, Dad?" Tamara asked with a shaky voice.

"No!" Douglas threw the answer over his shoulder, and added, "Call Pastor Heritage. And pray!" His voice was firm.

River and Chenoa climbed into Douglas' black Bonneville, and they headed down East Drive.

"Your father hit a patch of ice on Route 77 and lost control of the car." Douglas explained, "He skidded into the path of a tractor-trailer rig hauling steel and was killed instantly. He didn't suffer."

Chenoa clutched the back of the front seat and tried to fight for control. River hung onto her arm; his dark eyes filled with tears. Barbara sat in the front seat crying.

"What about..." Chenoa stammered, wiping the tears from her cheek. "What about my mom?" Chenoa guessed from the fact that they were racing for the hospital at breakneck speed it meant Anna was still alive...but for how long?

"Your mother has sustained massive head trauma and internal injuries," Douglas said. "I won't lie to you, Chenoa; it doesn't look good. She's at Aultman Hospital in the emergency room."

Aultman Hospital was thirty minutes away but Douglas must have broken all kinds of speed records; they made it under twenty minutes. As they rushed into the emergency entrance a tall, blond haired woman wearing white slacks and a flowered shirt met them.

"I'm sorry, sir, but I can't let children back here," she said, her voice cold and business-like.

"I'm Dr. Ream," Douglas said firmly. "I'm here to see Anna Gray Owl. These are her children."

"Doug!" A male voice called out behind them. "Doug, it's good you're here."

Chenoa turned to see a doctor about Douglas' age in green surgical scrubs approaching. He was tall and slender with gray hair.

"Hello, John." Douglas gripped the doctor's arm and pumped his hand in a firm handshake. It was apparent they knew each other quite well. Douglas turned to Chenoa and said, "Chenoa, this is Dr. Morrison, he's your mother's doctor."

"Where's my mom?" Chenoa sobbed. "I want my mom."

Dr. Morrison's green eyes were kind and a slight smile formed on his dry lips, but only briefly. "She's back this way. Follow me!"

He led them down a short distance to a sterile room. Chenoa's heart pounded against her ribs and she could almost hear it echoing in the quiet hallway.

Anna lie quietly in bed, her entire head swathed in white bandages. Her right eye, swollen shut, had turned a deep purple and her left arm was in a cast. The only sound in the room was the erratic blipping of the heart monitor as it recorded her weak heartbeats. The two IV tubes going into her right arm were connected to a bag suspended over the bed by a pole. One bag contained blood plasma and the other a clear fluid with life saving drugs and painkillers.

Chenoa rushed to Anna's bedside and gently took her hand. "*Shimaa,*" she cried, choking back a sob.

Anna slowly opened her good left eye and she smiled weakly. "Hi, Honey," she rasped.

Douglas and Barbara came to Anna's bedside with River. Douglas picked up River and held him.

River held out his hands. "*Shimaa!*" he wailed. He struggled to get down but Douglas held him firmly. River whimpered.

Dr. Morrison stood off to one side. Watching. Waiting for the inevitable.

"Chenoa," Anna rasped, "I want you and River to be good for the Reams." She paused, struggling for each ragged breath. "They're going to be your legal guardians."

Chenoa shook her head. "No!" she barely whispered. She didn't want to stay with the Reams.

"Do you remember last summer?" Anna reminded Chenoa. "The will?"

Chenoa remembered she said she wanted stay close to her father's family and get to know them. Aunt Lisa and Uncle Ray had large families, and they couldn't take in anyone else. Since the Reams lived in Ohio, Chenoa and River could stay with them and they would help with transportation.

Chenoa shook her head. "No!" she sobbed. Chenoa's own words sealed River and her fate. She laid her head on the bed and cried.

"The children will be well cared for," Douglas promised. "They'll want for nothing and they'll be treated as part of the family. That's my promise! Moreover, they'll have absolute freedom to visit their people in Whiteriver and Kill Buck. That's the promise we made you when we agreed to be named as legal guardians last December and we'll stand by that agreement."

"Please, raise my children in the Christian faith." Anna rasped.

Barbara smiled encouragingly. "Yes, we'll raise the children in the Christian faith, just as we did our own children. It'll be done, Anna, I wouldn't raise them any other way."

"*Shimaa*, don't die!" Chenoa cried. "You have to fight!"

"Hush, child," Anna said with gentleness and love. "I'm not afraid to die. I know I will be with my Lord and Master. You must turn to God for guidance. Trust Him."

Her words were like a slap in the face. How can I trust someone who's taking my best friend away, Chenoa thought? God was a loving God and merciful! Where is that love, that mercy?

"I foresee great things for you, Chenoa," Anna rasped. "I'm only sad because I won't be there to share them with you." By the time she finished talking she gasped for breath.

"Yes, you will, *Shimaa,*" she pleaded.

Anna's grip tightened on Chenoa's hand and she smiled weakly. "No!" she rasped, "it's out of my hands. Please, be strong and brave. I love you," Anna sighed.

Chenoa smiled through her tears and kissed Anna cheek. "I love you, too, *Shimaa*."

Then the heart monitor's erratic blipping turned into a long, continuous shrill squeal. When Anna's breasts were stilled there was the most beautiful smile on her lips and her face filled with radiance.

"*Shimaa!*" Chenoa screamed.

Dr. Morrison stepped forward and flipped the button on the heart monitor and the screeching machine was silenced. "She's gone," he said, "I'm truly sorry."

It felt like a trap door had sprung open in Chenoa stomach and she collapsed onto the cold hard floor. She welcomed the quiet darkness that enveloped her.

CHAPTER 15

Chenoa stared out the window Thursday morning and wiped a tear from her cheek. I can't believe Mom and Dad are gone, she thought. Mom was my best friend…the only person I could share my troubles. Why would a loving God take my mom away and still claim to be loving?

Chenoa heard River crying downstairs and climbed off the window seat. It was the wail of a broken heart. She knew well. As she descended the stairs, his wailing grew louder. She found Barbara sitting in the rocking chair trying to comfort River but failing miserably. He was wrapped in a blue blanket and one of his bunny house slippers lie beside the sofa. Chenoa picked up the house slipper and placed it on his foot. "*Doo ncha da* [don't cry].*" she whispered in his ear. "*Shi nzhoo* [I love you].*"

"He misses his Mom," Barbara said.

Chenoa sighed. "Come here, River." He was her brother and she would take care of him.

River wiggled out of Barbara's arms and the blanket fell away. He was still clothed in his pajamas with little rocking horse designs. Her arms encircled him, and he practically melted into Chenoa's breast. Once he was settled, he got quiet and sucked on his thumb. He hadn't done that since he was two years old.

"How are you holding up, Honey?" Barbara asked. Chenoa shrugged and didn't give a verbal response. "Your grandparents will be arriving this morning and will be here for the funeral. Douglas is paying their way."

Chenoa remained silent and cuddled River. It would be nice to have her grandparents attend the funeral.

"If you would like you could help me get the guest room ready. It might help if you had something to keep you occupied. Then maybe we could have hot chocolate and relax. "Okay?"

Chenoa nodded. "I'm taking River upstairs and get him dressed." Quietly she carried him up the stairs and into the room he was given to sleep in. "It's okay, River. I'm here for you," she said taking his pajama top off and putting a shirt on him.

"You won't go away, will you?" he whimpered.

Chenoa forced a smile. "No, I won't go away. I'm staying right here with you."

"Promise?"

"Yes. Forever and ever."

Chenoa quietly helped Barbara get the guest room ready for her grandparents' arrival. About eleven thirty, Douglas came through the front door with a suitcase in each hand. He was followed by Isabel and Lou Tinilzay.

"I'm here, grandchildren," Isabel said hugging the children.

"Mom's gone," Chenoa whimpered. "What will we do?"

"You will go on, Child," Isabel said firmly, but quietly. "Sometimes life isn't easy and we must make the best of whatever situations come our way. Do you understand?"

Chenoa nodded.

After lunch, Chenoa was sitting on the window seat feeling numb. She hated that feeling and she wished she could snap her fingers and feeling would go away.

A knock at the door snapped her out of her blue funk. "May I come in?" Isabel asked.

Chenoa nodded.

Isabel entered and sat on the edge of the bed. "I know it's hard to see a loved one leave us. My mother died ten years ago, and sometimes I still grieve. I don't think that's ever going away. I remember her words and that's what helped me through. Even though your parents are dead, they'll always be a part of you, because you can't forget them."

"Does the pain ever go away?"

Isabel nodded. "In time, child, in time. Death is a part of life and it comes to everyone. One day I will no longer be here."

"No, *Shiwoye!*" Chenoa sobbed and flung her arms around the old woman. "Don't say that."

"Shh!" Isabel said. "Now you have a responsibility to guide River."

"How? I'm a child!" Chenoa protested.

Isabel cupped Chenoa's chin in her hand, lifted her face to hers and looked her straight in the eye. "No, you aren't," she said firmly. "I've seen you take responsibility before and I know you can do it. The

Great Spirit has chosen this path for you and you must walk it no matter how difficult life gets."

"Did you know it would happen soon?" Chenoa questioned.

"Their death?" Chenoa nodded. "No. However, I fell asleep and right about the time that Douglas told me she passed, I had a dream. Your mother came to me and said good-bye. That was when I knew and my heart hurt. It wasn't a physical pain, but an emotional one because she regretted leaving you and River behind. I told her she had to go. Everything would be all right. She is the first of my children to die and as much as I hated to let her go, I knew I had to because she was going where she wanted to go. She disappeared into a bright light and there was a peaceful look on her face." As Isabel related this to Chenoa, a tear slipped down her cheek.

"When she died she had a smile on her face." Chenoa sighed and wished her grandmother had told her mother to stay. Why didn't she call her back? Chenoa wondered. Why did she let her go? "I told her to stay. I thought if she loved us she would fight harder."

"Child, that is not so. It was her time to go. You must let go of her. Moreover, you must let your father go, also. You must make the transition from needing them to caring about them when they are absent. You will never forget them."

"It's hard, *Shiwoye*."

Isabel smiled and hugged Chenoa. "I know. I must take my own advice. Out of my six children, Anna and

I were very close. However, we must go on and you must be strong for River. When your grieving is over, you must love him and instruct him about life. As I said before you left the rez, you must teach him about our people, and keep the stories alive in his heart and mind.

River burst into the room and flung his arms around Chenoa. She wrapped her arms around him and cuddled him like a safe cocoon. "I want Mommy," he whimpered.

Isabel took the child onto her lap and comforted him. "Your mother went to be with the Great Spirit, but she will always be in our hearts. There are things in this life we don't understand, but as you get older and wiser, some things you will understand, some you will not."

"Did Mommy and Daddy go to heaven?"

Isabel nodded. "They are happy. The Great Spirit will protect them now." She kissed his chubby cheek. "You must be a good little boy and always listen to Chenoa. Be the best little brother you can. Will you do that in memory of your mother and father?" River nodded. "Good. When I return to the rez, we will stay in touch."

"You aren't staying, *Shiwoye?*" River pleaded.

"No, I must go home, but I will be here for the burial of my child."

Isabel talked a while longer with the children, then returned to her room.

In the evening, Grandfather Lou gathered the children around him in the living room. A big blaze burned in the stone hearth.

"Grandchildren, don't be sad. Life and death is one never-ending circle. The sun dies each day and is born again in the morning. Plants wither in the cold of winter only to rise up from the earth in the spring. Therefore, it is with people; their spirits travel the path to where all loved ones have gone before them. Your parents aren't dead but have gone to another place.

You must be strong, Grandchildren. How you do that is up to you, and you will find the answer in your heart. Death comes to us whether we are young or old. Don't be angry about death because there was nothing you could do. Loosing your parents is terrible and you think everything has ended. Grandchildren, you must think of those who remain and go on. Chenoa, you must take care of River. River, you must help your sister."

"It's hard," Chenoa admitted. "I looked up to Mom and we talked.

"Yes, I know," Lou said. "It'll take time. You have to know these things, Child. Working through it is a part of life, each one at some point in their lives have gone through it. I was with my father when he passed to the other side. They always say that when they die their spirit leaves them, and that spirit goes back to the place where they love to be. I know that to be true because my uncle was out hunting and he felt the wind caress his face. He said that was my father's spirit. They were close and they always hunted together.

"Your parents are gone. But we know we have your parents here," He said putting his hand over his heart, "Not physically, but spiritually. They are still with us and you must believe in that. I'm going to speak to the Reams and ask them if they could get their minister's permission for you children to observe an Apache tradition during burial. It's important that you remember the things you were taught and not let them fall by the wayside."

That evening, after Chenoa had fallen asleep, she dreamed.

Chenoa stood in a field full of flowers back in Whiteriver and was alone. She saw her mother walking from afar dressed in a flowing, white robe. When she stood before Chenoa, she smiled and said: "I've come to tell you I will always be with you and watch over you. When you feel the wind against your cheek, you will know it is I. When you solve a problem you will know that I helped you."

"Are you truly happy where you are, *Shimaa?*" Chenoa asked.

Anna just nodded. "Understand, Daughter, the things I've taught you. Know that you are not alone in your walk. I understand that I could not stay with you. As much as I wanted to it wasn't meant to be. Whenever you have a problem, talk to Jesus."

"Grandfather said your spirit would always be with us."

"Yes, my spirit will always be within you. I am a part of you now and forever until we meet again."

With those words said, her mother's being turned into a wisp of white smoke. It swirled above Chenoa's head and then went into her chest. Her mother's energy warmed her and she was at peace.

Chenoa awoke from the dream and sighed. What is the meaning of that dream? she wondered. When I was younger, Mom and I walked in that field and we talked. Is her spirit in that field or in me?

The next morning, Chenoa found Isabel in the guest room so she could talk to her about the dream.

"*Shiwoye,* I had a dream and I don't understand it."

Isabel gave Chenoa her full attention. "What was the dream about?"

Chenoa told her about the dream. "Is her spirit in the field where we walked?"

"No, child, she's within you. The fact that she met you in that field of flowers is because it was a special place for both of you. She led you there to reassure you. She entered you to let you know she will always be with you. Cherish her memory within you and you will find strength."

CHAPTER 16

A cold north wind chilled those gathered at Mount Peace Cemetery Saturday morning. The overcast sky looked ominous. Low, thick clouds looked as if they could spew snow at any time.

Pastor Heritage said a few words then allowed Chenoa and River to observe an old Apache custom.

Chenoa took River's hand and led him to their parents' graves. She pulled a small leather pouch out of her pocket, opened it and said. "We need to put these ashes around Mom and Daddy's grave. Okay?

River nodded.

Chenoa and River sprinkled ashes around their mom's grave. Then circled their dad's grave, too.

Chenoa offered a brief prayer: "Great Spirit, welcome our parents into *yaa ka'yu*.* May our little sister Sage meet them and guide them into a better land that awaits them. Amen!"

Chenoa knelt in front of River and the cold hard ground bit into her bare knees. "When we leave, we have to leave separately."

River threw his arms around Chenoa and wailed. "No!"

"It's all right," Chenoa whispered. "We have to or Mommy and Daddy's spirits will want to follow us and not want to go to *yaa ka'yu*."

"No!" he wailed stubbornly.

Isabel stepped out of the crowd and took River's hand. "Go, child," she said to Chenoa. "It will be all right.

Chenoa kissed River and stood up. As she walked away, River wailed behind her. She didn't look back and headed for the car. Her tears blinded her but she kept walking.

Dear Diary,

I haven't written anything for a while. The last three days have been...well...a blur, and I cried all the way through them. I'm only now beginning to emerge from the black void and I'm feeling numb. We buried Mom and Dad today and I still can't believe they're gone. I'm not sure what I'll do without them, especially Mom!

Before death didn't seem real. You know in your heart that you or a loved one will die, but you don't really feel it in your heart. You see death all the time on television, in a video, or in movies, but that's not real death. It's pretend! Death is real, something to be taken seriously. Most of the time, I didn't think about my parents' dying until they were old and white-haired with many grandchildren.

Life will never be the same. Life is all down hill from this point.

Chenoa glanced out the window and a bleak wintry feeling began to settle into her heart, it was overcast and the lake looked sad, the way she felt.

She opened her hand and looked at the turquoise prayer stone Isabel had given her before she left Whiteriver. Since it hadn't given her strength or courage, she laid it down on the window seat beside her and sighed.

I'm alone, Chenoa thought. The Great Spirit has abandoned me. Why would he do that?

River burst into the room still wearing his suit and tie and threw his arms around Chenoa as if he were afraid to let go. "Chenoa, will Mommy and Daddy come home soon?" he asked, his voice small and afraid. "I know they're dead but will they be home for dinner?"

Ruffling his hair, Chenoa sighed wearily. She couldn't forget how much he looked like their mother and he had her sensitive nature. Anna said he'd be handsome and a real heart breaker when he grew up. It saddened Chenoa knowing Anna would never see that day.

"No, they'll never return. Do you remember what we talked about last night?"

He bowed his head in remembrance and sorrow. His dark eyes met Chenoa's. "Why?" he whined his voice pleading with her to bring them back. Chenoa wished she had that power.

At once Chenoa pushed her sorrow aside as a tiny tear trickled from his eye, down his cheek, and fell on her black sweater dress. "Because, they've gone to Heaven to be with God and Jesus."

He blinked. "But we put them in the ground," he said. "How could they go to Heaven now? Didn't Mommy and Daddy want to stay with us? Were we bad?" He started crying.

Chenoa didn't know which question to answer first. River asked questions about everything and she wanted to answer them like Anna and Victor did, but these questions she wanted to shove aside for now, because she didn't know the answers, not even the ones that would comfort her own aching heart.

"We weren't bad," Chenoa said gently reassuring him. "Mommy and Daddy wanted to stay with us. They loved us more than anything."

"Why do Mommies die?" he asked with sad puppy dog eyes.

Chenoa wiped a tear from her cheek. "I don't know," she said, as she tried not to cry.

River looked up at Chenoa with a woeful expression on his face. "Chenoa, will you go away like Mommy did?" he asked wiping a tear from his right eye.

His question pierced Chenoa's heart like an arrow as she fought the deluge of tears. If she started crying again, she'd never stop. Chenoa hugged him close because she didn't want him to see how uncertain she was of their future. "No, I won't go away until I am old and white-haired." She wanted to keep that promise even though their mother couldn't. She would protect him from the bogeyman and things that go bump in the night.

Quietly glancing out the window once again, she sighed. Yes, the lake looked dark and gray like it was sad for River and her.

There was a reason for their parents' deaths, though she didn't know it then and perhaps never would. Their role as parents was over and by legal authority; the

Reams were now their guardians. Some day that, also, would end as their parents' lives had ended.

It's just a legal arrangement, Chenoa thought. It'll never be like a real family.

Later that afternoon, Chenoa was sitting on the window seat looking out at the lake thinking about the past several days.

She hadn't written in her diary for three days because she couldn't deal with her feelings. She didn't get to say good-bye to her dad since he was pronounced dead at the scene of the accident. Nor did she get to see his body at the calling hours or at the funeral. He was really messed up and the funeral director wanted to spare the family. They put her father's picture on his casket.

Saying good-bye to her mother was the hardest thing she ever had to do in her life. When she died, Chenoa wanted to slam her fist into the door of the emergency room. When the rage was gone, all she did was cry.

Chenoa heard a noise and saw Barbara enter the room, her face flushed from climbing the stairs. She usually walked gracefully with perfect posture, but today her shoulders drooped and she walked as if there was a great weight on her, a sad reflection of today. Her dark eyes had lost their sparkle and were red from crying.

Barbara sat in the chair near the window and Chenoa caught the familiar fragrance of her perfume. She smoothed out the wrinkles in her black dress, the right pocket bulged with tissues. "How are you doing, Chenoa?" she asked.

"Uh, I'm doing okay." That was a lie. The nerves in her stomach were tied in knots and she thought she'd throw up.

"It's all right," Barbara said. She gave Chenoa's hand a gentle reassuring squeeze. "I know how you're feeling," she said, as if she knew she lied. "Now that the funeral is over I hope you'll feel at home with us. If you need someone to talk to I'll be here for you." She smiled and touched her cheek. "You'll be staying here; this will be your room. I never thought it would be used again except for a visiting grandchild."

Chenoa looked around the room and cringed mentally at the thought of occupying it. The room contained many memories and none of them hers. "Thank you," she said.

"Good! "I'd like you to come down and join the family. Douglas and I would like to talk to you."

"Okay," Chenoa said. She didn't look forward to it. She felt more like tiptoeing through an emotional minefield with a dull emptiness gnawing at her soul. "Give me a few minutes to change into something comfortable," Chenoa added, stalling.

Barbara patted Chenoa's hand and a look of inner anxiety clouded her eye. "Of course, dear." She sighed, rose from the chair and with much effort walked out of the room.

After a moment, Chenoa slipped out of her dress and dropped it on the floor. Getting into her jeans and a blue pull over sweater seemed like it took all her energy. Chenoa felt that she was moving in slow motion as she examined herself in the mirror. Her baggy clothes looked shabby and her eyes looked red and swollen from crying. She wished she had a magic paintbrush to paint the happy color back into them. Chenoa grabbed her hairbrush, brushed her hair, and tied it up in a ponytail with the blue satin ribbon the Reams had given her for Christmas. With a spasm of grief, she forced herself to go downstairs. Her knees felt like half-set Jell-O.

Descending the stairs, Chenoa walked into the living room where she found the Reams. Barbara sat in the rocking chair and held River on her lap. Douglas stood by the hearth caressing his beard in silent reflection and Tamara sat in a chair, her face masked of any emotion. Chenoa had no idea what she was thinking or feeling. Her grandparents sat on the sofa drinking coffee.

"Please, have a seat, Chenoa," Douglas said. Chenoa sat in a chair and waited for him to continue. His pale blue eyes were filled with sympathy. "I'm sorry about the loss of your parents. We, also, feel your pain and sorrow. Barbara and I want you and River to feel at home here with us. We'll try to make the transition from reservation life to living here as easy as possible. I'm sure this isn't what you're accustomed to but we're all making necessary adjustments."

Chenoa didn't know what to say, so she said nothing.

"Douglas told us about the arrangements your parents made with them," Isabel said. "We will honor their request. We know the Reams will do whatever they can to fulfill their promise."

"Yes," Douglas said firmly. "It will be done. As we promised your mother on her deathbed, and I say it in front of your grandparents, you'll have complete freedom to visit your people in Whiteriver and Kill Buck. Perhaps in April, you and River may want to accompany me. As you know, I volunteer two weeks out of the year to help at the medical facility there in Whiteriver. Helping the Native American is still a priority for me as it was with my late father. He was a doctor on the reservation for almost twenty-five years. I've always shared his concerns for your people."

Chenoa nodded. "Thank you," she mumbled.

"Know this," he continued, "I am a man of my word."

"Maybe we can work something out," Barbara said, "so you can spend part of the summer in Kill Buck and the rest of the summer in Whiteriver."

"Absolutely!" Douglas concurred, "We'll work it out later."

"Thank you," Chenoa said softly. "I'd appreciate that."

Douglas looked pale and bewildered as if he didn't know how to phrase what he had to say. "As we promised your mother, you and River will be treated as part of our family. If you need or want anything, we'll be here for you. If you have any problems, feel free to come to us. Ha'an dah!" He ended, spreading his arms out wide as if embracing them into the family.

Chenoa sat trembling inside, feeling ill and wishing her mother were there. She looked over at Tamara and thought she saw a sneer on her lips. Chenoa knew Tamara didn't want her around.

After supper, Chenoa sat on the window seat trying not to dwell on the fact that life wasn't always pleasant. Her mother's death made a void in her life. She missed her mother very much. She used to tell her mother what bugged her, and her mother knew how to fix the problem. If she couldn't, she'd tell her, to "talk to Jesus" because He understood and He would straighten it out.

Hugging her knees, Chenoa glanced out the window. If I talked to Jesus, she thought, what would I tell him? When does the hurt go away? Mother's death is like a dark cloud over my head and a big chunk of my heart is gone.

Chenoa sighed heavily and felt the weight of the whole world on her shoulders. She buried her face in her knees. If you're there, God, send me back to Whiteriver, please?

Chenoa sighed once again. She could almost smell the aroma of Isabel's venison stew that had been simmering all day, almost taste it with her favorite seasonings. Chenoa could hear Lou's strong voice ring out with story telling. She gulped back a convulsive sob.

Why did this happen? she thought. I was looking forward to returning to Whiteriver but now I'm hopelessly stuck in Ohio. My parents made that dumb

Will and I can't do anything about it. Why? Am I being punished for something? Is this some cruel joke or a conspiracy to make my life as difficult as possible? If it's a joke, I'm not laughing.

The doorbell rang downstairs and Chenoa heard Bach barking a warning to the visitor. She thought it was a neighbor come to chat with Barbara. Instead, Barbara called up from the bottom of the stairs, "Chenoa, Dakotah Little Eagle is here to see you."

Chenoa wondered why he wanted to see her. She remembered Thursday that he was trying to teach her how to ice skate. After studying her reflection in the mirror, Chenoa decided she was a mess, but there wasn't time to do anything about it. Going downstairs, she met Dakotah in the foyer. "Hi!"

Dakotah nodded and smiled slightly. "I'm sorry I missed the funeral this morning," he said, "I had to work and my boss wouldn't let me have time off."

"That's all right, I'm sort of a mess right now. I'm ashamed to be seen."

Dakotah smiled understandingly. "That's all right, I don't mind. I thought you might need a friend. Mary would have come, but she has the flu."

"I'm sorry to hear she's sick. Tell her I hope she's feeling better soon." Chenoa felt bad for Mary. Mary was a nice person and she liked her.

"I will. She'll be happy knowing you wished her better health." He touched her hand gently and his fingers lingered there for a second. "Is there a place where we can talk, privately?"

"We can go into the family room." Chenoa led the way down the hallway. Tamara came out of the kitchen with a plate of chocolate chip cookies and a glass of milk. She gave Chenoa a scorching look that gave her chills. Chenoa pushed Tamara's insecurities from her mind as Dakotah and she walked into the family room and sat looking at the black screen of the big television.

Dakotah placed his hand on hers and said, "My family and I are praying for you and River."

"Thanks. I appreciate your prayers."

"If there is anything I can do to help let me know," Dakotah said patting her hand. "I'll do whatever I can."

Can you turn back the clock about a week? Chenoa thought. Can you bring my parents back?

"Dakotah, how am I going to adjust to living with a white family?" The thought made Chenoa tremble. What if I forget that I am Indian and I don't want to go back home? What if I'm gone so long my Indian family won't know me or have anything to do with me?

Dakotah smiled. "Chenoa, I'm sure you'll find a way to bridge the cultural differences. You just have to be open and honest with the Reams and let them know where you stand. Don't be afraid to do something new, life is full of new beginnings."

"I can't do it," Chenoa said quietly and shook her head. I hate change. I want my life to stay the same and never change. What good is there in change? I feel safe on the reservation.

"Yes, you can. Look at it this way, Chenoa; the Reams are probably as uneasy about raising two Native children as you are about living with white people.

Don't let fear block your mind against moving ahead and learning life's biggest lessons. Ask God for guidance."

"I don't think He's listening to me,"

Dakotah squeezed her shoulder. "Sure He is. I'm your friend and I'll be praying for you. I see a lot of me in you." Chenoa looked at him in surprise. "That's right. I was thirteen when my family and I left the rez; I was really unsure of myself and fearful of the answers to life's questions."

"What do you do when you don't even know what the questions are?"

"Only you can find the answer to that question. Right now don't force them to the surface, let them come gradually. Then you'll be able to find the answers."

CHAPTER 17

Sunday, December 30, 2001
Dear Diary,

Mom said the Apache view of the afterlife has been meshed with later Christian ideas about heaven. The People believed in a life after death that was similar to the life on earth, where they dwelled together with their families in perpetual peace, joyously repeating the pursuits of the living. They spoke of four corners of heaven, all beautiful, from which the deceased woman might choose her permanent rest.

It's been five days since Mom died. When does the pain go away?

Chenoa grew tired of sitting in her bedroom. She had gone with the Reams to the airport to see her grandparents off. It was a sad farewell.

She went downstairs and saw Barbara and Tamara taking the decorations off the Christmas tree. River was sitting on the floor coloring in his coloring book.

Barbara looked Chenoa's way and smiled. "Hello, Chenoa. Would you like to help us?"

Chenoa shook her head. "No," she said as she went to the hall closet and took out her coat. "I want some air."

Chenoa went outside. Big snowflakes were beginning to fall. Bach bounded up to her, but she ignored him as she trudged over the snow-covered ground. Eventually she found herself down by the lake. Chenoa brushed the snow off the white wrought-iron

164

bench and sat down. She sat by herself for what seemed a long time, but it was actually five minutes. When she felt a hand on her shoulder Chenoa looked up with a start and there stood Dakotah, smiling down at her.

"Hi!" Sitting down next to her, he asked, "How's everything going?"

Chenoa took her time answering because she wasn't sure how everything was going and she didn't want to be whining. "I guess I'm feeling okay again," she finally said with a sigh. "Is that a good or bad thing? I'm slightly confused."

"It's a good thing," he answered putting his arm around her. "If you stopped all feeling and never felt anything again, that would be a bad thing."

"I don't want to feel."

"Why?" he asked as he took her hand. "You just lost both parents. It's normal to grieve but the way you handle it is important."

"Have you ever lost anyone important?" Chenoa asked. She hoped she wasn't unfeeling. Until a person has lost someone, they don't know how it feels.

"Everyone in your life is important. Yes, I've lost someone recently…in a way."

Chenoa looked at him wondering what he meant. "Who?"

"I took a positive step, and broke up with Janie the other day."

"I'm sorry," Chenoa said averting her eyes. One part of her heart was sad for him, yet the other part was happy that he had the courage to take that important step.

"I'll be okay," Dakotah said, keeping a positive attitude. "Janie didn't take it too well, though. I'm ready to move on." He squeezed her shoulder. "We'll just hang out together and support one another, you and me."

"You don't want to be around me when I'm sad," Chenoa warned him. "I cry buckets of tears and there aren't enough tissues to hold them."

Dakotah chuckled softly. "You haven't seen my tissues," he said patting his chest over his heart. "Tell me how you're feeling."

Chenoa sighed and shrugged. "I don't think you want to get me started."

He cupped her chin in his hand, lifted her face to his. Chenoa saw the tenderness in his dark eyes. "You'll feel better if you talk."

Fat chance of that happening anytime soon, she thought.

Chenoa took a deep breath and spoke about what was in her heart. "It hurts! It hurts real bad." She wiped the tears from her cheek. "It hurts during the day, in the middle of the night and in the pit of my stomach. When Mom died, it didn't feel real. I thought everything would be all right in the morning but it wasn't. When I got up the reality of her death was there and I felt numb." Chenoa sighed as she felt the rush of emotional pain overtake her.

Dakotah squeezed her hand reassuringly. "You're doing fine, Chenoa," he said. "Keep going."

Chenoa shook her head. "I don't want to talk about it, Dakotah," she pleaded.

"Yes," he said, "but you need to get those feelings out in the open." Chenoa closed her eyes and shook her head. "Yes, you can," he added, trying to encourage her.

It was a long time before Chenoa had the courage to speak.

Dakotah waited. He had the patience of Job.

"If death is beautiful," Chenoa said, "Mom went without questioning why. She had the most beautiful smile on her face when she died." Chenoa paused, feeling as though she couldn't go on. She hated talking about the fact that her mom did go so willingly. She sobbed and buried her face in his chest.

"I don't know," Dakotah said in a gentle voice. "I suppose when we get to Heaven we'll find the answer." Chenoa felt his arms tighten around her and felt comforted. "You've lost both parents whom you loved deeply. If you thought about it, what life lesson do you believe your mom and dad would have wanted to leave with you?"

Chenoa thought a moment, and then answered, "My dad always told me to have courage to stand up for myself and never back down when others challenge me for whatever reason. He believed in God and said He made us equal. No one should think they're better than you because of your race."

"And your mother?" Dakotah asked. "What did she teach you?"

Chenoa smiled. "Mom taught me many things, but if I had to choose…she always told me to talk to Jesus whenever I had a problem. Mom prayed about everything no matter what it was. She said if it was important to her, it was important to God."

"All those things are important," Dakotah said. "I've only been saved for four years and I've learned out of all the information my parents told me, having faith in God is what's important. However, what you do with that information is what forms your character."

Monday and Tuesday zipped right along, and nothing much happened on Wednesday. Chenoa lie on the bed most of the morning and cried. Since her mother's death, she had her good days and bad days. This was a bad day.

She remembered the long talks she and Anna used to have, and they had a lot of them. The reason she was so sad was that there wouldn't be anymore going to Anna for advice. She didn't have anyone there to help her. Anna wouldn't be there when she fell in love, had her first date, when she graduated from high school, when she got married, and Anna wouldn't be there when she had her first child.

Barbara would be there for her, but she was not her mother. They hadn't yet formed a relationship but she would never take the place of Anna.

"Why God?" Chenoa cried. "Why did you take her from me? She was my best friend!"

God didn't answer. He was silent as usual.

Later that afternoon Dakotah showed up. He got permission from Douglas' to take Chenoa for a drive and treat her to an early dinner.

"Are you all right?" Dakotah asked, caressing her hand as they ate in a small restaurant.

Chenoa shrugged. "I'm getting through it. I finally realized Mom's gone and I can't change that. I'll never see her again."

"I know it hurts," Dakotah said comfortingly and squeezed her hand. "I'm trying to put my stormy relationship with Janie Long behind me and move on."

"We'll have to look ahead and never look back. The past is gone and lost forever. My grandmother told me that."

"We can still hold onto the memories, at least the good ones."

They picked up their water glasses and clinked them together. "Here's to looking ahead."

"Amen!" he said, smiling broadly. "To the future!"

When they pulled into the Reams' driveway about eight o'clock they sat quietly for a few minutes in the silence.

"Dakotah," Chenoa began, "how come when I talk to God he doesn't answer me?"

"God does answer," Dakotah said, "Sometimes we don't hear him because we're not listening. Other times His answer doesn't come as fast as we want it to or the answer isn't always what we want."

"How do I listen for the answer?"

"Be silent in God's presence and be ready to hear him. The answers will come but you need to be patient."

On Thursday, Chenoa's school records and some important papers arrived from Whiteriver. The Reams had written to Chenoa's grandparents and requested the materials in order to enroll her in school.

A letter addressed to Chenoa from Isabel was enclosed. Chenoa sat down with River and read it to him. It was filled with news from home and at the end of the letter she wrote:

Grandchildren, don't dwell on the past, but look ahead! Hold your parents memories close to your hearts. The Great Spirit has so ordered your new path and your moccasins must walk a different road. Chenoa, whatever answers you are seeking now, you must get on your own. They are within you. Remember, have courage and you'll soar above any problems that come your way. First, trust in The Great Spirit and then trust in yourself.

Chenoa wondered what the next to the last sentence meant. What difficulties lie up ahead for me? Butterflies tickled her stomach. Why would Grandmother give only a partial message when it would cause anxiety?

CHAPTER 18

Monday, January 7, 2002
Dear Diary,

This will be my first day attending class at Lake High School, a predominantly white school. I'm nervous about it. I would rather face a storm of hungry fire ants or have a tooth pulled without Novocain than get on that school bus. However, Mary Little Eagle has promised to show me around.

Chenoa slipped her diary under her pillow, went down to the kitchen and forced herself to eat breakfast. The doorbell rang and she opened the front door. Mary stood on the other side of the door smiling.

"Hi!" Mary said. "Are you ready to go,"

"Yeah!" Chenoa said with a reluctant sigh. She wanted to get it over with. A whole host of butterflies gathered in her stomach. Chenoa slipped on her coat, and then took the old black and brown backpack, she'd found in her bedroom closet, and slipped it onto her back. It wasn't heavy because it held only two notebooks and her lunch.

Mary and Chenoa walked along the wooded pathway that led to the bus stop on Congress Lake Road, the main road leading into town. About half way to the bus stop Mary said, "Lake High School isn't such a bad school. Just stick with me and I'll help you find your way around."

"Okay."

They reached the bus stop and waited with several older girls and a tall, skinny boy with a pimply face. At 7:15, the yellow school bus pulled up with its red lights flashing. As they boarded the bus, the big, gruff looking man stared at them and chewed on the toothpick in his mouth. He reminded Chenoa of a beaver chewing through a twig making it ready for his dam. His gray hair was chopped off short and he had a five o'clock shadow that looked out of control; his whiskers were also gray.

Mary and Chenoa sat near the front of the bus. The bus continued down the road about forty feet and then made another stop. A white boy about sixteen years old got on; he looked a dreadful sight. Chenoa thought he could have passed as a 1960's flower child strung out on drugs. Whatever the definition, he fit the part. The old blue sweatshirt with a stain on the collar was half tucked into his jeans that were fashionably torn at the right knee. He had a red bandana on his head and his long blonde hair stuck out from beneath it. As he sauntered past Chenoa he stunk of tobacco, and she wrinkled her nose in disgust.

He noticed Chenoa and his blue eyes had a wild expression. He flashed her a wicked grin. "Oooh, more Injens!" he said and his tone sounded nasty. "Quick, boys, circle the wagons!" He guffawed and his intense gaze seemed to range freely over Chenoa. It felt like a trap door had sprung open in Chenoa's stomach and she couldn't help feeling violated.

Is that how it's going to be, she thought, having white boys leering at me.

Chenoa saw him run his tongue slowly over his cold, cracked lips as he grinned at her. He puckered up and blew her a kiss.

"Who's that?" Chenoa asked Mary in disgust.

"Zach Heritage," Mary answered. "He's Pastor Heritage's son and kind of the black sleep of the family. I've never felt comfortable around him."

"Why?"

"He's *wenoih!*"* Mary made the crazy motion with her finger. "Last summer he threw red paint on some cars and wrote obscenities in the paint."

Zach poked Chenoa on the shoulder. "What's your name, cutie?" he asked demurely. His rank breath was hot on her right ear. "I think I'm in love. How about an itsy bitsy kiss?"

Chenoa ignored him hoping he'd take the hint.

"Hey, Betty, did you hear about…" a skinny blonde haired girl across the aisle asked as she turned to the girl behind her.

Mary leaned closer to Chenoa and whispered, "That's Sally Kingston. She's the school gossip queen, a walking newspaper. Steer clear of her if you value your privacy."

The bus soon arrived at Lake High School, a one-story brick building built in 1970. Several small trees grew around the campus and well-manicured shrubs surrounded the building. As the students walked into the school Chenoa couldn't help but notice Zach Heritage following her. He made her skin crawl.

Mary took Chenoa to the main office where she introduced her to Mr. Wallace, the principal. He was a short, gray-haired man wearing a neatly pressed blue suit, which was, a black tie and big round glasses that reminded her of an owl. He promptly gave her a list of her classes and said, "Welcome to Lake High School."

Chenoa couldn't help noticing that history was her first class. The only positive note so far today was that Mary and she had some of the same scheduled classes.

After homeroom, Mary led Chenoa toward their first class. When Chenoa walked into history class, there were at least twenty students noisily taking their seats. Tamara sat in the first seat of the first row by the windows. Zach Heritage of all people sat in the third seat in the second row. His blue eyes followed Chenoa as she looked for a seat. The only empty seat was behind Zach. Once she was seated, he turned in his seat and leered at her.

"Hi, Babe," he said.

Chenoa ignored him and concentrated on the blackboard in front of the class. The words: DECLARATION OF INDEPENDENCE was written in large letters with chalk. The man seated at the big desk in front of the blackboard rose and faced the class.

Mr. Augustine, the history teacher, was somewhat ugly and bug eyed, his blonde hair looked like someone had covered his head with a bowl and cut around it. It reminded her of an Amish haircut. He had a short, square, blonde mustache and looked like a blonde-haired Adolph Hitler. She wondered if the kids made fun of him and gave him the Nazi salute behind his back. The drab, brown tweed suit he wore worn in many places and like it needed to be donated to the Good Will.

Mr. Augustine droned on and on about the Declaration of Independence for sixteen minutes to a bunch of kids that didn't look like they cared. The boy in the seat beside Chenoa had his head on his desk and snored softly.

"Who can tell me when the Declaration of Independence was signed?"

None of the students raised their hands. Several shrugged.

Mr. Augustine frowned and started picking students at random. His green eyes settled on Chenoa. "Miss Gray Owl, can you tell me when the Declaration of Independence was signed?"

Chenoa felt her arm pits start to sweat. History wasn't her favorite subject. "Uh…I…" she stammered. "I guess it was signed in 1780."

Mr. Augustine frowned. "Miss Gray Owl," he said indignantly, "I don't want guesses, just the facts." He looked at Zach and asked: "Mr. Heritage, what's the right answer?"

Zach shrugged. "Don't know," he said with a snicker, "I wasn't there."

The students burst out laughing. Zach grinned, pleased with himself.

Mr. Augustine looked annoyed. "Class, doesn't anyone listen to me or am I not speaking English?"

It got so quiet Chenoa could have heard crickets chirping inside everyone's heads. There was a nervous snicker from the back of the room.

"Class, it was signed in 1776," Mr. Augustine said, thinking, What's the use, I'm teaching a bunch of morons. "It'll be on the test. Don't count on me giving you the answer."

Mr. Augustine continued to drone on about the Declaration of Independence. Chenoa tried to concentrate on his boring lecture and busied herself taking notes.

When the end-of-the-class bell rang, all the students started filing out accept Zach. He turned to Chenoa again, "How about a date?" he asked for the third time.

"No, I don't date white boys," Chenoa said backing away as his hand went toward her hip.

"Ouch!" he said mockingly, "I'm so hurt." He grinned and touched her arm.

Chenoa shuddered. "Bug off!" she hissed. "I have a boyfriend." She didn't really but he didn't have to know that. She was hoping he'd think she did and leave her alone.

"Who is it?" he asked, looking at Chenoa as if he didn't believe her. "What's his name?"

Chenoa hadn't counted on him asking that question. "Dakotah Little Eagle!" she snapped and pushed passed him. Technically, they weren't officially a couple until Dakotah asked her out. Chenoa followed Mary out of the room and headed to their next class.

When Chenoa arrived in English class, she discovered Carissa Ann was the teacher. Carissa Ann explained to the class the difference between adverbs and adjectives.

"An adjective," Carissa Ann, said, "is a class of words that function as modifiers of nouns. Typically by describing, delimiting or specifying quantity such as the word 'nice' like 'a nice day' or 'other' as in 'other person'."

As Carissa Ann taught the class, she walked up the aisle Chenoa sat in and smiled pleasantly at her. Touching her shoulder Carissa Ann said, "I usually don't pick on the new students on their first day, but, Chenoa, would you please define the adverb and explain what it does?"

Chenoa was happy to give her the definition of an adverb. "An adverb is a group of words that act as modifiers," she explained with confidence. "They're used with verbs or clauses and express some relationship of place, time, manner or degrees. The adverbs usually end in 'ly'."

Carissa Ann patted Chenoa's shoulder and then caressed it gently. "Very good, Chenoa," she stated as she moved on down the aisle and spoke to the whole class again. "Now let's list several adverbs. Quinton, please, give me an example of an adverb,"

Quinton, the boy Chenoa saw at the bus stop that morning, looked a little shy. She didn't think he had the answer.

After a moment, Carissa Ann called on Chenoa again. "Chenoa, please, give me an example of an adverb."

"Acutely," Chenoa answered.

"Correct, Chenoa!" Carissa Ann said, and by the tone of her voice, Chenoa knew she had a smile on her face. Since she stood beyond her line of vision Chenoa could not see her face.

After class, Mary and Chenoa walked into the crowded girls' locker room to prepare for gym. Most of the girls present were bigger than Chenoa. One girl, whose name she learned in one of her previous classes, was Nancy Little. Little didn't describe her truthfully, being built like a defensive end; she out weighed Chenoa by seventy or eighty pounds. She had long, red hair and a blotchy face that always seemed to be in a constant sneer. Chenoa knew Nancy was trouble the first time she saw her.

Nancy met Chenoa with a withering stare and her violet eyes looked angry. She lumbered up with her portly waddle and sneered in her face. She stood 5 feet tall, and she scowled down at Chenoa. "Well, if it isn't the Indian Princess," she said with a sneer and her breath smelled nasty. "You're pretty dumb when it comes to history, but got smart in English. Don't pretend to be smarter than me or I'll rearrange your face." She ground out her words through clenched teeth and shook her fat fist in Chenoa's face.

Chenoa sized her up. Hmm, she thought being a fair judge of human character. All mouth and no action. She could probably outrun her in a windstorm running backwards uphill.

"I don't have to pretend," Chenoa quipped. "It just comes naturally."

Several of the girls gasped. Sally, the gossip queen, looked scared.

Nancy blinked incredulously. "Why you little..." she began making a threatening move.

"Let her be," Tamara said. "Pick on someone your own size."

A wisp of a girl with short, naturally curly black hair stepped out of the crowd. She looked as thin as a reed, the nervous type who saw shadowy figures in the night and cowered in fear. "Cool it, Nancy," she said in a squeaky voice, her hazel eyes darting around the room. "Do you want Miss Nixon to come down on you again?" Her frantic eyes seemed to search the room again.

"What do I care?" Nancy erupted. The small girl shrank away in fear. "I ain't afraid of any of you sniveling cowards." Her violet eyes smoldered and Chenoa could feel the heat from them. "Watch yourself," she growled.

The girls changed into their gym suits and sneakers and met Miss Nixon in the gymnasium. Chenoa felt sorry for her because she was so flat chested she could have passed for a man. If it hadn't been for her long nutmeg brown hair Chenoa would have thought she was a man.

"Okay, girls, you all need to practice shooting hoops," Miss Nixon said in a musical voice. "You have sixteen minutes to practice."

While the girls were practicing hoop shots, Nancy pushed Chenoa roughly and grabbed the ball from her hands.

"Hey!" Chenoa exclaimed defensively and gave her a scorching look.

Nancy scowled down at Chenoa and her violet eyes flashed a willful look, trying to intimidate her. "Yeah, what do you want?" she snarled. Chenoa thought she enjoyed making people uncomfortable.

It didn't work with Chenoa. Chenoa glowered at her. "It was my turn," she snapped and grabbed for the ball. Nancy wasn't going to push her around. Her dad had taught her to defend herself.

Nancy shoved Chenoa viciously and she landed on her butt. None of the other girls made an effort to take sides. They were probably afraid of her.

Chenoa grabbed both of Nancy's fat ankles and jerked her feet out from under her. Her butt made a phhlatt sound as she hit the floor and Chenoa swore the earth moved.

Nancy looked surprised and grunted.

Miss Nixon ran up to them with concern on her face. "What happened?"

"I think she tripped," Tamara said. "Chenoa fell down and Nancy tripped over her."

Miss Nixon studied the girls for a minute. If she didn't believe Tamara's explanation, she didn't say. "Is that true, Nancy?" she asked.

Nancy winced as she struggled to get to her feet. She looked like she was going to cry.

"Y-yeah, I guess so," she mumbled, looking humiliated.

"Okay," Miss Nixon said, "let's get back to practice."

The girls went back to practicing but Nancy kept her distance. Chenoa knew Nancy didn't know what to think of her.

Chenoa never thought to thank Tamara for sticking up for her. She should have.

Before lunch, Chenoa walked to her locker, alone, to put some books in it. She ran into Dakotah and he walked with her down the main hall. They turned down a long hallway where lockers lined the walls on both sides. Dakotah held Chenoa's backpack as she applied the locker combination.

"So, how's your first day at school?" Dakotah asked.

"It's all right, I guess," Chenoa answered with a reluctant sigh. "It's not what I'm used to back in Whiteriver, but I can't change that."

Dakotah smiled. "It'll get easier as time goes by."

Chenoa didn't share his optimism and gave an indifferent shrug. "Yeah," she said half-heartedly.

Dakotah handed Chenoa her backpack and she took out the books that she didn't need. When she looked up at him, he had a silly smile on his face. Chenoa wondered what he could possibly be thinking.

"Oh!" he said, snapping out of whatever zone he was in. "I wanted to tell you that my mother is having a surprise birthday party for Mary on the twenty-first of this month. She wanted me to invite you."

Chenoa smiled. "Really? I'd like to come to the party."

Dakotah's dark eyes danced. "Good, I'll tell Mom to expect you."

Before Chenoa could respond, he bent down and kissed her gently on the lips. It wasn't a friendly kiss, but one that meant a boy was interested in a girl. Chenoa felt the heat rise in her cheeks but she enjoyed the kiss.

"I'll see you around," he said. "Okay?" His dark eyes twinkled and danced, and Chenoa knew he enjoyed the kiss, also.

"Okay."

Dakotah turned and walked away. After he disappeared around the corner Chenoa looked away. As she reached into her locker to put her books inside, the locker door nearly slammed shut on her fingers. "Hey!" she exclaimed, jumping back.

Chenoa looked up at a very angry white girl about seventeen years old with curly blonde hair. She was pretty, but wore so much make-up she looked like a painted clown. Her blue skirt was so short that it almost didn't cover her and the white blouse was thin enough to see she wasn't wearing a bra.

As she glowered at Chenoa, her electric blue eyes seethed. "I just wanted to see for myself," she said savagely as she looked down her up turned nose at Chenoa, "the little witch who stole my boyfriend."

"Huh!" Chenoa thought dumbly, Could this be the infamous Janie Long?

An exasperated sigh escaped Janie's throat. "Oh don't act so innocent," she snapped. "Me and Dakotah were doing great until you came along. You're nothing but an ugly little witch and I don't know what Dakotah sees in you." Her pretty face became hard and pinched with resentment, even though her voice was loud and demanding. She was bossy and Chenoa didn't like people barking orders at her.

"Uh...I...don't..." Chenoa stammered, trying not to let Janie's aggressive body language intimidate her. Janie's manner was clearly different from Nancy Little's aggression. An ugly scowl contorted her face and she looked like a lioness ready to protect her young.

"Don't look so innocent!" she snapped again. "You're nothing but a boyfriend stealer. I hate you!" she screeched and her shrill voice nearly pierced Chenoa's eardrums.

"Hey, Janie!" a tall, thin girl with curly ash blonde hair called as she walked up unannounced. She wore short, red culottes and her long, thin legs looked like beanpoles. The blue platform shoes she wore made her look taller. "Come on! You can fight for Dakotah later."

I wish she wouldn't have said fight, Chenoa thought, feeling panicky.

"All right!" Janie threw over her shoulder. Glancing at Chenoa, Janie's blue eyes shot daggers at her. "Beware!" she said with a snarl, "You haven't heard the last of this."

"Come on, Janie," her friend urged.

"All right!" Janie spat impatiently. She turned in an exaggerated huff, and Chenoa felt the breeze as she stormed off with her long legged friend. She had such a voluptuous sway that Chenoa thought her rear end would fly off from the rest of her body. It rather reminded her of a female hippopotamus in heat.

Mentally, Chenoa tried to dismiss her encounter with Janie Long but she left such an impression on her that it was hard. Man, she thought, I'm going to try to stay out of her way…if that's possible.

She gathered her wits about her and went to meet Mary in the cafeteria. The cafeteria doubled as a study hall. The front that faced the hall had a heavy retractable curtain for use as a study hall. Now it was drawn back and the dining area was crowded with students eating and talking.

While Mary and Chenoa were eating, a white girl soon joined them and it was clear the two of them were good friends.

"Chenoa, this is Tiffany Long," Mary said introducing Chenoa to her friend. "Tiffany, this is Chenoa Gray Owl."

Long! Chenoa thought. She can't be Janie's sister because they look nothing alike. Thinking of Janie made her shudder.

When Tiffany smiled Chenoa saw that she wore braces on her teeth, but it was a kind smile. "Hi!" she said happily.

"Hi!" Chenoa said. Talk about opposites, she thought. How can someone as pleasant as Tiffany have a sister so nasty?

"You're the one who stood up to Nancy Little," Tiffany said.

Chenoa smiled. "Yeah, that was me."

"Way to go!" Tiffany and Chenoa gave each other the high five.

Chenoa thought Tiffany was friendly; her bright blue eyes were like mirthful crescents. She could tell Tiffany's long blonde hair was soft because when she moved her head it flowed easily.

"Are you any relation to Janie Long?" Chenoa asked.

Tiffany visibly cringed and she made a face. "Yikes! You've met the she devil."

Chenoa nodded reluctantly. She wished she hadn't had the pleasure. "Yeah."

"Yes, she's my sister, but only by adoption. Thank God! We're both adopted."

That explains it, Chenoa thought.

"You'd better steer clear of her," Mary warned her. "She's crazy!"

"Yeah!" agreed Tiffany. "She's meaner than a junkyard dog with distemper and has a temper just as wicked. I guess it comes from the fact that she's a result of her real mom being raped and all. Her mom didn't want her and put her up for adoption. I guess her father was ill tempered and a real goof ball. Not many people know her background. If they did, they'd understand."

"Oh," Chenoa said.

"Where are you from, Chenoa?" Tiffany asked, thankfully changing the subject.

Chenoa told her from and the reason she was living in Hartville.

"I'm sorry to hear about your parents dying." Tiffany said with a note of sincerity.

"So, Tiffany," Mary said changing the subject to something else, "has your mom had 'the talk' yet? You know, about dating."

Tiffany chewed nervously on her bottom lip. "No, I'm not looking forward to it." She sighed, her face growing pensive.

"Mom and I haven't either," Mary admitted, "It would be nice to be able to date, but I'm not allowed until I'm sixteen."

"Are you interested in anyone, Chenoa?" Tiffany asked.

Chenoa shrugged nonchalantly. "I haven't been here that long," she said quietly. Chenoa didn't want to talk about her feelings for Dakotah, especially in front of his sister. Nor was she going to tell them about the kiss.

"Speaking about boys," Mary said, "I kind of have a crush on Mike Webster. He's the cutest white boy here at Lake." She sighed. "He has the dreamiest blue eyes, I could get lost in them."

Tiffany laughed; it was a bubbly laugh. "There she goes again. If Mike knew he was the object of her delight..." her voice trailed of and her cheeks turned pink.

"Maybe if we hurry and finish eating," Mary said, "we can go to the gymnasium and I'll point him out to you. The guys are shooting baskets and he's really tall."

CHAPTER 19

Tuesday, January 8, 2002
Dear Diary,

I received a letter from Erica Lupe. It was full of interesting news from Whiteriver. She said she missed me. Erica wrote this about Paul Alchesay:

"I talked to Paul yesterday and he told me he really has it bad for you. He wanted your address and I told him I'd ask you for it. From what you said in your letter before Christmas, I wasn't sure if you wanted to continue to be friends with Paul."

Chenoa decided to write a letter to Erica and grabbed her notebook. She flopped on the bed and wrote Erica a long letter. She included this in answer to her question about Paul:

It's all right to give Paul my address; at least we can still be friends. Yesterday Dakotah kissed me. I felt embarrassed, but if he likes me the way, I like him...well...I'm waiting to see what will happen next. I'll keep you posted.

After supper Wednesday evening, Dakotah came by to see Chenoa. He had called earlier that afternoon and said he'd drop by later.

"I wanted to ask if you'd be interested in going to a night class at the school Friday. Mr. Turtle holds a class for the Native American students in the area that wants to stay in touch with their heritage. Would you like to go?"

"Yeah, I guess so." Chenoa really liked that idea. If she could be with Dakotah in any situation, she'd take it. "We'll have to ask Douglas first."

"Would you like me to ask him?" Dakotah offered.

"Okay."

Dakotah and Chenoa went in search of Douglas and found him in the kitchen pouring himself a cup of coffee. Dakotah explained to Douglas about Mr. Turtle's class on Friday night.

"I've read an article on those classes in the 'Hartville News," Douglas said. "I'm all for it! Chenoa gave up a lot when she left the reservation to live here." Douglas smiled. "You may go with my full support."

"Thank you," Chenoa said gratefully.

After Dakotah left Chenoa went upstairs to study in her room. She ran into Tamara in the hallway. Tamara stood with her hands on her hips.

"I can't believe you're moving in on Dakotah like that," she said bitterly. "I told you how I felt about Dakotah, but you took him anyway." Angry tears were in her eyes.

Chenoa looked at Tamara helplessly. "I didn't have anything to do with Dakotah choosing me."

"Oh, you didn't!" Tamara sputtered. "You backstabbing little…" She clenched her teeth and her face turned red. "Why don't you go back to the reservation where you belong?" she screeched.

Douglas rushed up the stairs and looked from Tamara, to Chenoa, and back to Tamara. "What's all this yelling about?" he asked calmly with a firm tone.

With tears streaming down her cheeks, Tamara pointed at Chenoa and sobbed, "She knows!"

Douglas' pale blue eyes turned a stormy gray. "Calm down, Tamara. What's this all about?"

"I hate her!" Tamara sobbed as she stormed into her bedroom.

Douglas looked puzzled. He took Chenoa into her bedroom and shut the door. "Chenoa, what's all this about?"

Chenoa shrugged helplessly. She wasn't about to drag him into this madness. "I don't know," she lied.

Douglas looked bewildered. He sighed and brushed at his beard. "I'm going to get to the bottom of this sooner or later." He turned and walked out of the room.

Chenoa got ready early and put on a yellow sweater and a pair of brown slacks. She knew she was too dressed up for class, but she liked Dakotah and she wanted to impress him.

Dakotah came by the house Friday evening around six o'clock and they went to the school to attend Mr. Turtle's class.

As they strolled out to the car, he said: "You look pretty tonight."

Chenoa averted her eyes. "Thank you. It pays to ditch the tomboy image occasionally."

Dakotah and Chenoa arrived at school and settled into their seats with the other twenty Native American students. They listened to Mr. Turtle talk about maintaining Native American identity in the white society. He encouraged student interaction through a question and answer discussion. It was an interesting two hours.

Dakotah took Chenoa to McDonalds after class and treated her to a cheeseburger and a diet cola.

Dakotah touched her hand and asked, "Did you enjoy the class?" Chenoa nodded, yes. "Good! Do you think you'd like to go next week?"

"Yeah."

"Good. We'll plan on it."

"Why didn't Mary come tonight?" Chenoa asked, sipping her diet cola.

She's babysitting for a neighbor, but she wanted to come." Dakotah caressed her hand and changed the subject. "So, what's new at home?"

Chenoa sighed. "I don't think you want to know."

Dakotah's hand tightened on Chenoa's. "There's a rumor circulating in school that you're a boyfriend stealer. I want you to know you're not. I've also been told that Tamara and Janie have been talking and I find that odd since Tamara doesn't want anything to do with Janie. Do you know anything about that?"

"Will you keep a secret?" Chenoa asked. Oh brother! she thought. I'm beginning to sound like Tamara. Secrets, I hate them!

"You know I can."

Butterflies gathered in Chenoa's stomach as she debated with herself about telling him why Tamara and her were at each other's throats. "Well, when I first got here, Tamara told me she had a crush on you." Dakotah's eyebrows arched in surprise over her comment, but he remained silent. "I guess she thought once I went back to the rez her secret would be safe. She told me once you dumped Janie she was going to start dating you."

Dakotah burst out laughing as if Chenoa had told him the funniest joke in the world. When she gave him a questioning look, he sobered up.

"Do you want to know a little secret, Chenoa?" he asked in a serious, adult tone.

What's this, trade a secret day? Chenoa wondered.

"Yeah."

"Dating Tamara Ream would be extremely boring," he confessed. "We have absolutely nothing in common. Aside from the fact we're both Christians there isn't any chemistry between us."

"What do I do about that nasty rumor Janie is spreading about me?"

"Forget about it," he said in a firm voice." Janie doesn't know how to treat people. She'll soon stop her foolishness and go onto her next victim."

On Saturday morning, Barbara gave Chenoa some money to buy flowers for her parents grave. She drove River and Chenoa to Giant Eagle where they looked at the flowers on display. When they went to pay for their purchase, Chenoa ran into Dakotah. He was the cashier who rang up her purchase.

"Hi," Chenoa said, handing him the money.

Dakotah smiled. "I get off work at two o'clock, I'll drop by and we can talk. Is that all right?"

"Okay, about two-thirty."

Barbara drove River and Chenoa to Mount Peace Cemetery where their parents were buried. The siblings laid the flowers on their mother and father's graves and then stood in silence for a moment.

River looked up at Chenoa with sad puppy dog eyes. "Will *Shimaa* be happy in heaven with Daddy, too?"

Chenoa smiled and hugged him. "Yes, they'll be there to greet us when it's our time to go there."

"I miss them!" he sobbed.

Chenoa hugged him tighter. "I know. I do too."

That afternoon Dakotah kept his promise and dropped by the house after work. They walked along the lake rather than stay in a stuffy house.

"How's everything going with you?" Dakotah asked, as they walked hand in hand.

"All right. River and I put flowers on our parents graves' this morning."

He put his arm around her. "Are you okay?"

Chenoa shrugged. "You'll see your parents again. You can have that assurance."

"How?"

He looked out across the lake and pointed to the opposite shore. "Do you remember the story about the sled and the other side of the lake? If the other side of the lake is Heaven and the only way to get there is by getting on it, then you need to make a decision. You have to resolve that Jesus is your guide."

Chenoa thought about the questions that she'd asked herself when he first told her that story. Maybe it would be a good time to ask them. "What if I find a crack in the ice and it gets bigger as we pass over it?"

"Don't look at the crack, Chenoa. The cracks are trials in your life and you need to keep your focus on the sled, Jesus. Keep your eyes on the sled and the distant shore. Keep your focus on Jesus and trust him."

As Dakotah and Chenoa continued their walk, Chenoa did some thinking. She didn't know if she could put her life in God's hands. It seemed so scary to blindly follow Christ.

Sunday afternoon, after lunch, Dakotah showed up. He got Douglas' permission to take Chenoa on a Sunday drive and to invite her to his house for dinner. As they drove through the countryside, they chatted endlessly. It was strange how relaxed Chenoa felt with Dakotah. Dakotah drove by a pasture and she saw a strawberry roan horse.

"Stop here!" Chenoa said excitedly. "I want to see that horse."

Dakotah pulled over without questioning and shut off the engine. They walked up to the fence.

"Come here, boy," Dakotah called to the horse and held out his hand. "Come on!"

The horse snorted and walked to the fence. It wasn't in any hurry and took its time. The horse nuzzled Dakotah's outstretched hand.

"He's beautiful," Dakotah said with a smile. He stroked the horse's long nose, patted his cheek and scratched him under the chin.

Chenoa reached out and patted the horse's neck. "He reminds me of the horse my grandfather had when I was ten years old." Chenoa ran her hand through its gorgeous, well-groomed blonde mane. "I rode him quite often."

"Really?" Dakotah asked. He looked interested in her story. "Did you ride horses a lot?"

"Whenever I got the chance, but I miss it." Chenoa sighed and swallowed the big lump in her throat.

Dakotah held Chenoa close. "I'm sorry," he said gently. Then in his gentle manner, he cupped her chin in his hand and lifted her face to his. His dark eyes searched Chenoa's. "May I tell you something?"

"Yeah."

"The first time I saw you I felt something I didn't understand at first, but I did some praying. I know God is leading me toward something, but I have yet to find out what that may be. I don't know why you're in my life but I guess I'm bound to find out eventually. I've had more fun getting to know you than I ever did with Janie."

"Really?" Chenoa didn't know where this conversation was headed, but if she ventured a guess, she'd say he was interested in her. He didn't make a commitment but she was hopeful.

Dakotah was about to kiss Chenoa but the strawberry roan snorted and nudged his shoulder. Dakotah chuckled and patted the horse's nose, then walked her back to the car.

That evening Mrs. Little Eagle served up a delicious dinner of baked chicken, mixed vegetables and mashed potatoes.

"Dinner was good," Chenoa said to Mrs. Little Eagle.

Mrs. Little Eagle smiled. "Thank you, Chenoa. I hope you saved room for my cherry pie ala mode later."

Chenoa's mouth almost watered. "Mmm!"

"Hers is the greatest," Dakotah whispered in Chenoa's ear.

As they left the table Dakotah asked, "Would you like to listen to some CDS, Chenoa?"

"Sure!"

Dakotah led Chenoa to his bedroom, and she sat in his chair. He put a CD in the player, pushed the play button, and then lie back on the bed. Rich Native American voices mixed with music filled the room.

"I'm glad we share an interest in my music," Dakotah said. "Janie and I shared very little interest in anything."

Thinking cautiously before she spoke, Chenoa asked, "What's the story about Janie?" Chenoa knew she was heading toward dangerous ground and she didn't want Dakotah to think she was being nosy. "I'm just curious."

An invisible shadow crossed his face, "I don't have a clue, Chenoa. I really did want to be able to help her understand me, and possibly get her to come to church now and then. Lately she's been unreasonably angry and I don't know why."

"Did you love her?" she asked. Chenoa realized she had asked a very personal question not knowing if she was ready for his answer, but it was too late to take it back.

Dakotah grunted and answered carefully, "That's a hard one to answer, Chenoa. Maybe at one time there was a flicker, but it went out a long time ago. She was pretty and...well, we have absolutely nothing in common. She's not a good listener, and it's not beneath her to slap someone around, maybe not always physically but surely emotionally."

"Oh?" Chenoa was surprised. Of all the things he could have said, that statement was about the farthest thing from her mind.

Dakotah looked at Chenoa with the saddest dark eyes she had ever seen. His throat muscles were working overtime, and he was having difficulty swallowing. When he finally managed to do so, his Adam's apple bobbed several times.

"She slapped me once or twice because she thought I was being unfaithful and ordered me never to speak to another girl. No one tells me who I can talk to or not."

"Wow!" Chenoa expressed in a loud voice. "I always thought it was the boyfriends who were the abusive ones."

"That's a misconception, Chenoa," he stated with a wary sigh. He shook his head in disbelief; he couldn't believe it either. "There are girls, that is, certain ones, that can be as abusive as boys and she's one of them."

"I can see why you broke up with her," Chenoa said. "You're too nice of a guy to be slapped around by a girl. Any girl in her right mind would be happy to have a kind guy like you for her boyfriend."

Dakotah smiled, propped himself up on one elbow and said, "Bless you for saying that and thanks for being a wonderful listener. At least I can move ahead with college and not be influenced by her negativity."

"I have a suggestion about college. Well not about college but afterwards."

"What's that?" he asked, looking eager to hear what she had to say.

"Instead of being a guidance counselor, you might want to work with Indian children on the reservation. Since you care about people you might start with those of your own."

Dakotah sat on the edge of his bed. "Hey," he exclaimed and his face brightened, "that's a great idea, Chenoa!"

Chenoa was glad he liked her suggestion. "Yeah, our young people need the right motivation to stay in school and work towards a positive goal. I figure if they see one of their own people be successful, then they'll know it's possible they can, too. Too many Indian students drop out and seem to give up on their education, let alone better their situation."

"I agree! I am going to do some praying about this between now and graduation. I want to make sure it's God's will. I want to stay open to his guidance." He knelt beside Chenoa chair on one knee and gave her a kiss of gratitude. When their faces were inches apart, Chenoa saw something in his dark eyes that she couldn't read. Then he smiled and kissed her deeply.

Chenoa responded to his kiss, maybe a little too eagerly as she ran her hand through his long jet-black hair. His hair felt silky smooth against her skin and she loved its feel.

Dakotah grunted and pulled away from her. In his eyes were a mixture of all the emotions he must have been feeling and trying to control. He looked unsure what his next move should be and his Adam's apple bobbed up and down so many times he nearly swallowed it.

"I think we s-should stop," he said in barely a whisper.

"Maybe, I-I should go home," Chenoa said, not wanting him to feel uncomfortable.

His eyes seem to plead with Chenoa to stay but he said, "Y-yeah." His voice cracked. "I'll drive you."

"No," Chenoa declined his offer. "I'll walk." She got out of the chair and went downstairs. No one was present in the living room, so she grabbed her coat out of the hall closet and fled out the front door.

CHAPTER 20

Monday, January 14, 2002
Dear Diary,

I'm not sure what happened between Dakotah and me last night, but I know one thing, our souls connected. I can't explain how or why it happened but it crept me out. Why do I feel so strongly for Dakotah when I didn't toward Paul Alchesay? Sometimes I think my heart is conspiring against me and it's a battle of wills. My heart turned into a stranger that delights in making me miserable. Do I let it control me, or will I gain the upper hand and slap some sense into it. Who are you, heart, and what's your game plan?

Chenoa put her diary under the pillow and walked out of her room to go down to breakfast. Tamara emerged from the bathroom and gave Chenoa an icy stare. Things between them weren't getting any better and her icy stare told Chenoa something was going to happen eventually; she opted for sooner rather than later.

Chenoa hurried down to the kitchen and rushed through breakfast, barely tasting her food. She met Mary and they walked to the bus stop. On the bus, Sally Kingston sat across the aisle buzzing about the latest school gossip with the girl behind her. The girl on the receiving end looked Chenoa's way several times and that made her uncomfortable.

Are they talking about me? Chenoa wondered.

At the next stop, Zach Heritage got on the bus. He blew Chenoa a kiss and his devilish smile made her nervous.

Once they arrived at school, it was business as usual. As Mary and Chenoa walked toward homeroom, Nancy Little got in Chenoa's way with her usual sneer. "Make way for the Indian Princess," she said drooling contempt.

Chenoa didn't know if she wanted to get into it right there or not, so she just ignored her and kept walking.

After homeroom, Dakotah met Chenoa at the door with a big smile. "Let's talk," he said taking her hand started walking down the hall. "I'm sorry about last night," he apologized, "somehow I feel like I took advantage of you."

"You didn't," Chenoa added choosing her words carefully, "and I enjoy your company." Chenoa felt him put his arm around her and he gave her shoulders a gentle squeeze.

"I like you too," he confessed." I-" His words were cut off when someone shoved him from behind.

"You dumb jerk!" Janie snarled as Dakotah and Chenoa turned around.

"Janie!" Dakotah said. "What's going on?"

"I hate you!" she spat.

"I'm sorry you feel that way, Janie," he said patiently. "I don't hate anyone, not even you."

Janie grunted. She gave Chenoa the evil eye that made her wonder if she should be intimidated. "Do I mean that little to you?"

"Janie, I will never treat you any differently than I treat my friends. I'm sorry things didn't work out between us, but I want to part on friendly terms. Hopefully, you'll find someone who will share interests with you."

The students passing by turned their heads but nobody stopped. Several of the kids wore wary expressions but many of them were eager to get to their classes.

"Yeah, right!" she snapped clenching her fists into tight balls, "Why did you let that boyfriend stealer come between us?" She jerked her thumb toward Chenoa.

"Chenoa," he began, "didn't come between us, nor is she a boyfriend stealer. We both knew it was coming to this break up. I'm sorry if you thought we'd always be together. I'm not sure what kind of personal problems you were having but I would've sat down with you and talked about them. That's what friends are for."

Janie's electric blue eyes snapped and sparked like a downed live wire. Then she bared her teeth and stormed off.

Dakotah put his arm around Chenoa and they continued walking down the hall. "Janie's a very troubled soul," he said.

Chenoa nodded. She thought Dakotah's willingness to sit down and help Janie with her problems showed his compassion. The scene between them could have been worse, but he calmly took control of the situation and spoke from his heart. She respected and admired Dakotah.

When they reached the door of Mr. Augustine's history class, Dakotah stopped and smiled at Chenoa. "I'll see you later, okay." Chenoa nodded. "Bye!" he said and walked away.

Mr. Augustine announced that there would be a history test on Friday. That bit of news was met with a lot of boos and "Oh no's!"

Before lunch, Chenoa went to her locker to unload her backpack, because she wanted to get ready for afternoon classes. When she started to put the books inside, she was physically pulled away and her books spilled from her arms.

"Hey!" Chenoa exclaimed. The offender spun her around, and she came face to face with Janie Long, and Tamara Ream. They both glowered at her. Janie kicked her history book down the hall with such force that it hit a locker and put a dent in the door. Then she turned to Chenoa. "You're in trouble," she said with a snarl.

"Huh?" Chenoa grunted looking at both of them. They looked like they were out for vengeance.

"Yeah!" Janie snarled, "I'm you worst nightmare!"

"What did…" Chenoa began anxiously looking for a way of escape. There wasn't any. Even though there were only two of them, they had every possible escape route blocked.

"Do you think you can steal someone's boyfriend and get away with it?" Janie asked savagely.

"Normally," Tamara said, "I don't side with Janie, but you crossed the line when you stabbed me in the back. I told you I had a crush on Dakotah and you stole him from me."

"I didn't steal him from you," Chenoa retorted. "You never had him to begin with."

"No thanks to you!" Tamara spat with bitterness. She put her hands on her hips. "It's all your fault."

"Yeah! Janie spat the word out. "We're angry! I won't let anyone come between my boyfriend and me. I'd even fight her over Dakotah." she added jerking her thumb in Tamara's direction.

Chenoa didn't know if they were going to give her a verbal warning or if they were going to gang up on her and beat her black and blue. She didn't think Tamara had it in her, but she wouldn't bet the farm on Janie.

"But...I...Uh..." Chenoa stammered not really knowing what to say in her own defense. Her armpits started sweating.

"Don't stand there and look so innocent," Janie snarled with maliciousness emanating from her electric blue eyes. "You're in deep, deep trouble. You're branded a boyfriend stealer." Then she spat a few choice words in Chenoa's face that would make a sailor squirm. Chenoa's ears burned.

"What's going on here, girls?" the voice of someone behind them asked.

The girls turned to see Carissa Ann walk up the hall. She scooped up Chenoa's history book and surveyed the damage to the locker door. Chenoa heard

Tamara mutter something under her breath although she didn't know what she said.

"Janie, is there a problem?" Carissa Ann asked.

"Uh…no, ma'am," Janie said trying to sound innocent, but failing miserably. The fact that her face was hot and pinched with anger was a dead give away. "We're just discussing something."

Carissa Ann didn't look like she believed Janie. "From the tone of your voices, I don't think you're trading recipes," she said. "It's time for lunch so I suggest you go eat."

"Yes, ma'am," Janie said obediently. She shot Chenoa a warning look, then took off like a frightened rabbit and disappeared around the corner.

Tamara remained and glared at Chenoa. That was her first mistake. Carissa Ann didn't look intimidated by her little sister's staring contest.

"I guess the Cavalry is here," Tamara said in anger. That was her second mistake.

Carissa Ann looked at Tamara sternly. "I don't know what's going on here," she said as she handed Chenoa her history book, "but I have a pretty good idea. You'd better behave yourself, Tamara Marie."

"Oh, butt out, Carissa Ann!" Tamara sputtered.

Carissa Ann gave her sister a warning look. "Need I remind you, Tamara, that we're on school grounds? I'm first your teacher. Therefore you're to treat me with a little respect."

Tamara put her hands on her hips. "How little?" she quipped. Once the words left her mouth, she must have realized her third mistake talking back to a teacher even if it was her own sister. She bit her bottom lip and waited for her punishment.

Carissa Ann's bright blue eyes became livid. "Mom and Dad are going to hear about this," she said calmly, wagging her finger at Tamara. "I don't think they'll approve of you hanging around known troublemakers like Janie Long and spawning whatever mischief you two are hatching up."

Tamara looked like the wind had been knocked out of her sails. "Sorry," she squeaked.

"I suggest you go to your next class," Carissa Ann said.

"Yes, ma'am," Tamara mumbled and hurried down the hall and disappeared around a different corner.

Carissa Ann looked at Chenoa and sighed. "I don't have to ask what this is all about," she said kindly. "I've heard the rumors, nor do I think the problem will be resolved with violence."

"I didn't steal Dakotah," Chenoa said in her own defense.

Carissa Ann smiled and put her arm around Chenoa. "I know," she said, giving her shoulders a slight squeeze. "Janie has been like a time bomb ready to explode and everyone knows it. It was time Dakotah got out of the relationship while he could. As for my little sister, I'm not sure what her problem is, but she hasn't been acting very Christian-like."

Chenoa really didn't want to have this conversation. "I need to go to lunch," she said, hoping to be excused from the conversation.

Carissa Ann nodded. "Yes, go to lunch. I'm sure everything will work out."

Chenoa gathered her books and placed them inside her locker, Carissa Ann walked away. Chenoa stuffed some books in her backpack, turned around and saw Zach leaning against the lockers a few feet away. Her heart nearly stopped beating.

"I can make your problem go away if you want me to," Zach said with a wary smile.

"What problem?"

"Janie Long." Zach touched Chenoa's arm; it gave her goose bumps.

"What do I have to do?" That was a stupid question, she thought. I might not like the answer.

"If you agree to go out on a date with me, I'll get Janie to back down. Everyone will be happy, especially me."

"I'd rather eat glass!"

"Aw! That wouldn't be pleasant. We'd be great together." He tried to take Chenoa in his arms, but she backed away.

"Stay away from me."

He smiled devilishly. It was a game to him. "Are you playing hard to get? I kind of like that." He moved toward Chenoa again, and she stomped down hard on his foot. He nearly jumped a mile. "E-e-e-yow!" he howled and hopped around on one foot. Chenoa heard him grumble something under his breath. "What's wrong with you?"

"I won't date you!" Chenoa spat.

"Why not?" he asked, rubbing his injured foot. "I really like you!"

"I don't like you. You're too freaky. You're intolerable and you smell."

"Aw," he said mocking Chenoa. "I'm so hurt, Baby."

"If you don't leave me alone I'll tell Dakotah, and he'll make you leave me alone."

Zach guffawed. "You'll regret that decision." There wasn't any humor in his voice. It was an ominous warning.

"I'll take my chances."

Zach shrugged. "It's your party," he said grimly and limped away.

As Chenoa sat on the window seat in her bedroom that afternoon, she penned these words:

Zach's been acting strange. Today he practically told me there is going to be trouble. I wonder what he knows. I can't afford any more complications in my life. Lately it's been one thing after another. What else could possibly go wrong?

Chenoa reread the last sentence and made a face. I shouldn't go looking around corners thinking trouble is there, she thought. Zach's just a strange person, that's all. I'll scratch the last sentence from my diary. There, it's gone! No problem!

She decided to go over to Mary's house after supper. They were going to study for the history test coming up on Wednesday.

Dinnertime was quiet. Tamara wasn't very talkative, probably because her parents had grounded her for two weeks. Chenoa knew she wasn't her favorite person.

She was about to leave, but she had to decide what to do with her diary while she was gone. The night before she discovered the diary shoved up against the headboard and the pillow scrunched up. She usually placed the diary under the center of the pillow leaving it nice and neat. If Tamara were reading her private thoughts and feelings, she'd have to make her slip up.

Opening her diary, she hastily penned these words:

Tamara says she's a Christian, but I think she's a phony. I'm not sure why she thinks Dakotah would want her and I'm not sure what she and Janie Long are hatching up against me, nor do I care. If Tamara has sunk to Janie's level of operation, what does that say about her walk of faith with Christ? Her faith seems shallow to me.

She closed her diary, slipped it under the pillow as usual, and straightened the pillow. If she's reading my diary, she thought, I'd catch her.

Putting her coat on, Chenoa grabbed her backpack and coat and went downstairs. She met Barbara in the foyer. "I'm going to study with Mary. Is it all right?"

Barbara smiled. "Of course, but don't stay too late."

"Okay," Chenoa went out the front door and trudged over to Mary's house. She rang the doorbell.

Mr. Little Eagle opened the door and smiled. "Hello, Chenoa," he said with a cheerful smile. "Come in!"

After Chenoa entered the house, Mary joined them in the living room. "Let's go to my room. We'll have less interruptions there."

Once they were settled in Mary's room, they studied.

"I'm not sure what method you used to study by, but we'll do whatever works best for you." Mary said.

Chenoa told her how she used to study with Erica back in Whiteriver so they studied like that for an hour. They took a break and went down to the kitchen for milk and cookies.

"What's new at home?" Mary asked, dunking her chocolate chip cookie in the milk.

Home, Chenoa thought. Living with the Reams was far from home. Tamara didn't make things easy.

"Tamara talked back to Carissa Ann in school today," Chenoa answered. "Her parents grounded her for two weeks."

"I heard a rumor going around that she has a crush on my brother." Mary took a bite of her cookie. "Is it true?"

"Yes, it's true. She told me about it after I got to Hartville last month."

"Oh really?" Mary looked surprised.

"Yeah. We started out on friendly terms, but it changed when Dakotah and I became friends."

"She asked me some questions about Dakotah a couple of times. I had no idea why."

"She hates me because I stayed here after my parents died." Chenoa's heart felt tight when she thought about her parents. "She hates me because she thinks I stole Dakotah away from her and she hates me because she was grounded. Like that was my fault."

Mary squeezed Chenoa's hand. "Those three circumstances weren't your fault, so don't blame yourself. If Tamara's filled with hatred, she needs to deal with it. Don't hate her in return, hate only brings alienation."

"I don't hate her," Chenoa confessed with self-doubt. She wasn't exactly fond of Tamara either. She still hadn't figured out Tamara's problem.

After they finished their snack, they went back to their studying. About eight forty-five Chenoa told Mary she had to go home. When she got home, she went up to her bedroom to finish her homework. As Chenoa sat on the bed, she noticed her diary laying on the bedside stand. She remembered putting it underneath the pillow before she left the house.

Chenoa sighed in aspiration and thought, isn't anything private any more? How dare she invade my privacy?

She marched across the hall, didn't bother knocking and opened the door. Tamara looked up from her glowing computer screen. When she saw Chenoa, her blue eyes turned as stormy gray and her mouth crimped with annoyance.

"What do you want?" Tamara asked; her tone defensive.

"Have you been reading my diary?" Chenoa asked, not wasting time with pleasantries.

Tamara's blue eyes flashed her anger. "No," she mumbled, looking back at her computer screen.

"I found it on the bedside stand. That's not where I keep it."

Tamara grunted but kept her eyes on the screen and pretended to be reading. "Maybe you just forget to put it under your pillow."

I knew it, Chenoa thought. It was she! I have her now!

"I never said anything about it being under the pillow," she said, happy she had caught Tamara in a lie.

Tamara's head jerked in Chenoa's direction and her lip curled with disgust. "You had no right writing those things about me," she said, her voice dripping ice.

"You should know better than to snoop in other people's belongings," Chenoa said, her tone matching Tamara's. "Next time you read someone's diary you'd better do a better job at hiding the evidence."

"Get out!" Tamara growled. She leaped from the chair like a cat pouncing on a mouse but her right foot was caught on the desk and she tripped. She landed face first on the carpeted floor an angry growl stuck in her throat and she just whimpered like a whipped puppy.

Chenoa was satisfied that Tamara was humiliated, so she backed out of the room, closed the door and let Tamara wallow in her self-pity.

CHAPTER 21

Tuesday, January 15, 2002
Dear Diary,

I thought about what Mary said last night about hate or anger causing the alienation. I tried to reason with myself that I didn't hate Tamara Ream, that things had just gotten way out of hand. How did that happened? Jealousy over a boy seemed so juvenile, but is it my fault that Dakotah showed an interest in me? I 'm glad that he did because I really like him. I hope that he'll ask me out on a regular date soon. Dating Dakotah would be the ultimate high.

Downstairs she took time to eat a bowl of oatmeal and a piece of toast. Tamara sat at the table like an iceberg and Chenoa knew that the trouble between them wasn't over and it would only get worse before it got better.

A car horn honked out front and Chenoa perked up because she knew it was Dakotah. He promised to drive her to school and talk some more. She had a few questions she wanted to ask him. She grabbed her coat and backpack, and hurried out of the house slamming the front door. As she raced across the front yard, she slipped in the snow, picked herself up, shook the snow off her jeans and climbed into the car beside Dakotah.

"How's your morning starting out?" Dakotah asked.

"Chilly! I think there's a new Ice Age coming."

"Oh," he said, as he pulled the car out of the driveway and headed down East Drive. "Are we talking about a literal Ice Age? If it's a literal Ice Age I have to get a new wardrobe started."

Chenoa didn't laugh at his joke. "No, Tamara is acting like the ice queen."

Dakotah sobered up. "I see," he said with genuine concern.

Chenoa looked at Dakotah and changed the subject. "Dakotah, when I'm riding on the sled what do I do when I fall off? Is that the end of the ride?"

Dakotah reached over and took her hand in his. "No, Chenoa, that's not the end of the ride. You ask God's forgiveness, get back on and continue your journey."

"Have you ever fallen off the sled?" she asked, searching for answers.

"You seem like such a good person and…"

"Chenoa," he said firmly, "I'm not perfect so don't put me on a pedestal, I don't deserve it."

"Have you?" she asked feeling verbally chastised.

"Yes, I've have, several times," he answered, his voice gently softer now. "I hurt a friend but I was able to make it right between us."

"Wouldn't it be easier to go around the shore to the other side?"

"No, there are no shortcuts."

They rode the rest of the way to school in silence. When they arrived, Chenoa saw several girls giving her the strangest looks as if she had blue hair or something. On the way to her locker Chenoa walked by a boy and girl who were seniors. The boy glanced Chenoa's way, and the girl jerked his face back toward her.

"Hey, you're with me," she grumbled. "Don't you dare look at that boyfriend stealer."

Chenoa just kept walking and decided not to confront them. She thought she smelled peanut butter. As she went further down the hall, the smell was stronger. When Chenoa reached her locker, she gasped. She saw peanut butter smeared all over the locker door. Some one wrote: "Boyfriend stealer," in the goop.

She marched to the principal's office and found Mr. Wallace looking through a desk drawer. "Excuse me," she said tapping him on the shoulder.

Mr. Wallace looked up and smiled. "Yes, Chenoa, what is it?"

"I have something to show you, would you, please, come with me?"

"Okay," Mr. Wallace complied.

Chenoa led Mr. Wallace to her locker and showed him the mess on the door.

"Hmpf!" he grunted, putting a hand on his hip. He pushed back his glasses. "Did you see who did this?"

"No." She had a good idea but she didn't voice her opinion.

"Hmpf!" he grunted once again. "I'll have maintenance clean it up. Go to class."

"All right." Chenoa walked into Mr. Augustine's class late and he looked displeased.

"Miss Gray Owl," Mr. Augustine said with a stern tone, "I don't tolerate tardiness. I ought to send you straight to see Mr. Wallace."

"I just came from talking with Mr. Wallace," Chenoa grumbled.

"Does his wife know?" an unidentified male voice said. "She might want to…"

"Enough!" Mr. Augustine barked. "I'm not in the mood for such childishness, Miss Gray Owl, sit down and let's concentrate on the test tomorrow."

Ugh! Chenoa thought. I don't want to take a stupid test tomorrow.

Chenoa took her seat and listened to Mr. Augustine cover what was going to be on the test. She looked at Mary and Mary smiled. At least she was on her side throughout this madness. When the end- of-the-class bell rang, Chenoa gathered up her books and shoved one of them into her backpack.

Mary walked up to Chenoa and touched her shoulder. "Are you all right, Chenoa?"

Chenoa shrugged. She hadn't been "all right" since her parents died. She felt as if she was in limbo, and that wasn't a good feeling.

"Look," Mary said. "I heard what the others are saying about you. Tiffany and I are behind you one hundred percent."

"Thanks," Chenoa mumbled, slipping into her backpack harness.

"I mean it, Chenoa. I know Janie's behind that nasty rumor going around."

"She won't get away with it," Chenoa vowed as they walked out of the classroom.

"Chenoa, you can't sink to her level. You're better than that."

"Someone plastered peanut butter all over the front of my locker door and wrote in it."

"What did it say?"

Chenoa fought back the angry tears. "Boyfriend stealer! What else?"

"Come on," Mary said, taking hold of Chenoa's arm, "let's go. We'll try to think of something."

Mary and Chenoa walked to their next class in silence. Chenoa tried not to let the stares get to her, but by lunchtime, she'd had enough. Approaching a drinking fountain, she accidentally bumped into a girl.

"Hey!" she exclaimed, whirling around. "Watch it!" It was Sally, the school gossip queen. She wasn't pretty and her large eyes were the color of smoke.

"I'm sorry," Chenoa apologized, wondering if she'd made another enemy.

"Hey, you're the boyfriend stealer!" Sally exclaimed. Chenoa didn't know if she was being defiant or simply stating a fact.

Janie and her stupid lies, Chenoa thought. I want to reach out and claw those blue eyes out of her head. Janie needs to feel the same frustration I feel.

"Look, I'm no more of a boyfriend stealer than I'll become Miss America in 2025," she said holding her temper in check.

"Huh?" Sally looked puzzled.

"Just because Janie Long is a sore loser she has to pin a label on someone." Then Chenoa remembered Tiffany's story surrounding Janie's conception and birth. "I have a story about Janie that would blow your socks off."

Sally looked interested. "What? What's the story?" she asked eagerly. "Huh! Huh! Tell me!"

She's too eager, Chenoa thought, but I have her full attention now. Should I?

"Tell me, already!" Sally sputtered. She was like a dog jumping for a bone that was held out of reach.

Something deep inside of her told her not to do it, but her heart rebelled, as she paid no attention whatsoever to that voice and threw caution to the wind.

"Janie's real mom got raped by some man she didn't know." Chenoa said. "He had a nasty temper and that's probably who Janie inherited hers from."

"Really?" Sally asked, looking like she was eating up the story.

"Yeah," Chenoa nodded. "He got Janie's mom pregnant. When Janie was born her mom put her up for adoption. I guess her mom didn't want her either."

"Wow!" Sally exclaimed.

"Don't tell anyone else this story," Chenoa added, knowing the rumor would start circulating within the hour.

"Yeah! Sure!" Sally scurried off.

Take that, Janie, Chenoa thought. She finally felt vindicated. However, deep down something inside her said it was wrong and trouble wasn't too far behind. The story, she reasoned, isn't a lie. It's the truth! Nevertheless, as Chenoa walked back to the table she shared with Mary and Tiffany, she didn't feel justified. She felt rotten to the core.

When Chenoa got home that afternoon, she sat on the window seat in her bedroom. Barbara had gone to the store and taken River with her, and Douglas was still at the clinic. Even Bach was hiding in some out of the way corner.

She picked up her history book from the floor and thought about studying for the history test. She didn't feel like studying for that dumb test. That story she'd told Sally would cause her trouble in the end. She wasn't going to wring her hands over it because she wasn't the hand wringer type. Rolling her prayer stone around in her hand, she caught herself trying to start a prayer but she had no idea of how or where to begin.

At bedtime, Chenoa went to the bathroom to brush her teeth and met Tamara on her way out of the bathroom.

"Boy, you're in really big trouble," she said in a huff. "Spreading that rumor about Janie wasn't smart."

"It's the truth!" Chenoa threw the words in her face. "It's the absolute truth!" That reasoning ate at Chenoa and her stomach felt sour, queasy, making her feel like puking.

"Yeah, maybe it is, but you told Sally Kingston knowing full well that she has a wagging tongue with a mind of its own. It was spiteful and mean!"

"Not any meaner than what she said about me," Chenoa said with ice in her voice. "If she would have been nicer person maybe Dakotah would still be dating her."

"Oh, you're a fine one to talk." Tamara stuck her chin out in defiance, "You've sunk to Janie's level. I didn't think you were that kind of person. I thought since your parents were Christians they would have taught you better. What would your mother think about her daughter being a miserable failure? You once called me a phony. Well, what does that make you?" Tamara turned stiffly and walked into her bedroom.

Chenoa felt sick to her stomach and started shaking inside. She made it to the bathroom in time to throw up in the toilet. After flushing the toilet, she crept back to her room. Her stomach hurt and she lay in a fetal position and cried for at least an hour.

I've messed up big time, she thought. I don't consider myself a bad person, but maybe I am. Maybe I'm no better than Janie Long is. If she's evil, what does that make me?

She squeezed her eyes shut to keep the tears from spilling out. No matter how hard she tried to shove those feelings from her mind, she kept hearing Tamara's harsh words repeated in her troubled mind.

She didn't get to sleep until well after midnight, yet when she did manage to fall asleep she had a horrible dream-the worst dream of her entire life.

She was riding a sled across ice on Congress Lake. The sled seemed so heavy that she imagined it caused the ice to crack. The crack kept getting bigger and bigger. Ignoring it as the sled glided over it she kept focusing on the opposite shore. Finally, the ice thinned and the weight was so heavy she heard a tremendous crack and the sled fell through.

She gasped as she descended down under the frigid water. No matter how hard she tried to resurface, she kept sinking.

"Help me!" she cried as she went further down beneath the ice into the darkness of an unknown realm.

From out of what seemed nothing a hand reached down through the water. "Take my hand," a kindly voice said calmly but with much authority.

"I can't," she cried. "I can't, I can't!"

"Don't be afraid! Take my hand!" The stranger's voice was insistent.

Chenoa reached out feeling for the stranger's hand. She barely touched his fingertips, she strained yet she couldn't grasp the hand and slipped deeper, deeper than she thought possible. It was then she saw the face of a bearded man in a long, flowing white robe. There was a look of sadness on his face as she slipped further out of reach. Chenoa tried and tried to grab his hand but could not find it. Something deep within the water just kept pulling her down into the murky depths.

She woke up with a jolt, covered in sweat; her heart pounding so hard she thought she was having a heart attack.

Oh God, help me, she cried. Her stomach hurt so badly she wanted to puke but couldn't. She cried out in short tiny gasps, "Oh God, my God don't leave me!" Realizing she was shouting aloud, she clamped her hand over her mouth and listened, intently. Hearing no sound from anyone else in the house, she sighed. She pulled the covers over her head and shook, finally falling asleep again.

CHAPTER 22

Wednesday, January 16, 2002
Dear Diary,

I've really messed up big time! I'm surely going to hell where I'll be tormented forever more than I am now!

Chenoa closed her diary and laid it aside. She was so tired from loss of sleep due to that horrible dream; she thought about asking Barbara if she could stay home. She didn't feel like facing Janie Long or her friends, who would surely grow to hate her.

She shuffled sleepily down to the foyer and waited for Dakotah to pick her up. She skipped breakfast because she wasn't hungry. Her stomach growled with pain but she couldn't look at food, the mere thought of it made her feel queasy.

"What's wrong, Honey?" Barbara asked, placing a comforting hand on Chenoa's shoulder.

Chenoa shrugged. "Nothing." She shook off Barbara's attempt to mother her. When she heard Dakotah honk the car horn she rushed out the front door to escape Barbara's questions. She jumped into the car and sat beside Dakotah, sullen, unspeaking like a rock. Dakotah drove down to the end of East Drive and parked the car.

"What's wrong, Chenoa?" he asked concerned. "You don't look your radiant self."

"It's nothing."

He reached over and touched her hand. "If you need too talk I'll be here for you." The tone of his voice was tender and compassionate, more than she felt she deserved.

She wanted to talk to someone but hesitated. She couldn't take the problem to the Reams. However, Dakotah seemed to know what to do because she saw how he handled the fight between Janie and him. She sighed and told him the whole story.

Dakotah put his comforting arms around she. "Chenoa, you aren't evil. Even though someone said something hurtful about you, and you got back at him or her, it's not the end of the world."

"It might as well be," Chenoa said with a heavy heart.

"I heard about that rumor going around about Janie. I dated her for over a year and I didn't even know that about her. I'm not your judge nor are you your own judge."

She didn't respond. She only sat there like a lump. It was comforting to have his arms around her holding her protectively, lovingly.

"Chenoa, our church youth group is having an ice skating party Saturday night, and I'd like to have you come as my guest. In the evening, we build a bonfire and roast hot dogs and marshmallows. During the roast-out, our youth pastor always has something positive to share. I'm sure you'd find it encouraging."

Chenoa looked him in the eye. "Why?" she challenged. "Dakotah, why do you care what happens to me?"

Dakotah's dark, serious eyes bore deep into Chenoa's soul. "I don't put much stock in love at first sight but it happens. I don't understand it myself. Whether we want to believe it or not we're soul mates."

Chenoa blinked in surprise. "And you believe that?"

"You're in my life for a reason," he answered, speaking with conviction. "Nothing happens by accident, there's always a reason."

"Dakotah started the car and drove toward the school. They didn't say anything more on the subject.

Again, Chenoa walked into history class late. She stopped in the girl's restroom to freshen up so she could face the day bravely, if that was possible.

Mr. Augustine's mouth crimped with annoyance when Chenoa walked in five minutes after the bell rang. "Late again, Miss Gray Owl?" he questioned sarcastically.

"Sorry," Chenoa mumbled.

"Being sorry doesn't cut it, Miss Gray Owl. That's why we have bells, to encourage you to make it to class on time. I thought you skipped out of taking the test like a few other students. Won't they be surprised when they have to take the make-up test?" He sounded sarcastic. "Take your seat."

Chenoa's dignity severely bruised, she sank into her seat. I wish I would have stayed at home, she thought wearily.

She glanced over at Mary. Mary gave her the sweetest smile. She smiled slightly and tried to concentrate on the test that Mr. Augustine plopped down on her desk with a thump. She answered the first two questions, and then came to the third question. "When was the Declaration of Independence signed?" Chenoa thought about the answer Zach Heritage gave in class, and wrote: "I don't know. I wasn't there." She was stuck on question four. Her mind wandered to what Janie was doing. Was she telling more lies, and Tamara helping her? The next thing she knew the end-of-the-class bell rang. It startled her.

"Turn your tests in before you leave," Mr. Augustine said.

As Chenoa walked past, she plunked the test paper down on his desk the same way he presented it to her ignoring his look of disapproval and walked away.

At lunch, she set her food tray before her on the table as she joined Mary and Tiffany. "I suppose both of you hate me," she said defensively. She'd heard the story she told Sally Kingston yesterday had spread faster than a prairie fire during a windstorm.

"No, I don't hate you," Mary said.

"I don't hate you either, Chenoa," Tiffany assured her.

"I'm just sorry this trouble got started in the first place," Mary said. "You're my friend, Chenoa."

"Yeah," Tiffany agreed, "but I kind of figured Janie had it coming to her. I don't know what her problem is lately, maybe PMS! This has been going on for two months and it's the longest case of PMS I've ever seen. She's been a real bear. A big, thousand pound angry grizzly bear fighting PMS."

"Yeah, Tiffany, we get the picture," Mary said.

"Steer clear of her, Chenoa," Tiffany warned firmly. "She hates you so much she might explode and take you along in the fireball. I'm not on her list of favorite persons either, because I told you her little secret."

"I'm sorry I got you in trouble," Chenoa apologized sincerely. She pushed her food tray away without touching the food. Even the pizza square didn't appeal to her. "I need some air, good, clean fresh air."

"Okay, see you later!" Mary said.

That's Mary, Chenoa thought, always cheerful in the midst of the storm.

Chenoa decided to stop by her locker and pick up her afternoon books. She rounded the corner when someone grabbed her by the hair. She came to a screeching stop. "Hey!" Chenoa exclaimed. The offender slammed her up against the lockers.

Janie Long shoved her snarling face within an inch of Chenoa's and she felt Janie's breath hot and heavy. "You'll pay for this," she vowed venomously. Her face grew red and it made the vein in her temple swell dangerously. Chenoa thought she'd have a stroke. "You won't know how or when, but you'll pay."

From the corner of her eye, Chenoa caught a glimpse of a narrow feminine hand with a class ring grip Janie's arm; the aquamarine setting shimmered in the overhead light. "Come on, Janie!" the feminine voice pleaded and her hand held on firmly. "Not here!"

Janie swung her face in her friend's direction and hissed through clenched teeth. It sounded like air escaping when a tire goes flat. "Let go!" she hissed fiercely.

225

Her friend shrunk away with genuine fear on her face, and threw up her hands in surrender. "Okay, Janie! Okay! Stay cool!"

Janie stuck her face toward Chenoa's again and bared her teeth. "Yeah, you're going to pay you little witch!" she snarled and her blue eyes seem to explode with anger.

Chenoa tried to swallow the lump in her throat but it wouldn't do down, it just stuck. She panted for breath, pleaded under her breath for mercy, but doubted she'd get it. She realized she was trembling.

Janie grabbed the collar of Chenoa's shirt and she couldn't breath. She gulped. "Beware! I'll get you and that's not a threat it's a promise!" She let go of Chenoa's shirt and disappeared around the corner with her friend.

The moment she let go of her collar, Chenoa gulped for precious air. She realized her heart was racing like a runaway train. Her stomach hurt so bad she wanted to throw up. She hardly remembered making her way to the girl's restroom, yet once inside she threw up all over the floor. She didn't know where it all came from and she didn't think she had anything left in her after puking her guts out the night before.

Sally Kingston and another girl were brushing their hair at the mirror and screeched as if they'd seen a mouse. Sally was kind enough to assist Chenoa to the principal's office.

"Mr. Wallace, she's sick," Sally said, disgust in her voice. "She threw up all over the restroom floor. It's disgusting!" Sally shuddered.

"Thank you, Sally," Mr. Wallace said kindly. "We'll handle it."

"You need to get the janitor to clean up the mess," Sally said. "I'm so not going in there again."

"Yes, Sally, we'll take car of it," Mr. Wallace said firmly. "Go to class."

Sally left quickly as if her shirttail was on fire.

Mr. Wallace knelt beside Chenoa's chair and placed a gentle hand on her arm. "Does your stomach still hurt?" She nodded. "You're not going throw up in here, are you." She shook her head, no, but she wasn't promising anything. "Would you like to go home?"

Finally, Chenoa thought, the question I wanted to hear. She nodded.

Mr. Wallace called Barbara, and she came to the school and took Chenoa home.

She didn't say anything in the car. When they got home, Barbara sent her to bed. She refused to eat when Barbara offered her dry toast. She slept until Douglas came home around four-thirty.

Douglas looked into Chenoa's room and smiled. "Are you feeling any better, Chenoa?"

"Kind of," she mumbled.

"Well, I want to check you out," he said, his doctor instincts kicking in. "Turn over and let me examine your stomach.

"Why?" she grumbled. She just wanted to be left alone.

"I want to rule out appendicitis. Maybe it's just a flu bug."

Chenoa looked at him. She didn't have appendicitis or the flu bug. She just wanted him to go away.

Douglas smiled kindly. "Humor me, Honey. I'm a doctor and I want to make sure you're all right. Once we file the papers with the court we'll become your legal guardians and I'd be remiss in my duties as a doctor and guardian if I didn't take care of you."

Chenoa didn't feel like being poked and prodded, but she didn't want to argue with him. The faster she got it over with, the sooner he'd leave her alone. Chenoa flopped over on her back and endured Douglas' thorough examination of her abdominal area.

Chenoa answered all of his, "Does this hurt or does that hurt?" questions with a negative shake of her head.

"Well, I don't see the problem. Judging from what you've been through, I'd say you have a case of nervous stomach."

"I guess so."

"Is everything all right? Are you having trouble here or at school?"

Chenoa shrugged. She wasn't sure how much she could trust Douglas to be objective. Since Tamara was his daughter, he'd most likely take her side.

Douglas looked puzzled when Chenoa didn't volunteer any information. "Chenoa, if you want to talk, I'll listen."

"Dakotah said the youth class is having an ice skating party on Saturday," Chenoa said, changing the subject. "Can I go?"

Douglas' bewilderment deepened but he didn't press the subject. "Don't you think you should wait until you see how you feel the next few days? Chenoa nodded. "If the symptoms disappear tomorrow I don't see any reason why you can't go." He patted her shoulder. "I encourage it whole heartedly." He didn't say anything more and walked out of the room looking thoroughly perplexed.

In the evening, Dakotah showed up and presented Chenoa with a bouquet of a dozen red roses. Barbara supplied a white vase and Chenoa set the roses on the bedside stand.

"They're beautiful, Dakotah," Chenoa said admiring them. "Thank you."

He sat on the bed's edge. "I hope they'll cheer you up." He gave Chenoa's hand a reassuring squeeze. "I heard you had a run-in with Janie. I'm sorry she won't let this problem go. She can be ruthless, and I don't know how to stop her. When I was dating her it was like trying to tiptoe through a minefield with big clown shoes on my feet." He sighed. "It's all over the school about Janie's mom getting raped and becoming pregnant."

"If you're going to preach to me about the evil I've stirred up, save your breath! I feel bad enough."

Dakotah patted her hand comfortingly. "No, I'm not going to tell you that because I know how you feel." He stroked her hair with gentleness and smiled.

Chenoa closed her eyes and could only sigh. She lie there like a rock, a big ugly rock. "How can you love me, Dakotah?" Chenoa heard the words in her mind but she didn't know if she said them aloud.

"Because, I just do," Dakotah said in a comforting voice, "and God does too." Chenoa opened her eyes and searched his solemn face. "It doesn't matter if you don't feel the same way about me. I'll wait."

Chenoa touched his face and smiled slightly. "You're sweet, Dakotah," she said softly. "Thanks for the roses, they're pretty."

Dakotah kissed her hand. "You're welcome. Are you coming to the ice skating party Saturday night?"

"Yes."

"Good! I'll pick you up early." He hugged and kissed Chenoa. "I hope you're feeling better soon."

After Dakotah left, she hung out in her room. She must have dozed off because River burst into the room and startled her. He jumped on her bed and huddled close to her.

"What's wrong, River?" Chenoa asked concerned.

"There's a monster trying to get in my room," he whimpered. Chenoa felt him trembling in her arms.

"It's probably just the wind."

"No! I heard it scratching on the window." He huddled tighter against her. "It had sharp claws."

Chenoa figured it was just a tree branch scraping on the window, but River was scared and she didn't want to downplay his feelings.

"Do you want me to chase it away?" Chenoa offered trying to show him how brave his big sister was.

He shook his head. "No," he whimpered. "It'll eat you for sure!" he added, his eyes big and round. "I don't want it to get you."

"Okay." Chenoa said softly as she kissed the top of his head. After a long moment passed, she asked, "River, would you like to go back to Whiteriver?"

He looked up at Chenoa with big, wondering eyes. "You mean to stay forever and ever."

"Yes."

"I don't care. I want to stay with you," he added in a small-frightened voice.

"Okay," Chenoa hugged him close.

"Are we going back to the rez?"

Chenoa sighed wearily. "Maybe," she answered, her tone was the way her heart felt. "We'll go back as soon as I can make arrangements."

Chenoa didn't believe the words coming out of her mouth. Nevertheless, her heart did-or thought it did-and it seemed happy. Almost!

Thursday, January 17, 2002
Dear Diary,

Was Dakotah speaking the truth when he said he loved me? When I think about his words about falling in love with me at first sight, it gives me goose pimples, and I want to run for the hills. That's how I felt the first time I met him. It's weird because I'm not sure what that means. I don't know who to talk to about it. It makes me happy and scared all at the same time. How can that be? I wish Mom were here to talk to me about it.

However, my feelings are shadowed by the problems I've been having at home and at school. I told the Reams I want to go back to the rez. My dad said once that if you say you want to do something, it is going to happen and you can't stop it. I'm not sure I want to stay. I'm not one to run away from my problems but I can't stay here either and face Tamara's hostility. Janie will never let go of her feeling for Dakotah and her hatred toward me. Therefore, it's better to leave than to continue to stir up all the hatred and jealousy of others.

How do I deal with my feelings for Dakotah? That's the hardest thing I have to think about. I want to stay because of him, but how do I do it? He's so sweet and I'm so evil. I've sunk to Janie's level...how can he love me.

CHAPTER 23

Saturday, January 22, 2002
Dear Diary,
   Now that I mentioned going back to Whiteriver to River, that is all I can think about. I don't see why I should stay in Hartville when I'm not happy due to all the things happening in school...well, it's a sure sign. Everyone will be better off when I'm gone. I want the simple, slow pace life I can only get on the rez.

Chenoa put her pen down and thought; when I'm gone, everything will get back to normal. No one will miss me.

The doorbell rang downstairs and Chenoa was snapped back to reality. As she hurried down to the foyer, she arrived just in time to see Douglas let Dakotah in.

Dakotah smiled. "Are you ready to go, Chenoa?" he asked cheerfully.

"Yeah!"

"Have fun!" Douglas said as they left.

Dakotah and Chenoa headed to church. Once they arrived, they had to wait for the rest of the kids.

Dakotah introduced Chenoa to a tall, blonde-haired man who looked to be in his early forties. "Bob," Dakotah said, "I'd like you to meet Chenoa Gray Owl. Chenoa this is Bob Greene, the youth pastor."

Bob smiled broadly and his friendly hazel eyes danced. "Hello, there! It's nice to meet you," he said as he stuck out his hand.

"Hello," Chenoa shyly shook his hand. He had a firm grip.

"Are you ready for some fun?" Bob asked.

"Of course," Dakotah answered for the both of them.

"Great!"

At three o'clock, everybody who was going had gathered by the green and white church bus. A total of fourteen were in the group, including Chenoa. Five minutes later, they all boarded the bus on their way to Nimisila Lake west of town. The kids sang spiritual songs.

When the group reached the lake, Dakotah and Chenoa sat on a log and he laced her skates.

Bob Greene walked up and squatted beside Chenoa. "I hope you two have loads of fun," he said with a friendly smile. "Have you skated before?"

"I'm teaching her how to skate. She's a good student."

Bob chuckled. "What kind of teacher is this young man?"

"Patient," Chenoa answered truthfully.

"Oh, just patient?" Bob asked with a teasing twinkle in his eyes. "Good! Maybe he can teach my baby sister to ice skate. She requires a bushel of patience because she has two left feet and she's not very coordinated."

Dakotah looked up from lacing up one of his skates and cracked a smile. "Do you mean she can't chew gum and walk at the same time?"

"Exactly!" Bob exclaimed jubilantly." She's her own worst enemy." He put his hand on Chenoa's shoulder, turned serious and changed the subject. "We're going to have hot dogs later, Chenoa, and I'm going to share a brief message with all of the kids. I hope you'll enjoy it."

Dakotah took Chenoa's hand and led her toward the lake where he instructed her about some things and then let her skate on her own. She did okay by herself for a few minutes. A couple of the boys and girls in the group clapped at Chenoa's progress and cheered which distracted her. Her feet went out from under her and she fell hard on her butt.

Dakotah skated up to her. "Are you all right? Did you hurt anything?"

"Only my dignity."

Dakotah helped her up. "Your dignity will be black and blue tomorrow."

"You're telling me," Chenoa rubbed her sore behind.

Greg Martin skated up to them. "Aw, she'll be a professional before you know it," he kidded.

"I'm glad you think so." Chenoa winced in pain. Maybe in the year 2050, she thought. Then I'd be too old to do it.

"Well," Greg said, "there's still a little time left. Maybe I can get a little more skating done. He pushed off on his left skate and quickly skated away.

"Let's skate," Dakotah said as he pulled Chenoa toward him and they started to skate, straight across the lake.

After the ice-skating was over the boys built a bonfire, and the girls brought out the hot dogs and buns. As Chenoa sat on a log watching their progress, Greg sat beside her.

"You're living with the Reams, right." Greg asked in a serious tone.

"Yeah."

"I heard about that mess in school; I don't believe what they're saying. I thought if Tamara wasn't carrying a torch for Dakotah I might ask her out."

"Why are you telling me about your feelings for Tamara?" Chenoa tried not to sound too snippy.

Greg shrugged. "I thought when this passes, and it will, you could mention my feeling to Tamara. Hey, sooner or later she'll have to drop this campaign against you and get on with her life."

"Why don't you call her and tell her yourself?" Chenoa didn't want anything to do with getting them together. That was something he had to do for himself.

Greg grinned like the Cheshire Cat in Alice in Wonderland. "I'm shy." He said the words as if he didn't even believe them.

Chenoa laughed. "I'm sorry," she apologized. "I don't believe that. You told me your feelings for Tamara. Besides, Tamara and I aren't exactly on speaking terms right now."

"If the right moment arises, will you try?" Greg begged. "Please?"

Greg must have had strong feelings for Tamara or he wouldn't have sounded so desperate. "I'll try, only because you're Dakotah's friend." Chenoa wished she wouldn't have promised Greg she'd do it. "I don't guarantee favorable results." He only nodded and smiled.

After the boys lit the bonfire, the group roasted hot dogs and toasted marshmallows. While they ate, Bob shared a message about living for God.

"Salvation," Bob said, "isn't what we achieve, but what we receive by God grace; it's a gift. God is rich in mercy and love. Even when we sin, he loves us. When Christ died and was later raised to life he proved it. God saved us by His special favor, and you can't take credit for this gift. It's a reward. We'd boast about that and that would be wrong. You must confess that Jesus is Lord and believe in your heart and you'll be saved."

Bob smiled. "Let's join hands and pray."

After the kids all joined hands, Bob said a brief prayer for each of them.

Bob looked at everyone present and his gaze lingered on Chenoa for a long, uncomfortable moment. Chenoa wanted to shrink back into the shadows, far away from the flickering firelight.

"Now," Bob said, "I ask-no, I implore-each of you to pray for one another. If you haven't done it yet, make turning your life over to Christ your top priority." Once again, his gaze made Chenoa uncomfortable.

As the bonfire died down, so did the party. Chenoa was walking toward the bus when Dakotah caught up with her. They boarded the bus and sat down in the front seat.

"I hope you'll think about what Bob said, "Choosing the right path is important. I know indecision is hard and I can't make the decision for you," Dakotah said.

"You're right!" she snapped. "You can't, so don't try, Dakotah."

"Huh?" Dakotah looked surprised.

"Why can't you accept me the way I am? If you loved me as you say you do, you'd quit harassing me."

Dakotah blinked incredulously. "But I..." he began.

"Dakotah," Chenoa interrupted, "I can't live off the rez and I'm thinking of going back, so forget me."

"No!" Dakotah tried to put his arms around Chenoa but she pushed him away. "I can't, Chenoa! Why?"

"Because I've made such a mess of things here. No one likes me and I've been branded a boyfriend stealer. White people can be so mean and hateful. You, Mary and Tiffany seem to be the only people who've accepted me. After I'm gone, you'll forget all about me. I belong with my family, my race, my people, and my religious beliefs."

Dakotah looked helpless and tears were in his dark eyes. "You don't know how wrong you are," he said, his voice thick with emotion. "I love you and it would tear my soul apart to see you walk out of my life. Abandoning me when I love you the way I do would be cruel."

Chenoa gave him a hard look. "Now you know how I felt when my mom died. Life is cruel, Dakotah. Accept it!"

"No!" Dakotah grabbed Chenoa by the shoulders and for the first time since she met him, he was rough with his grip. "No, Chenoa! Why are you giving up?"

Chenoa shook him off. "I'm not!" she spat, "I'm fighting back." She pushed him hard and he nearly fell out of the seat. "You're chasing a dream and I'm not it!"

For an instant Dakotah looked manic and wiped a tear from his cheek and Chenoa thought he'd take her in his arms and beg for her love, but he just turned and dashed off the bus. He disappeared into the darkness and Chenoa didn't know where he went. She sat for a long time trying to forget the scared look he had when he left. Since Chenoa couldn't forget, she sat in her seat and cried.

Half an hour later Dakotah returned to the bus just as the rest of the kids were getting on it. He paused a second when he reached Chenoa's seat, then went to the back of the bus and sat down. When they reached the church, Chenoa called Douglas and asked him to pick her up. She was grateful Douglas didn't ask her why Dakotah hadn't brought her home.

Chenoa walked into her bedroom and caught Tamara sitting on her bed in the act of destroying her roses. Red rose petals were scattered all over the bed. That despicable act made Chenoa see red with rage.

"Tamara!" Chenoa screamed like a volcano spewing molten lava. "What do you think you're doing?"

"Huh!" Tamara jumped about an inch off the bed. A thorn stuck her finger. "Ouch!"

"That's all you do is think about yourself!" Chenoa really wanted to rake her over hot coals.

Douglas and Barbara rushed into the room and Douglas gave Tamara such a scorching look of disapproval that she shrunk until she seemed an inch tall.

"Tamara Marie Ream, what on earth?" Douglas said with irritation. His pale eyes turned a stormy gray. "I thought I raised you to be considerate and respect other people's property. I've half a mind to ground you another week.

"I'm sorry, Dad," Tamara sobbed.

"As well you should be," he said fiercely. "I don't know what's been going on but it has to stop. And now!"

"Yes, Dad," Tamara said meekly.

"Go to your room, young lady. We will talk about this later."

"O-okay," Tamara stammered, hurrying out of the room leaving a trail of red rose petals behind her.

Douglas and Barbara remained in the room. Douglas closed the door and asked, "Honey, what's been happening between you and Tamara? Why didn't Dakotah bring you home after the skating party tonight?"

Chenoa ignored both questions. "I want to go back to Whiteriver," is all she could say.

Douglas and Barbara exchanged uncertain glances. "Why, Dear?" Barbara asked. "Aren't you happy here?"

That's the million-dollar question I've been waiting for someone to ask, Chenoa thought. What took them so long to ask it?

"Chenoa," Douglas said, placing a firm hand on her shoulder. "We'd like to be able to sit down and discuss the matter with you. If we aren't able to iron out the problems in a reasonable time frame, then you may go home. Is this plan acceptable?"

Chenoa wanted to say, "No, send me back now." Something in the tone of his voice told her it was a fair deal, so she didn't say anything and just nodded.

Sunday, January 20, 2002
Dear Diary,

Breaking up with Dakotah is the hardest thing I've had to do. We've never actually started dating and haven't formed a close bond, but my heart has been torn apart by my decision. However, I know I can't stay here and face my friends. I'm just an evil person. Eventually Dakotah would grow to hate me and I can't bear that.

I made Dakotah cry and I'm not proud of that. I didn't want to hurt him, but pushing him out of my life seemed like the best thing to do. How can he have deep feeling for me in a few short weeks? When I'm gone, he'll forget me. He has to! He'll find someone else worthier of him. He'll have to realize it wasn't meant to be...I have!

I've made a mess of things and it's time to cut out. I'll have to write my grandmother and tell her about the situation. Maybe they'll let me come stay with them on the rez. I belong with my people. White people can be so cruel.

If I'm going on a spiritual journey, why did God send me here? I don't understand God and never will. Why am I here? Couldn't He show me what He wants without uprooting me? Why didn't He let me stay where I was? Why didn't He just let me alone? I was happy...happier than I am now. Why doesn't He just let me be?

CHAPTER 24

Monday, January 21, 2002
Dear Diary,

The weekend was a total disaster! I'm not quite myself today. I mentally wrestled with myself all night over Dakotah. I hate seeing him in school because I don't know what to say to him. He's a great guy and I didn't mean to hurt him. He deserves better than me and when I spoke those words, "I want to go home to Whiteriver," hasn't helped any. This is a mess! Where do I turn? Things can't get any worse!

Chenoa reread the last sentence, made a face and thought; yeah things can't get any worse. Those are famous last words of a fool.

She sighed and slipped her diary under the pillow. Grabbing her coat and backpack, Chenoa went down to the kitchen where Barbara had warm oatmeal and toast waiting for her. Chenoa stomach was in such agitation she didn't dare eat for fear she'd throw it up.

Chenoa put her coat on and went out the front door. Mary waited for her at the end of the driveway with her usual smile. It wasn't painted; it was genuine.

"How's everything?" Mary asked. Chenoa shrugged. "Don't be too hard on yourself, Chenoa. It will work out."

I wish I had Mary's faith, she thought. Chenoa wanted to ask Mary how Dakotah was doing but she didn't have the courage. She loathed herself for some of the decisions she had made lately.

"Mary how is Dakotah? I didn't mean to hurt him like that." Chenoa said her voice sounding small and afraid.

Mary caressed Chenoa's hand with reassurance. "I know, Chenoa," she said with kindness in her voice. "He's a wreck right now, but he'll get through it. He's not a quitter, he really loves you, that much I know."

Chenoa broke down in tears. Mary put her arms around her and let her cry, which was something she hadn't let herself do.

"What do I do, Mary?" she asked, once her tears had stopped.

Mary drew back and smiled. "Everything will work out in time, Chenoa. I just know it. Come on we need to get to the bus stop."

Mary and Chenoa barely made it to the bus stop. The driver had a frozen look on his face because he had to wait for them.

"You're late!" he growled fiercely, chewing on his toothpick.

Mary smiled sweetly. "Sorry, Mr. Williams."

After Mary and Chenoa sat down, the driver continued down the road. At the next stop, Zach got on and sauntered down the aisle. He winked at Chenoa.

Sliding into the seat behind her, he leaned forward. "Hey, sweetie, we need to talk," he whispered in Chenoa's ear.

"I've nothing to say to you!"

"You will. I can make the problems you're going to have go away."

The problems I'm going to have, Chenoa thought. What did he mean by that?

Chenoa half turned in her seat and looked at him. "What do you mean?" she asked, a feeling of dread creeping over me.

Zach had a devilish grin on his face. "First, you have to agree to go out on a date with me."

"And if I don't?" Chenoa hated that question. Whatever answer he could give her would cause goose bumps to break out all over her arms.

He sobered up and his grin faded. "You don't want to know that, Baby. Just agree and your troubles will vanish."

"Agreeing to that would be like selling my soul to the devil," Chenoa said in a sharp tone. "And I've got enough problems without thinking about dating you. No, thank you!" Chenoa turned back around in her seat.

"Suit yourself," Zach said, with coldness in his voice. "It's not your soul I'm trying to save."

Zach's words left Chenoa chilled, butterflies tickled her stomach, and she felt queasy.

Once they arrived at the school Chenoa tried to put Zach's words out of her mind. She saw Nancy Little standing by the water fountain getting a drink. Nancy gave her a smoldering stare. Chenoa did her usual thing and ignored Nancy. She blew past Nancy and waited for a blow to the back of the head or something; it didn't come so she kept walking.

Mr. Augustine's deep frown greeted Chenoa when she walked into history class. Chenoa beat the bell by one minute. He passed tests back to the class. When he came to Chenoa's, she saw the disapproval chiseled into his face, but she didn't care. Chenoa noticed the big red "F" on the top right corner.

The rest of the morning went fast. When Chenoa went to her locker, she saw Mr. Wallace and several other men going through lockers. She'd never seen them there before. The butterflies in Chenoa's stomach increased and she had a bad feeling. As she got closer her heart quickened, and she could hardly breathe.

"Locker number 775 is clean, Mr. Wallace," said the tall, skinny man in the gray suit and black tie.

That's my locker, Chenoa thought, as she approached them. What's going on? Chenoa's first instinct was to turn around and walk away at a fast pace.

Too late, Mr. Wallace and the two other men looked up and saw Chenoa. Mr. Wallace was the first to speak.

"When's the last time you were in your locker, Chenoa," he asked in a matter of fact tone.

Chenoa's stomach felt queasy. "Uh…I put some books in my backpack this morning, I usually…Uh… what's going on?"

Mr. Wallace took Chenoa's backpack and handed it to the tall, skinny man who unzipped it and started rummaging through it. "We make a periodic drug search."

"Drugs!" Chenoa exclaimed. "I don't take drugs. I don't even like to take aspirin."

"We'll see," Mr. Wallace said. "I'm sure Officer Chambers from the narcotics department has heard every excuse in the book."

"That's a sad fact, ma'am," Officer Chambers said.

"It's not that I don't trust you, Chenoa," Mr. Wallace said. "I just don't want drugs in my school."

"Perhaps you'd wish for an aspirin." Officer Chambers pulled out a long funny white thing from Chenoa's backpack. "Now, what do we have here, do you suppose?"

Chenoa's heart flip-flopped. She swallowed hard. "It's not mine," she said in a shaky voice.

"That's what they all say, ma'am," Officer Chambers said.

"I swear it's not mine!" Chenoa said, pleading her case.

"Mr. Wallace, may I use your office to question the young lady?" Officer Chambers asked.

"Of course," Mr. Wallace said.

Mr. Wallace led the way to his office. They passed Janie standing in front of the girl's restroom, a gratified smirk planted on her lips.

"Busted!" Janie said with satisfaction in her voice.

Officer Chambers questioned Chenoa in Mr. Wallace's office with the principal present.

"Is this yours or is it not?" Officer Chambers asked, holding up the marijuana cigarette.

"No!" Chenoa flatly denied. "I didn't know it was there…honest!"

Mr. Wallace and the officer exchanged wary glances. Chenoa didn't think either one of them believed her.

Chenoa needed some air. Her instinct was to run, but her feet fanatically disobeyed her. Her heart pounded so hard she thought she had a tribal drum in her chest.

"It's not mine! Someone must have planted it there." Maybe if Chenoa planted reasonable doubt in their brains they'd drop it.

Fat chance! she thought. Moreover, the moon is made of green cheese.

"It's not mine!" she insisted.

Mr. Wallace sighed. "We'll determine that during the investigation. We'll have to notify your legal guardians."

It felt as if a trapdoor spring had opened in Chenoa's stomach. "Why?" she asked as her voice raised an octave. Her knees started to quake and it felt like a cold fist was closing over her heart.

"Calm down," Mr. Wallace said. "If you cooperate everything will go smoothly and the mystery will be solved.

Yeah, right! Chenoa thought chewing on her lower lip.

The Reams were notified and both Douglas and Barbara came to the school. They talked to Mr. Wallace and Officer Chambers for half an hour. It sounded like a lot of mumbo jumbo but she knew she was in deep, deep trouble.

When she left the school with the Reams, she didn't dare look back because she didn't want to see anyone staring at her.

Douglas, Barbara and Chenoa sat in the family room and talked about the suspension.

"No!" Chenoa said, feeling like she was being grilled in the Spanish Inquisition. "I want to go back to Whiteriver."

"Now, Honey," he said, "running away from your problems won't make them go away. We'll pray about it."

"No! Prayer doesn't work for me." Chenoa made up her mind. She chose not to pray about the matter because she knew God wasn't listening.

Douglas sighed. "Look, Chenoa, this is serious. We need you to cooperate with us or the situation will get worse."

Get worse! She thought. How could it get worse? This is as bad as it gets!

She sat on the sofa like a rock. She didn't want to talk about it.

Douglas finally threw up his hands in despair. "We're getting nowhere," he said in desperation. "I need to get back to the clinic. We'll have more time this evening to sit down and discuss this reasonably." He hurried out of the house like a fox being chased by hounds.

"Everything will work out, Chenoa," Barbara said. "Maybe if we find out who put the marijuana in your backpack the problem can be solved quickly."

"I wouldn't count on it," Chenoa grumbled.

Barbara hugged Chenoa reassuringly. "You'd be surprised once you start remembering a conversation." She sighed. "I need to get back to the laundry," she stated as she walked out of the room.

Chenoa went to her bedroom and nearly wore a path in the rug pacing back and forth. She thought about what Barbara said and remembered her conversation with Zach on the bus.

What does he know about the situation? How much does he know? Did he put the marijuana in my backpack, or was it Janie? The possibilities made her head spin.

She paced the floor until she was exhausted. She sat on the bed and put her head in her hands. I just want to go back to the rez. I hate it here. If the Reams don't send River and me back to Whiteriver, I'll take River and run away with him. We'd get to the reservation with or without their help.

She sat on the bed, her head in her hands and rocked back and forth. Her world was going to heck in a hand basket. She was too upset to cry.

River came into the room. "Chenoa, what's the matter?" he asked his voice sounding small and afraid.

Chenoa looked up. "I'm in deep trouble," she answered. Chenoa didn't expect him to understand.

River looked confused. "Why?"

"You wouldn't understand."

His confusion deepened. "Why?"

Chenoa wasn't in the mood for his endless questions. She knelt in front of him and asked directly, "Do you want to go back to Whiteriver? We can live there with Grandmother and Grandfather Tinilzay."

"Yeah," he said, sounding a little unsure.

"Good! That's all I needed to know."

Chenoa grabbed her backpack, dumped out the books and started stuffing some clothes into it.

"What are you doing?" River asked curiously.

"We're going back to Whiteriver." That's all he needed to know. "Stay here."

Going into the Reams' master bedroom she frantically searched one drawer after another hoping she'd find enough money to get them to their destination. Chenoa found an envelope with "vacation" written on it. Opening it, she counted out $450. Chenoa stuffed it into her backpack and returned to her room.

River still stood in the middle of the room. He looked confused and frightened. Chenoa didn't have the time to comfort him. She was on a mission to get them back to the reservation.

"Come with me," Chenoa said, taking him by the hand. She grabbed her coat and backpack. They went to his room and got his coat. After Chenoa got him ready, she decided to leave the Reams a note. She wasn't sure why she even bothered but she scribbled: Going back to Whiteriver, and laid the paper on her pillow.

Chenoa took River downstairs to the kitchen and opened the basement door a crack. She heard Barbara working on the laundry and humming "Amazing Grace." Before they left, Chenoa found a package of chocolate chip cookies in the cupboard and shoved them into her coat pocket.

"Chenoa…" River began.

Chenoa knelt in front of him. "Shh! We have to leave quietly. Okay?"

"How do we get to Whiteriver?"

"We'll take a bus," Chenoa answered, trying to keep her voice down. "I need to get to a telephone and call a taxi."

"What if we get cold?" he asked, pulling back.

Chenoa didn't have the patience for his questions. She didn't want to take the time to explain the details.

"We'll be all right, River."

"Do we tell Mrs. Reams good-bye?"

Another question! Chenoa's mind was ready to snap. *He takes after Dad. He'd make a great lawyer someday.*

"No," Chenoa answered, slowly losing it all together. "That's the whole point of running away, River. You don't tell anyone, not even the people you like. Let's go!" Chenoa took River's hand and they snuck out the back door.

As River and Chenoa sat on the snow covered picnic table in the woodsy Hartville Park, a clock in the bell tower of the town hall chimed eight o'clock. It was dark, and they were stuck. In her haste to grab the Reams' vacation money, Chenoa got all bills and didn't have any coins to make a telephone call. She couldn't risk being seen trying to ask for change. Police cars drove by the park a few times, but they were pretty well hidden and the police didn't see them.

Brilliant plan, Chenoa, she chided myself. *I have no plan at all. I guess I should have had a plan B or* something. On the other hand, she wished she just had a plan to begin with.

"Chenoa, I'm cold," River whined and tugged on her arm.

Chenoa cuddled River and kissed his cold cheek. "Eat your cookies," she said, trying to sound like she was in control.

"Nooo!" he wailed.

Chenoa held him closer and wished she hadn't brought him but couldn't imagine leaving him behind. Maybe it was wrong to run away without a better plan. My father always said I did stuff without making a list. Blast my spontaneity! she thought. As Chenoa wiped a tear from her cheek, she realized her own fingers and toes tingled from the cold.

Chenoa got up and took River's hand. "Let's go!" she ordered firmly.

"No!" he sobbed. "Carry me!" He stomped his foot and cried.

"No," Chenoa said firmly. "You need to walk. It'll keep the circulation flowing. "She had to coax him to walk. He cried so loud that a dog at a nearby house started barking. River nearly jumped into her arms. "It's okay." Chenoa carried him to the narrow road and had to put him down.

"Hold me!" River wailed.

Chenoa knelt in front of him. "You're too heavy!" she nearly yelled at him. "You'll have to walk."

"I want Mommy!" he sobbed.

"I know." Chenoa kissed his wet cheek. "I'll find a warm place for us to stay tonight."

"Nooo!" he wailed. "I wanna go back to the Reams!"

Chenoa took him roughly by the shoulders. "No! We can't do that!"

I wish I knew what I was doing. This day can't get any worse.

"Yes!" he screamed in her ear. He whacked Chenoa in the ear with his little hand and the blow made her dizzy.

River bolted out into the middle of the road. He froze when he saw the headlights of a car come over the hill.

"River!" Chenoa screamed as she ran out into the road and pushed him out of the way. She failed to get out of the way herself and the car hit her. She felt the impact, heard the sickening crunch in her left leg and felt a pain so great it nearly astounded her. The car sped away without stopping. Chenoa lay on the ground hurting with every breath, and her left leg pained her something awful.

She heard River crying next to her, and she felt him pulling on her coat. "Chenoa, get up!" he sobbed. He sounded afraid and she wanted desperately to hold him but she couldn't move. She felt so weird, like she was floating on an ocean.

"Chenoa!"

"River," she sighed. "Don't be afraid."

"Chenoa!" he wailed, still tugging on her coat. "I'm cold! Chenoa!"

She wanted to comfort him, but she couldn't move. His voice seemed a million miles away. A strange and scary darkness loomed over her. Eventually blackness enveloped her.

Am I dying? She thought. When death came for Anna was she at peace? Where is that peace? God, help me!

A bearded man in a white robe knelt beside Chenoa; a great light illuminated him. He smiled and gently took her hand. "I'm with you, my child," he said as his voice comforted her.

"Don't leave me," Chenoa pleaded, trying to remember where she had seen him before.

He squeezed her hand. "I'm here," he said. "I will never leave nor forsake you. Peace is with you."

Then Chenoa remembered the dream she had about falling through the ice. He was the man reaching down to her. He was sad when she didn't reach up to him.

"Are you Jesus?"

The bearded man smiled lovingly and nodded. "I am! Rest now."

The thought that Jesus cared enough to come down from Heaven to be with her, gave Chenoa peace. Chenoa let the darkness envelop her. She welcomed it.

CHAPTER 25

When Chenoa opened her eyes she was in the hospital and the doctor in green surgical scrubs stood by her bed smiling down at her.

"Good morning, young lady," he said. "You've had a serious accident but you're going to be fine in time."

She shook the mental fog from her brain and said, "It's morning? What morning?"

"Tuesday January 22nd," he said.

She remembered her leg hurting last night and she had a million questions to ask. "M-my leg…"

The doctor squeezed her hand and said in a reassuring voice, "Honey, you have a broken leg, several bad breaks I'm afraid. I'm an orthopedic surgeon and was on call last night. I did emergency surgery and put a pin in your leg. You're lucky you didn't lose your leg."

"Will I walk again?'

"Yes, but you'll be in a cast for two months," he answered, giving Chenoa his verdict.

Chenoa snorted. "It beats the alternative," she said thinking about going through life without a leg. What would people think of me then? she thought. I'd be damaged goods that nobody would want.

"I agree, it does beat the alternatives," the doctor said. "Looks like the Man upstairs was smiling down on you."

"What man?" Chenoa asked, wondering what he meant.

"The main Man, God!"

"Yeah, I guess so," Chenoa said remembering seeing Jesus in her dream-like state. Was he finally listening? she thought. However, I haven't called on him, yet. I guess I should count my blessings that I wasn't zapped unwillingly into oblivion.

"I'm going to let you rest now. Have a pleasant morning."

Chenoa didn't offer a response; she was too tired and weak.

Looking back over the past several weeks, she had done many hateful things that would probably leave Anna shaking her head and remarking, "Is that my daughter?" Maybe if Chenoa had "Talked to Jesus" all her troubles could have been avoided.

Will God forgive me? she thought. Will Dakotah forgive me?

Chenoa wiped a tear from her cheek. "I don't deserve their forgiveness," she said to herself. "I'm strictly beyond all hope." She was concerned about her future, the suspension, and just how that marijuana cigarette got in her backpack.

By early afternoon Chenoa was beginning to feel abandoned. No one came to visit her; therefore, she was depressed. Abandoned, she thought, how did you let this happen to me? Am I being punished? I thought you were a loving God who cared about people and helped them.

At lunchtime, an orderly walked into the room and set Chenoa's food tray on the bedside table without saying a word. He didn't even smile but rushed off to complete his busy schedule.

Lunch didn't appeal to Chenoa so her food tray went untouched.

Shortly after the food tray arrived, Dakotah tiptoed into the room with a bouquet of red roses and a present. He smiled as if last Saturday had never happened.

"Hi!" he said cheerfully as he placed the roses in Chenoa's arms and kissed her. "These are for you. I hope they brighten your day. When they're gone, I'll bring you more."

Chenoa sighed. "You're the last person I expected to see here. After what I said and did Saturday night I didn't think you'd ever want anything to do with me."

Dakotah took her hand. "I couldn't stay away, Chenoa, I love you."

"I don't deserve your love," Chenoa grumbled, her mood turning dark.

"Tell my heart that," he said with a solemn sigh and patted his chest. "When the Reams told me you ran away and took River, I nearly freaked out. I drove all around town hunting for you, the Reams and the police did, also. When I found you mangled and bleeding in the road I pleaded with God to let you live. Luckily, my father had loaned me his cell phone. As soon as I got the bleeding stopped and made sure you were warm, I called 911. Then I comforted River. he was so scared, and he didn't want to stay in the car even though it was warm."

Chenoa wiped the tears from her cheeks. "Stop it, Dakotah!" she sobbed. "I don't need to hear how horrible I am. I don't want to hear how I put my own little brother in danger. I'm evil! Yes, I'm an evil person."

Dakotah held Chenoa so close she could hear his heart beating. "No, Chenoa, you're not evil. Sometimes we feel so lost we do the wrong things."

"How can you be so understanding?"

"God alone understands."

"What's God got to do with it?" Chenoa asked snidely.

"He's got plenty to do with it. Why don't you face the fact that God has you right where he wants you, flat on your back and nowhere to run? He'll take your confusion and hurt away. He's the answer to all your questions. God knows you're confused about all that's happened to you lately, yet he's trying to tell you something. Listen to Him! The accident at the park was no mere accident. Remember me telling you God has a purpose for everything? He'll knock you down so you have to look up. I'm positive he has something better planned for you."

"Like what?" Chenoa really wanted to know if life had a better meaning than it did now.

"First, he wants you to give Him your whole heart, mind and soul. Second, He just wants you to trust Him completely." Dakotah took her hands in his. "He's the only one who can take your sins away and replace them with joy. John 3:16 says: 'God so loved the world that He gave his only begotten son that everyone who believes in Him will not perish but have eternal life.'"

"Chenoa, you need to trust God," Dakotah said lovingly but firmly. "Get on the sled, now, before it's too late." He forced Chenoa to look at him. "You need to do it."

"How, Dakotah?" Chenoa's heart pounded so hard she thought it would burst out of her chest or explode trying.

"You need to pray," he said, and then smiled. "Or as your mother would say, 'talk to Jesus.'"

"I don't know how to pray," Chenoa said tearfully. She felt helpless and she hated that feeling.

"I'll help you," Dakotah offered. His dark eyes searched Chenoa's for an answer. "Are you ready?"

Chenoa swallowed the big lump in her throat. She wiped the tears from her cheek. She knew she had to do it because there had to be a better way of life than the route she was taking. It felt as if she was in the woods, walking in circles and never finding the right way out.

"Okay," Chenoa nodded.

Dakotah and Chenoa bowed their heads, closed their eyes, joined hands and prayed.

"Dear Heavenly Father, Chenoa knows she's a sinner and we ask You to forgive those sins today and cleanse her heart. Please, show her a better way. Take all the bad and replace it with good. As she surrenders all to you, her heart, mind, and soul, we ask you to make her a new person in Christ. We ask this in Jesus' name. Amen!"

"Amen!" Chenoa wept unashamed and felt washed clean inside. She felt an indescribable peace come to life within her soul.

Dakotah hugged Chenoa and smiled. "Trust God, Chenoa." She nodded. He handed her the present. "I want you to have this. Go ahead, open it."

Chenoa tore the wrapping paper off and discovered it was a Bible with a white cover. "Oh, Dakotah, I don't know what to say, except thank you."

"Read it!" he stressed. "Read it everyday, ask God to help you understand it."

"I will," Chenoa vowed. "I promise."

"Chenoa, I talked to the Reams while you were in surgery last night," he said solemnly. "I told them everything that was happening in school. Douglas asked me, and I had to tell him."

"I couldn't tell them," Chenoa confessed. "I couldn't trust them to be fair and help me because Tamara was involved. I thought if I got them involved Tamara would really hate me."

Dakotah caressed her hand. "They're coming in later and they want to talk to you. It's important. I suggest you listen to them with an open heart."

Butterflies tickled Chenoa's stomach. "I will," she promised.

"I'd like to stay longer, but I have to go to work," he said as he hugged her gently. "Tell the Reams about your decision to follow Christ. Trust God! He'll take care of the rest. I'll drop by later, if not tonight maybe tomorrow." He kissed her and left.

Chenoa picked up the Bible and opened it. She began reading in Genesis, chapter one.

Fifteen minutes later, the Reams walked in. It didn't look like either one of them had slept. Barbara sat on the bed and Douglas sat in the chair beside the bed.

"How are you feeling?" Douglas asked pleasantly.

"Okay," Chenoa answered.

Barbara touched the vase of roses. "Where did you get these lovely roses?"

"Dakotah delivered them in person and he gave me this Bible," Chenoa said smiling happily as she proudly showed off the Bible.

Barbara smiled. "How nice," she said, patting Chenoa's hand.

"I gave my heart to God today. I want to follow Christ."

Barbara caressed Chenoa's hand. "That's wonderful, Chenoa! "I'll be praying for you."

Douglas touched Chenoa's hand. "We sure will," he said with a smile. He then changed the subject, "Chenoa, we talked to Dakotah last night," he said getting to the point. "He told us everything. We wondered why you didn't trust us enough to share your problem. We would have been more than willing to sit down and work those problems out with you."

Douglas sounded like he was scolding her. I guess I deserve I, she thought.

She sighed wearily. "I guess I was being stupid."

"That's an unfair assumption, Chenoa," Douglas said firmly. "There's no point in beating yourself up over past decisions because we learn from our mistakes."

"Yes, dear," Barbara said kindly. "We must learn to trust one another. We know we can't replace your parents and we wouldn't try, but you will be living with us and we consider you part of the family."

"Now," Douglas changed the subject, "there is the matter of you and River returning to Whiteriver. If you still want to go back, as we said in the beginning, we won't stand in your way. We just ask that you first wait until you're well enough to think about it clearly. You've just had major surgery and right now you need to concentrate on getting well. Will you promise us that you'll agree with this?"

It sounded like a fair request. "Yes," Chenoa said with a nod.

"Good!" Douglas answered. "Now that that's out of the way, there are the matters of your suspension and the police investigation we need to be concerned about."

"How's the investigation coming?" Chenoa asked curiously.

"Slowly, I'm sorry to say," Douglas answered with a shake of his head. "If you cooperate with the police maybe the mystery of who put the marijuana in your backpack can be resolved. This is where you must trust God and allow Him to work in your favor."

Chenoa looked at Douglas, then Barbara. "Do you believe that it wasn't mine?" She needed a reason to trust them. This was where their belief in her was important as it had a great impact on how much she thought she could trust them.

"Yes, Chenoa," Douglas said firmly, "I believe you."

"And so do I," Barbara said with a firm nod.

"Thanks," Chenoa said with relief.

"Tamara will stop by tonight," Barbara said. "She wants to talk to you. She's really upset about the events over the past several days."

Chenoa nodded. "Okay." She couldn't be as upset as Chenoa. She thought about her little brother. She couldn't get his frightened cries out of her mind. "How is River?" she asked with concern.

"Well, he's understandably upset," Douglas said. "Dakotah stayed with him while he waited for the ambulance. River needs the assurance that you'll be all right. I'm going to work something out with your doctor and see if he'll allow us to bring River in to visit you. Right now you need your rest."

"We'll return this evening," Barbara said. "Is there anything we can bring you?"

"My diary," Chenoa answered.

Tuesday evening. No Dakotah. He had to work but he called during his break just to say, "I love you." That was sweet of him.

Dinner consisted of yucky mashed potatoes and chicken that lacked flavor. The cherry jell-o was so-so.

The Reams along with Tamara came in at six thirty. Barbara gave Chenoa her diary. They chattered briefly and then they left Tamara and Chenoa alone.

Tamara sat in the chair and didn't say anything for two long minutes. She must have been nervous because her hands shook.

"How's your leg?" Tamara asked.

"It hurts a little," Chenoa admitted. "But look at the bright side, at least I still have my leg."

Tamara sighed. "Look, I'm really sorry about everything. I...I never meant for anything like this to happen. I just...well I wanted Dakotah and I was just mean and stupid."

"I won't disagree with that," Chenoa said, "but like your father said, we all make mistakes. That's how we learn."

"I guess so. Anyway, Mom said you were saved today. That's really swell and, if it's true then maybe you'll find it easier to forgive me."

Tamara sounded sincere and Chenoa understood why she was so nervous. Asking to be forgiven and meaning it wasn't easy. She remembered reading in the Bible that if she didn't forgive the one who hurt her, then Jesus wouldn't forgive her. This must be the first step toward spiritual healing.

Chenoa reached over and took her hand. "I will forgive you, if you'll forgive me, too."

"What for?"

"For being a jerk. Moreover, well I didn't ask Dakotah to fall in love with me. I know what it's like to have a crush on a boy, and I didn't mean to trample all over your feelings, believe me."

"Okay, I forgive you. Sunday, when Pastor Heritage gave the alter call, I went up front and prayed

about what was going on in school and my part in it. I
hated teaming up with Janie Long. She's ruthless and
evil and I felt I was selling my soul to the devil. I tried
several times to go to your room, but I felt ashamed."

"It's all right, Tamara, I'm willing to work on being
friends."

"Me too." She hugged Chenoa.

Chenoa touched her hand. "But, I don't want my
relationship with Dakotah to cause you any pain."

"It's funny how things work out. Greg Martin
called me last night. He's a good friend of Dakotah's.
We talked a while, he's very nice, and at least I think
so."

"I talked to him Saturday night. I wanted to tell you
about him but I had that fight with Dakotah and I was
upset."

"Greg said you suggested he call me. I had no idea
he felt that way about me. We've talked in church but
…well, he asked me out and I've accepted.

"I hope it works out for you. He seems like a nice
guy."

"Yeah." Then she got serious. "Chenoa, my parents
told me you want to go back to Whiteriver. That's
crazy! For what it's worth, I hope you consider staying
as I really would like to get to know you better."

"I promised your parents I'd pray about it."

"Fair enough."

"Tamara, do you know who put the marijuana in my
backpack?"

Tamara shook her head. "No, I wasn't in on that
because I had a big fight with Janie on Monday

266

morning. She called me a weak-kneed prissy with no backbone...and a few other choice words I don't care to repeat. Chenoa, Janie's dangerous and she frightens me. Stay out of her way, please."

Wednesday afternoon Dakotah walked in wearing a big, cheerful smile. "Hi!" he said, his eyes dancing. "How are you feeling today?"

"I'm feeling a little better."

"I was praying about the problem in school and wondering if you could remember anything about Monday.

Chenoa shook her head. "No, I can't."

Dakotah took her hand in his. "Are you sure? Think about it a minute."

Chenoa did think about it and remembered Janie threatening her. She told Dakotah about all the stuff Janie said to her, like when she was carted off to Mr. Wallace's office and passed Janie in the hallway, how she said, "Busted". Chenoa told him about the way Zach Heritage was acting.

"Oh?" Dakotah asked dubiously. "Really?"

Chenoa nodded. "Yeah! He practically warned me there was going to be trouble. He told me if I dated him he'd make the problems go away."

"The dates of those drug searches aren't made public, only Mr. Wallace knows about them. I'm trying to think if any of Janie's friends help in the office. It could be they snooped into his files or something."

"Ask Sally Kingston."

Dakotah looked at Chenoa. "Huh?"

"She knows everything, maybe someone bragged."

"Yeah," Dakotah nodded, "She might know. It's worth a shot. That narcotics officer is still poking around school and asking questions, maybe I can give him the information. I'm sure he'll be interested. You did great, Chenoa."

"I'll say a prayer for you. That's all I can offer from my bed."

"I'll take whatever help I can get, especially from above. You'd be surprised how much you can help from your bed."

Friday. Chenoa was reading her Bible when Dakotah walked into her room looking troubled.

"What's wrong, Dakotah?" Chenoa asked, closing her Bible.

Dakotah dropped into the chair as if a great weight sat on his shoulders. "Janie was rushed into the emergency room last night," he said wearily. "She had a miscarriage."

"Huh?" Chenoa asked dumbfounded. "I didn't know she was pregnant."

Dakotah sighed. "Me either."

"Who's the father?"

Dakotah shrugged. "Beats me!" he exclaimed bewildered. "It's not mine! She said she didn't know who the father was, but one of her friends told me she's been hanging around Zach Heritage."

"Wow!" Chenoa exclaimed remembering how hard Zach tried to get her into his clutches. "How's she doing?"

"She'll be fine physically. Emotionally, I'm not so sure. She was two months along which explains the bizarre behavior."

"Wow! She nearly sank her fangs into my jugular vein because you broke up with her and she was cheating on you."

"Yeah! Go figure!"

"What have you learned about what we talked about the other day?"

"I talked to Officer Chambers and he said your information was helpful. I haven't talked to him today."

"Did I hear my name mentioned?" came a voice from the doorway. Officer Chambers entered the room. "I hope you're feeling better, young lady."

"I'm getting there," Chenoa said. "If you have any good news it would really make my day."

Officer Chambers smiled. "Then I just might make your day. I've been doing some thorough investigating and trying to get to the truth. It reads something like a soap opera."

"A soap opera?" Dakotah looked puzzled. "How?"

"Yes," Officer Chambers nodded. "I learned Janie Long was carrying Zach Heritage's child. I've been told she lost the child. Anyway, Janie threatened to tell Zach's father about it if he didn't put the marijuana in your backpack. She wanted to get even with you for breaking up her and Dakotah."

"That's crazy! Chenoa wasn't the cause of our break up."

"Well, I won't debate that. Frankly, it's none of my business. Anyway, Zach confessed he didn't want to do it because he liked Chenoa, but he didn't want his father to know about the baby. Sorry to say Pastor Heritage sat in on my conversation with Zach."

"Brother, that is a soap opera," Dakotah said with a bewildered sigh. "What's going to happen to Zach and Janie?"

"That's up to the judge. I've already spoken to the Reams since they're your legal guardians. Now, have I made your day?"

"You bet!" Chenoa exclaimed. "Thank you! Thank you ever so much."

"No," Officer Chambers said, "the information you gave me about your conversations with Zach, and Janie's threat to get even, broke the case wide open. I should be thanking you." He glanced at his watch and added, "If you'll excuse me I hope you kids have a pleasant day. Good-bye." Officer Chambers turned and waved as he walked out the door.

Dakotah hugged Chenoa and said, "You did it!"

"No, He did it!" Chenoa didn't have to say God because Dakotah knew what she meant and nodded.

Saturday, January 26, 2002
Dear Diary,
I am glad that everything worked out and Officer Chambers found out who stuck the marijuana in my backpack. I kind of figured Janie was behind all of it. She must really be evil to want to get back at me in that manner. I just hope she'll be okay and recover from the

miscarriage. I would never want to wish anything bad on her.

I guess I have a lot to think about. I'd really love to go back to the rez and be with my people, but if I ran away from all my problems like I did this one...well... My dad said you should never run away from your problems because they just get bigger and bigger. The bigger they get the harder it is to face them. When you face them and conquer them you grow stronger.

I'm not sure why but I have a desire to stick it out and see where this all leads. I'm the curious type. As scary as it is, Grandmother said I was put here for a reason. I just hope she's right. I'm happy Dakotah forgave me for hurting him and has agreed to stand by me. If I had to go it alone...well I don't even want to think about it. I have to face it...we're soul mates. I know that now. In addition, even if it is never meant to be my life is richer for him being in it.

271

EPILOGUE

Sunday, January 27, 2002
Dear Diary,
    I've called the Reams and asked them to come early to the hospital because I have something important to discuss with them. I've made my decision.

Chenoa busied herself while she waited for the Reams to arrive by reading some important scripture passages in her Bible. It was comforting reading all of God's promises. One promise stood out more than any other did. It was the one stating that God would always love her. After her parents died, she didn't think He loved her but He did. Chenoa remembered her grandmother saying she was going on a spiritual journey and she had to walk that journey alone. She didn't understand why her parents had to die for God to get her to this point, but she was there.

She lost track of time and before she knew it the Reams walked into her room at eleven o'clock. They looked anxious as they stood around her bed.

Douglas brushed at his beard and was the first to speak. "I'm very curious why you summoned us so urgently."

"Yes, dear," Barbara said, "I've been praying for good news. Has the doctor said when you'll be released from the hospital?"

"No," Chenoa said. "I know I promised you I'd wait until I got better and out of the hospital before I made a decision about what I wanted to do. I've made

272

a decision. I've decided to stay here in Ohio. I know I've made a mess of things but my father always told me not run away from my problems. Then Grandmother told me of a dream she had. She told me that the Great Spirit was going to send me on a spiritual journey, she also told me not to fear change but welcome it. I'm not sure why I am in Ohio, but I know I'll find out eventually. Putting my future in God's hands seems scary, but I'm going to try." Chenoa looked at them intently, not saying a single word.

Douglas smiled. "You can count on our prayers," he said, squeezing her hand. "You and River are welcome additions to our family. We'll go ahead and file the petition for legal guardianship. We're honored to have you as part of the family."

"Yes, Chenoa," Barbara said smiling, "we couldn't be any happier about your decision."

"Thank you," Chenoa said smiling.

Knowing that was how the Reams felt about River and her was fantastic. It was a new beginning, and a new family loved her. Nevertheless, best of all, God loved her, and Chenoa loved Him. That's all that really mattered.

GLOSSARY

The words and phrases used in this book are of the Western Apache language. The spellings are taken from the *Western Apache Dictionary* by Edgar Perry and his staff at the White Mountain Apache Culture Center. Also, translations were provided by Mr. Perry.

Daa got'ee *[dah-ah goh-tah ah]*-Greetings

Daant'ee *[dah-nah-tah ah]*- How are you?

Doo dansht'ee *[doo dahn-shah-tah ah]*-I am fine

Nadistinyu bikeh hi daa *[nah-dee-stee na-yoo bee-kah-hee dah]*-Follow the right path.

Na go dihii *[nah goh dee-hah]*-Storyteller

Ni at e' hii nlt eego antee le *[nee ah tah ah nah-tah aah-goh ahn-tah lah]*-Be true to your heritage.

Shichoo *[shee-choh]*-grandfather

Shimaa *[shee-mah]*-mother

Shiwoye *[shee-yoh-yah]*-grandmother

Yaa ka'yu *[yah kah-yoh]*-Heaven

BIBLIOGRAPHY

Bolton, Martha. "Saying Good-bye [When You don't Want To]."
Ann Arbor, Michigan. Servant publications. 2002

Haley, James L. "Apaches: A History & Culture Portrait." Garden
City, N.Y. Doubleday & Company Inc. 1981.

Herbst, Mrs. Mark, Mrs. Donald Ream & lair Stilwell. "History of
Congress Lake Club." Hartville, Ohio. Knowles Press, Inc. 1964.

Mumford, Amy Ross "It Hurts to Lose A Special Person."
Colorado Springs, Colorado. Cook Communications Ministries. 1982.

Stark County Bicentennial Committee Bicentennial Story
1776-1976" Volume I. Canton, Ohio. Zepher Press.

Staff of the White Mountain Apache Culture Center. "Western
Apache Dictionary". Fort Apache, Arizona. White Mountain Apache Culture Center. 1972.

Golston, Sydele E. "Changing Woman of the Apache". New

York, New York. A division of Grolier Publishers. 1996.